SCOUNDRELS

SCOUNDRELS

A
PHOENIX QUILL
ANTHOLOGY

Edited by Ashley Cyr

SCOUNDRELS: AN ANTHOLOGY

Copyright © 2017 Ashley Cyr

Cover by: John Ryers

ISBN: 978-0-9952890-4-8

Bushmead Publishing
www.bushmead.com

Printed in U.S.A.

To anyone weird enough,
clever enough,
or rebellious enough
to be called a Scoundrel.

TABLE OF CONTENTS

An Introduction

Well, this is our third time around in this series now. We've learned so much from these authors who have worked with us, from those who we've shared their stories with, and from the world in general. In the previous editions, we've dealt with things that are a little more stark, though the amazing writers we've worked with have been able to come up with some amazing spins to keep them from being quite so black and white. With Scoundrels, we've really embraced those antiheroes, those villains, and those who are really just misunderstood. We could go on and on with this, but who really reads introductions, anyways? On to the rogues, thieves, con artists, and other stories about scoundrels.

- From someone, somewhere in Canada, November 2017

MINIATURE YOU

BY LINDA G. HILL

I love you, you know. I wish I had a miniature of you, for when I'm afraid and sad and lonely. Something to cuddle when we hang up the phone after hours of reluctantly saying goodnight. A tiny you to squeeze when I need to feel you by my side. Something to squish when I'm mad at you. When I hear a girl giggling in the background and you insist you're home, even though there are traffic noises competing with your voice. Something to stick pins in when I know you're lying.

A miniature of you.

One for all occasions.

OCEANITIDES

BY LAURA JOHNSON

"And on your left, you'll see Nethuns, also known as Poseidon or Neptune to you Terrans. But he goes by any of those names, of course." Finn, Lena's tour guide, chuckled, but his laughter had the staleness of a joke told many times before and his breath stank of fish. A few of the other tourists, all human, cracked smiles. His Neeric accent added a musical quality reminiscent of a wooden xylophone, which Lena found pleasing to the ear. Finn scratched his beard, the gray hairs curled so tightly that they resembled barnacles. Perhaps they were. "Created by Aquatimeus during the early Rediviniation Period..."

The mosaic depicted the trident-wielding god, his chariot pulled by dolphins. Orange tentacles splayed over his shoulders in a cuttlefish cloak. The ocean boasted whitecaps as jagged as shark teeth, and spray misted the background in the form of tiny white tiles. Except for one corner blackened by mould, the mosaic was wonderfully preserved, its details exquisite. It was as if it had been commissioned that decade and not, as Finn had rightly said, during the Rediviniation Period, when an interest in the ancient gods had resurfaced.

Homesickness tugged at Lena's heart like a fishhook. She wished it were pleasure, not business, that had prompted her visit to Tethyea. She was only here because of a mandatory field trip for history students at the Oceanus University for Offworlders...

or so claimed her fake ID chip.

In truth, she was a thief.

She suddenly yearned for her IRIS communicator, which she'd left in a storage locker at the aerodrome. Then she could have snapped some high-res photos to show her father — Aquatimeus had gotten the nose all wrong, and were those gill slits on his neck? But before the descent, Finn had instructed everyone to leave their electronics behind. The air was humid, and photography was forbidden. They wouldn't get signal, in any case. However, digital photos were available in the gift shop for memorabiliacs, as well as laminated postcards for the nostalgic paperphiles. Lena was neither. Her father had raised her not to be sentimental, although he had given her a pair of handcrafted trident earrings for her birthday. Clinging to the past, he said, was like refusing to abandon a sandcastle at high tide. Everything was ephemeral.

Well, almost.

As she fiddled with one of her earrings, Lena looked at a video camera in the upper corner and waved. She'd tampered with the security system earlier that morning. All they would see was footage of one of Finn's other tours. She was as good as invisible.

Although she *did* catch one of the tourists, a well-dressed man in his late twenties, tilting his head and looking at her strangely, scowling, with glittering sea-green eyes. A conch shell hung at his belt. Had they met before? Doubtless he thought her odd, waving at the cameras as if fame-starved. Normal people ignored them.

"Note the green sheen on the stalactites above the entryway. When this temple was still in use, its guardians would grow bioluminescent fungi on them to ward away would-be thieves. Or perhaps unsettle them enough to make them easy targets. A superstitious lot, they were. When these caves were discovered a few clicks from Atlantis, we found over a hundred skeletons in it, either intruders or sacrifices." Finn's dorsal spines quivered with excitement as he pointed at clusters of needle-like stalactites. His gill slits fluttered. "Any questions? No? Then let us continue."

Atlantis had another name in the native tongue of the Neeri, but to encourage inter-planetary tourism, the Tethyean government had re-branded everything: "I ♥ Atlantis" had a much better ring to it than "I ♥ Eurynomos." The older merchandise in the city-wide gift shops were all collectors' items now, but Lena wasn't a collector. There was only one item she wanted: the trident. After a treasure hunt of an intergalactic scale, she'd finally tracked it down. It was here, she could feel it. *Not at the university. Not in the museum. Here, in the Temple of Nethuns.*

Tucked away in an air-filled cavern, the Temple of Nethuns was only accessible via a maze of winding coralline tunnels. There were no detectable currents inside the tunnels, no sense of up and down. Just cold, never-ending darkness. On the shuttle ride there, Finn had said that since the temple's discovery, there'd been over two hundred and sixty disappearances, both humans and Neeri. As such, it had been given the Grim Reaper warning sign, which they'd adopted from Terran divers. Every single missing diver had drowned — even the Neeri, who respired equally well through their gills or vascularised swim bladders. Consequently, visitations now required an official guided tour, and permission was difficult enough to obtain as an offworlder. So unless she stole the trident today, Lena would have to return solo. And despite her strong swimming ability, affinity for water, and internal GPS system, she distrusted caves. They reminded her too much of her uncle's place.

Lead on, Macduff, she thought.

As Finn opened an airlock with a keycard, Lena wondered how many people had tried to move the trident before they'd learned the hard way that it was a bad idea. Eurynomos — Atlantis, now — had been the epicenter of more earthquakes than any underwater city on Tethyea. And drownings, of course.

She squeezed past the guide, bumping into him with an apologetic smile as she stepped into the temple proper. Nothing of value in his pockets. While waiting for the others, she followed the vaulted arches with her eyes and tried to determine whether there was a pattern to the tiles on the ceiling. It arched so high, you wouldn't know you were hundreds of metres underwater. A silver trickle raced down one of the arches and escaped through its base. Traces of algal moss lingered there despite obvious cleaning attempts. The air was thick with moisture, and Lena's skin tingled. The other tourists were panting. Sweat stains darkened their armpits. Their puffy red faces shone, reminding her of raw salmon.

Finn, however, seemed perfectly content, his wide mouth split into a fishy grin. *Probably humid enough for him to breathe through his gills!* Lena thought. The Neeri paused in front of a seven-foot tall marble statue. Completely intact and fully painted, it seemed untouched by time, unlike its stark-white counterparts housed in Terran museums.

"It's near-miraculous, actually," he gushed. "With the saline air, you'd have expected mould or algae to have at least taken hold, like in the mosaic we saw, but it's pristine. The paint has neither chipped nor faded, insofar as we can tell."

It was, she assumed, meant to be a likeness of Nethuns, but she could see where the Neeri had imposed their own features on the statue. Its turquoise skin was flecked with green, akin to patches of scales. Its lips were wider, its eyes rounder, and its nose — it was as if the artist had not known what to do with it! Lena was suddenly reminded of a unicornfish. Her father would laugh if he saw this.

"An Eridanos," Finn said with a nod, as if that explained everything.

Then she spotted the trident. The statue (Lena refused to refer to it as Nethuns) clutched it in its right hand. Or so it seemed at first glance. The golden artifact was actually leaning against the curled fingers. A tenuous hold; it didn't belong there. A careful hand could slide it right back out again. She stepped toward the trident, transfixed by the jewelled nautilus shell embedded below the prongs.

Something gurgled behind her.

"Excuse me," said her tour guide, waving frantically. The

webbing between his fingers splayed out like a fan. "Please refrain from touching the statue. The oils on your hands..."

"My apologies," murmured Lena as she returned to the group, but that fishhook lodged in her heart twisted as they exited into a side chamber. Her head thrummed, as if she'd put a conch shell on each ear and the ocean had flooded into her thoughts. Sea salt permeated her nostrils.

I'm not leaving here without it. The words erupted in her mind like a geyser. *I won't get this chance again...Not in this century.* Coins glimmered on the floor around her, but she wasn't interested in such petty things. Let the Neeri have what belonged to the Neeri, and Nethuns what belonged to Nethuns.

Lena drifted to the back of the group. They paused at a copper horse statue untouched by oxidization. Finn's butchery of the Neeric myth made her shake her head. Horses that size weren't even native to Tethyea! They'd been brought by Terrans long ago — the native equines were only slightly larger than a dog, useless for working or riding. Anyway, according to the real story, Nethuns didn't create horses but seahorses in his quest to woo the lovely Anemone, the Neeric goddess of aquatic fauna and flora. Nobody told the stories right anymore; she'd learned them on her father's knee. Still, she supposed it was a miracle they contained as much fact as they did.

The man with the sea-green eyes was scowling. He too, then, knew the real version of the myth. Lena's stomach churned, an eddy of unease. Something about him struck her as familiar. Had she seen him on the same ship to Tethyea, or perhaps the shuttle from the aerodrome's hotel?

When Finn began talking again in that excited manner of his, barely acknowledging his audience's existence, Lena slipped away. Her slippers muted her footsteps. Back in the cella, she gave the statue one last pitying glance before wrapping both hands around the trident. Beads of moisture dribbled down the grooved shaft. She slid it free of the statue's grip, careful not to snap off so much as a thumb. Her fingers warmed, and soundlessly the trident shrank until it was the size of a pendant, as she knew it would.

Snippets of Finn's voice continued to carry into the room. So he hadn't discovered her absence yet. Good. She then hooked a gold chain around the prongs of the miniaturised trident and clasped it around her throat.

It even matches my earrings. How lovely. Everyone would simply believe she'd had a pendant all along, if they even noticed. Nobody would believe the truth. *And that's just the way I like it.*

Her objective completed, Lena tiptoed back to the tour group. On the edge of the semi-circle of tourists stood the strange man who kept staring at her, but he wasn't focused on the guide. Instead, he was turning his head, watching for something.

A minute later, Finn announced their relocation to the next room. Quiet as a cuttlefish, Lena stalked behind her mark as the tourists bottlenecked in the doorway. Amid the jostling of elbows and hips, she slipped her fingers into the man's bulging back pocket and procured a communicator.

How had security not confiscated this? A breath later she almost laughed — there wasn't even a passcode. Within seconds she had accessed his information. It was odd that most of his files were in Ancient Greek. But if it was a code to keep people out, why not at least password-protect the device?

Curiouser and curiouser.

She pondered what she had learned. He signed all his emails with the alias "Triton." He'd contacted the museum to arrange a tour only a day after Lena had landed. His interplanetary flights were the same as hers. Recently he'd purchased an apartment on Tethyea. In Eurynomos, to be precise. An odd place to live for a human, even if the city was encased in a waterproof dome.

When they stopped again, Lena tapped Triton on the shoulder. "You dropped this," she said. He didn't even thank her.

Then she sidled to the front of the crowd. Once Finn had finished his spiel, she asked a poignant question about the artifact before them, as if she had never left. The guide smiled at her, the inquisitive lover of art, but she caught the strange man — Triton — looking her way. If he'd been scowling before, he was glaring

15

now. He certainly hadn't noticed his pocket being picked; her touch was so light that sometimes her father joked she had ties to Hermes somewhere on her mother's side. This man had no reason to look so affronted.

Let him be affronted, then. I got what I came for.

Now all that remained was the getaway. Easy as ambrosia.

"And that, my land-loving friends, is the end of the tour." They passed under an archway and back into the cella now, not far from the statue. "Once we return to the museum, you will find yourself in the gift shop..."

Someone grabbed Lena's shoulder and pulled her backward. A gruff voice said, "Where is my trident?"

"Let go of me," Lena said, "or I'll scream." The currents in her mind whipped into a frenzy of thought. She knew that voice! Turning, she stared through the illusion at the man: yes, those were gill slits on his neck, and the hand on her shoulder flickered between human and crustacean, but the guise was convincing. "And it isn't *your* trident. Just because Dad didn't choose you for this assignment doesn't mean you can hijack it. You're as lazy as a remora, scavenging another's leftovers. All your years of life and you still don't know how to haul your own catch."

So much for a quiet escape. Damn him to Hades. Older or no, Triton was *not* going to one-up her in front of her dad.

"I am not bringing it to Father. It is my inheritance, and I have waited long enough for it!"

"Don't make me call down the wrath of Poseidon." To prove her point, she clutched the tiny trident and pointed it at him. Her fingers warmed. Water jetted from the prongs, slamming Triton in the abdomen. He crumpled to the ground and went still. Sympathy stabbed her like a fish fork. Yet she rearranged her expression into a scowl and fled to the cella.

Dad should have warned me.

"Sorry," she said to Finn, who was waiting by the airlock. "I just had to get one last glimpse of that mosaic..."

"Don't worry. We're still waiting on one other individual."

Dammit, he's not going to leave without every tourist, is he? Lena suddenly wished she were silver-tongued like some of her cousins. Triton would not be incapacitated for long, and when he came after her — which he would, if he'd pursued her this far — he wouldn't care if a shuttle of humans drowned. They were just blips on the radar. Collateral damage.

An idea came to her.

"I can't...breathe," Lena said as she stepped through the airlock to the docking bay. Emulating hyperventilation, she took noisy, shallow sips of air. Tears welled up in her eyes. She collapsed, as if her legs had given way. Sobs burst from her lips. One of the women helped her back to her feet. Seizing the tourist's arm, Lena dug long fingernails into her skin.

"The walls are closing in. The temple's going to collapse on us. We're all going to *die!*" Lena shrieked in the sharp, woe-filled style of a harpy.

The woman shoved Lena away and rubbed her arm. "No way am I getting on board with her," she proclaimed, pointing to the tiny half-moons in her skin. Several other tourists murmured in assent. Finn appeared on her side of the airlock, wringing his webbed hands.

"We paid for a full tour," snapped one of the men. "I'm not having it cut short because some girl didn't consider her claustrophobia beforehand. When we get back, I *will* complain—"

"Sir, this *is* the end of the tour—"

"If I didn't come I'd fail the course," Lena wailed, drowning them out. "But I need out of here!"

She screamed again, this time clinging to Finn, fish-breath and all.

"Don't panic, miss. If you can hold on, we'll send a team in to—"

"I need to get out *now!* I'm going to suffocate!!"

Take the bait, fish boy.

After another six seconds of Lena's pseudo-panic, Finn

relented. "Okay, okay," he said, his webbed fingers splayed over her forearm. "Come with me. I'll take you back to the museum and call for a separate shuttle to pick up the others. Is that all right?"

The tourists nodded stiffly. Lena sniffed and wiped the tears from her eyes, although she continued the hyperventilation charade. The two of them boarded, and as the vessel slipped beneath the water, she relaxed, or tried to.

"You seem calmer now," Finn observed a few minutes into the journey. "Are you feeling better?"

Lena hadn't planned on making conversation. "I hate caves. At least in here I can breathe easier." Lies, lies, and more lies, but what could she do but add to the murky thickness of the deception? *Actually, Finn, my half-brother has been stalking me so he can steal something from me that I stole from you, which your kind stole from my father...*

Behind them glowed the docking bay, but ahead was near-darkness punctuated by stalactite shadows that revealed themselves only when the shuttle's headlights shone on them. It was wrong to use Finn's gullibility in this way, but with Triton so close a threat...

She tapped her foot against the floor, willing Finn to go faster. He likely couldn't — not safely.

Ten minutes into the journey, the trumpeting of a conch shell echoed around them, followed by a low, deep rumble. Triton had regained consciousness. Lena pressed her face against a window. In the dim light, she made out the ripples of a shockwave. Bubbles appeared in a flurry. The water turned milky from the disturbed sediment. Vibrations shook the vessel, and a slew of Neeric curses escaped Finn's mouth.

The rumble became a deafening roar. Keeping in character, Lena shrieked.

"Stay calm. It's just a tremor. We're minutes from the mouth of the tunnel now." The quiver in Finn's voice betrayed his own unease. Earthquakes and the Temple of Nethuns had a deep and dark history.

Something crashed into the top of the shuttle. A stalactite, perhaps, thrust by the violent current that had manifested. Then another. And another — until the cacophony of scrapes became normal. The ship halted; the tunnel before them had collapsed in on itself.

Lena closed her eyes and pictured the ocean around them, let its energy seep into her. You might be older and more powerful, Triton, but I'm ten times as clever.

It was Triton's anger churning the water, agitating it. In a battle of wills, Lena lacked the strength to combat him. The ship scraped against the rough sides of the tunnel, thrown like a child's toy. Finn lifted his hands. "We're stuck. I'll turn us around and head back. I'm so sorry, Lena. You must be terrified."

The conch horn sounded again. Finn jumped in his seat.

Lena ignored him and placed one hand on his scaly shoulder, the other on the shuttle wall. In front of them, the tunnel seemed to grow, the rocks becoming larger. A passage opened up where a crack had been before. To Triton, their presence would be as insignificant as a minnow. It would be as if they'd disappeared. The vessel groaned, and she strained to hold the transformation in place. Mundane objects were not meant for such things.

"Don't ask. Just go," she said between clenched teeth.

And Finn did. Quiet as a cuttlefish.

"Don't go back to the museum," Lena said as they left the tunnel. "Take me directly to the surface." The sooner she got off-planet, the better. She wanted to put as much distance between her and her half-brother as possible.

"I—"

"Listen, fish boy," she said, faking the malice in her voice. She took off the necklace and expanded the trident to its full length. "Either navigate me to the aerodrome, or I'm going to turn you into a fish kebab, understand? Now drive."

She positioned the trident near Finn's gill slits, which began to flutter. The Neeri's eyes were so wide she thought they would burst. At the threat or the trident, she wasn't sure which. Oh, how she wished she didn't have to threaten anybody! But she had a ship to catch back to Earth. It didn't matter now if Finn knew of the trident. Speed was imperative. There wasn't another ship going by that solar system for a month, and she'd known timing would be tight before all of this.

She prodded him until he adjusted their course. "The government will track you down," he said calmly. "They're not going to just let you take a priceless artifact. Your civilian number, your residence — everything from your ID chip, we have a record of."

"As far as the government is concerned, I don't exist," said Lena. *And neither does Triton, likely.* As if she'd be stupid enough to use her real identity, her real home coordinates, during registration. Not that anyone would believe her if she told them. "And it doesn't belong to you anyway!" *Or Triton, whatever his delusions or desires.*

They reached the surface without incident. After shrinking the trident back to pendant size, Lena thanked Finn, who muttered something about liability.

As she made her way to the check-in counter, she smiled. When Triton blocked the passageway, he'd trapped himself inside, too.

The ride to Earth went smoothly and without incident, although Lena did receive several compliments on her jewellery. In the ship's restaurant, she took great satisfaction in cracking the shell and claws of the lobster she ordered. She billed the meal to her father. He owed her that, at the very least.

She hailed a cab as soon as the ship docked in Earth's aerodrome. Once home, she ripped the trident from her necklace.

Glaring, she threw it on her father's nacre desk, where it returned to its original size and pushed a stack of papers onto the floor. She didn't care that her blouse was stiff with sea salt or that her hair resembled Medusa's serpent locks. Let him see the trouble she'd gone through to get the darned thing.

Lena took a deep breath.

"Next time get one of your other bastards to run your errands," she snapped. "It's not like picking up your dry cleaning or mailing a package. Triton's got a chip on his shoulder the size of the Pacific. Honestly, what's the deal with you guys? Don't you have enough toys to go around without squabbling over an oversized fish fork?

"And would it kill you to drop a line to Mom now and then? A holochat. A voice call. An email, at least — it doesn't have to be a Homeric epic. Gods in Olympus, Poseidon, you're immortal! Take a couple of minutes."

The only difference between gods and boys is the size of their toys, Lena thought. Perhaps she'd go spelunking in Tartarus with her uncle, or enjoy a lovely picnic lunch with her aunt in the Elysian fields. She also had a voucher for a private ferry ride from Charon.

Anything to avoid being a delivery girl again.

TIES THAT LIE

BY TIFFANY WOODBECK

Her arms skimmed through the air. Over her head, around her body, her hands bent and turned in a graceful flow. She closed her eyes, letting her chest expand and deflate in a rhythmic beat. The plants surrounding her faded to the edge of consciousness while her feet slid across the cobbled walkways of her garden.

Estiel became aware of another presence, and she slowed. Her eyes landed on a young man, just over a year younger than her eighteen years. They shared the same high cheekbones, rounded chin, and thin eyebrows hovering low above their almond shaped, light brown eyes.

Raising her hands, she fixed the tie securing her hair. The odd shade of black held light auburn highlights—a trait found only in the royal household of Shandjal. She hid the sudden unease within her chest with an unfeeling smile. "Gaebrel, do you need something?"

His expression slipped into a narrow-eyed, smirking demeanor, vanishing as fast as it appeared. "No, Sister. I thought I'd come see what you were up to."

Eyeing him, she grabbed a mug and raised it to her lips. Both hands closed around it to hide all but her steady gaze. "You never stop by just to visit. What is it?"

She barely caught a sneer. "You think you rank high enough on my list for all that? Please."

Without lowering the mug, she stared, unblinking. "Then go away, Brother. I don't have the patience for your attitude."

With a gradual step, his arms hung limp. "And I don't have the patience for yours."

Footsteps sounded from the entrance to the garden, and another young man appeared. Luka and Gaebrel looked almost identical, though Luka shared his birthday with Estiel. His lips pursed when he spied their little brother. "Are you bothering our sister again, Gaeb?"

He flashed a smile that held no evidence of his earlier animosity. "We were merely talking."

Sighing, Estiel refrained from rolling her eyes. "Leave, Gaebrel. I don't want you in my rooms, let alone my garden."

"Ouch. Such a thing to say to your sibling."

Luka shifted to stand in front of him. "If there's no purpose for you being here, remove yourself, or I will."

A laugh met his words. Gaebrel wiped a tear from his eye, waving vaguely as he walked away. "You're both so sensitive. See you at dinner."

Estiel muttered beneath her breath, sighing when Luka enfolded her in a hug. "Thank you."

"Don't let his antics bother you, Esa. He's a rotten brat."

Through the humor in his words, she caught the slightest hint of anger. Pulling away, she drew in a breath. "Was there a reason you came by, or do I get the heir to the throne to myself for a while?"

The corners of his eyes crinkled. He shook his head. "I was sent to tell you Father wishes to see you."

Something in the way his body shifted made her frown. The tone of his voice betrayed nothing. "Whatever for?"

"You know how Father is. He wants to tell you himself." He stepped back and turned, pausing. "He wants you to freshen up and dress to greet. I'll see you later, Esa."

A frown formed as he disappeared into her receiving room. Glancing at her dirty, simple attire, Estiel obeyed the king's command.

◆ ◆ ◆

Estiel stepped through a set of wooden doors, engraved with ornate decorations and gilded in flakes of silver and gold. A guard closed the door behind her. She let her silken skirts swish around her legs as she crossed the floor. Beside a bay window stood the king, who turned at her approach. With a quick, inspecting gaze, King Gaebrel Evantriel I smiled.

"Estiel, thank you for coming so quickly."

Smiling, she wrapped her arms around his neck. They parted before she spoke. "Of course, Father. What did you want to speak to me about?"

She hid a frown as he swept a hand through his greying hair.

He only does that when he's nervous, she thought with a mental sigh.

"As you are aware, we have a few noble families staying in the palace."

Oh no.

Despite her stiffened reaction, he continued. "A powerful family has extended an invitation for betrothal to their eldest son."

With a deep breath, she shifted, hiding her expression with her hair. "I see. Which family, Father?"

The following pause left a tingle running between her shoulder blades. "The invitation came from Duke Shol."

Every muscle hardened. When she forced herself to speak, her words emerged tightly controlled. "Have you accepted?"

A sigh floated between them. "Estiel." He waited until she turned, shaking his head at her blank expression. "I know you and Alken have had your differences, but you must be aware of your position. As a princess of Shandjal, your duty is to the stability and wellbeing of this kingdom."

She winced as she nodded. Her hands clutched each other. "I understand. 'Differences' is a mild term though, Father."

Pursing his lips, he grasped her shoulders. "Marriage within the royal household is rarely what we would wish. Now, he will be here any moment. Lift your chin and be gracious, as befits a daughter of House Evantriel."

Estiel closed her eyes, then gazed out the window where an expansive city sprawled in a spiral toward the East. With each rotation, the city of Djalen lowered into a valley. Their elevation gave a clear view of the outer wall and the vast forest beyond. She remained still despite her urge to move, despite her need to calm her nerves.

When the door opened, she froze. Under the watchful eye of the king, she turned to greet the man she would marry.

Alken Shol crossed the distance between them. Performing a shallow bow, he offered a genial smile. He ignored the way his fine burgundy hair drifted around him. It settled around the base of his ribs. "Good afternoon, Your Majesty."

Lines wrinkled the areas around the king's eyes. "Good afternoon, Alken. You've met my daughter, Estiel."

"Of course." His eyes caught her own. Varying shades of blue and grey streaked through them. Bowing, he grasped her fingers to place a light kiss upon her knuckles. She smiled, doing her best to hide the unease growing in her chest. The relief when he released her almost slipped out in a sigh.

"I'm sure your father discussed this with you. It will be announced publicly at the next open court." At a nod, he crossed the room to his desk, retrieved a small stone, and stepped up beside them. The king linked their hands together, placing the stone in Estiel's upturned palm. A low aura of energy encompassed their hands. It sent a glow of warmth to spread up her arm. Their eyes connected; neither showed more than a polite mask. Her father let his hands drop, leaving a chill to rest between them. "Estiel, daughter of House Evantriel... in the Fates' name, I proclaim your betrothal to Alken Shol, heir to the Sholdrea Dukedom."

A cold trail of sweat trickled down her spine. The brief, traditional ritual brought her spirit to an abrupt halt. Still, she spoke as Alken slipped his other hand into hers. Her lowered voice held a smooth lilt. "I look forward to joining our two families."

"As do I." Again, he lifted her hand, his lips lingering. The energy around the stone encompassed their hands and a charming air drove the neutral expression from his face, nearly throwing her off balance. She could not keep her eyes from widening at his next words. "Perhaps we should let your father return to his duties and take a walk through the gardens?"

Staring at his sharp, elegant features, she inhaled and murmured a reply. "If it would please you, I would gladly accept your invitation."

Her father's approval radiated from him. Relief entered his voice as he took the stone from them. The warmth immediately vanished when it left Estiel's skin. "I'm glad your betrothal will start with a moment to get to know one another. We will speak more later." Placing a gentle kiss on Estiel's forehead, he moved away to sit at his desk.

Dismissed, she braced her resolve and allowed Alken to lead her from the room.

Thoughts flooded her head. She strode alongside him until they stepped through a huge, arched doorway. Plants rose all around them; ferns, flower bushes, and various small trees lined the pathways of the palace garden. He said nothing as they navigated the paths, only stopping once they reached an out of the way, neglected alcove.

Releasing her, he stood in front of a wild, thriving growth of tulips. One rested in his palm. "So, you are to be my bride."

Any semblance of her amiable nature left her expression. Her gaze drifted, settling on a fern overgrown with weeds. She answered with an uncaring tone. "It appears that's what was decided."

Before she realized he had moved, his hand gripped her wrist in a painful hold. She landed against his chest and stared into cold, unfeeling eyes. His burgundy hair framed their faces, revealing one blood-red diamond earring swinging beneath his left ear. Her irises frosted over, flicking to the earring as his gaze narrowed. "I don't care who your father is. You will show nothing less than the utmost respect."

Estiel stumbled, released with enough force to push her back. Holding her wrist, her words held a sweet, biting cadence. "Whatever you say, future husband."

The glint in his eyes sent a shiver up her spine. "Careful, Estiel. You might be the beloved princess, but I have purpose and power in this kingdom. And once you are my wife, you will be mine."

There was no malice, no anger, no emotion. He spoke the warning as fact alone. Her mouth stretched to the side, giving away nothing more than he had. "I know how marriage works, Alken." She silenced the rest of what ran behind her eyes, dropping her hands to her sides.

"Good. I have work to do." Without another word, he strode past her, leaving her to stare at the tulip he had held moments before.

Estiel's eyelids slid shut. A tiny smirk lifted the corner of her mouth before she followed in his wake. Whispered words fell around her. "You aren't the only one with purpose and power."

A day passed, and the sun shone high in the sky. Hair streamed behind Estiel, mingling with the mane of her dappled brown mare. They worked their way around an obstacle course within the palace walls. The princess felt her features flush as they leaned and turned, jumped and dodged, going through at a speed that caused the stable hands to chew their nails to nothing.

Their concern, though welcome, was unnecessary. She had to murmur a single word, or give a subtle command with her knee, and Maaji performed whatever she wished.

Laughing, she slowed Maaji at the end. Her chest heaved as heavily as her mare's sides. She enjoyed the momentary breeze easing the heat in her body as her feet hit the ground. Frazzled hair settled around her.

A shrill whistle brought her attention to a woman who, dressed in riding leathers, stood near the outer fence. Estiel led her horse over to her.

"Mother." Breathless laughter threaded through her words. "Did you come out for a ride as well?"

Light chuckling answered her, but Istrella Evantriel shook her shoulder length, curly red hair. "Yes. Oh, Estiel... my wild child." She reached up, smoothing Estiel's hair behind her ear. "You've always had my penchant for getting your blood racing. Come. You can walk Maaji while we speak."

"Of course." After a moment, she glanced at her mother, walking beside her. "Have you been to see Haithen? He asked for you when I left my magic theory lessons."

She blinked, glancing from the corner of her eye. "The royal sorcerer? No." Turning her head, she did not quite hide the way she pursed her lips.

They strolled around the outer edge of the course. When they reached a distance out of the way of prying ears, Istrella spoke. "Esa, did I ever tell you how your father and I became betrothed?"

Ah, that's why she wants to talk, Estiel thought.

Aloud, she kept her voice upbeat, her eyes trailing the fence. "I don't think you have."

"It isn't surprising. In this kingdom, women tend to be silent, or are silenced. Such matters are deemed too unimportant for social chatter." Silence met her words. She laughed. "At any rate, I was the youngest daughter in the Garol family, holders of the Garoldrae estate. My father, Barlen Garol, had five children."

"Duke Garol is your father?" Estiel fell silent. When she spoke, her mood had subdued into a fiery curiosity. "The dukes are all members of the king's counsel. I'm surprised I haven't heard this before."

"You know how marriage works, dear. When a woman marries, she severs all ties to her maiden family. It has been our way throughout history. It is the Patron Fates' design. Erah, the Patron Fate of Loyalty, spoke Their doctrine, as given to Her by Aelan, the Patron Fate of Guidance. In His infinite wisdom, He set the way."

"I know, but..."

"I had one sister, Idjora. When we were both of marrying age, our father brought us to the palace. I took any chance I could to be outdoors. At the time, your father was a rowdy young man. He and I met in this obstacle course. I was filthy from riding in the rain. He came along, on his way to sword training, and stopped when he saw me. With our fiery personalities and shared interest in the outdoors, we seemed to be a good match."

Her next words made Estiel halt.

"We hated each other."

"What?"

The surprise on her face brought a bubbling laugh from Istrella's core. "It's true. We may have been similar, but perhaps too alike. Our egos clashed immediately. And..." She closed her eyes, lowering her head. "Oh, no matter. The rest is in the past." Beaming, the queen reached out to grasp her hands. "Estiel, No matter how bleak the marriage may seem to you now, it may turn into a hidden gem. Alken is well connected. You will need that in the future." With that enigmatic comment, she strode off at a healthy pace, beckoning.

Wondering at the glimmer in the queen's eye, she complied. Neither spoke of marriage again. By the time they reached their beginning point, their laughter echoed beyond the open spaces.

The horse beneath her shifted with a steady gait. Estiel gazed at the sturdy wooden houses towering around them in the middle district of Djalen. Beside her, Luka rode his grey stallion. Maaji whickered and pranced, drawing a chuckle from her rider. She patted her neck as she glanced at her twin, raising an eyebrow when she found him watching her.

"You and Maaji have your own language, Esa."

Laughing, she let it fade. "I don't see your horse misbehaving."

"That isn't the same thing. He's been well trained. Your mare acts more like a close friend than a trained steed." Amusement grew in his expression as she rolled her eyes.

Changing the subject, she winked. "Are you ready for today's open court?"

"I've been handling them for two years now, since Father handed them off to me." He paused, glancing back at the contingent of guards. Alken rode among them, feigning interest in the ramblings of an elderly soldier. Not far in front of them, their little brother waved at the people they passed. Luka met her eyes again. His had sobered, but showed none of the unease she felt from him. "Are you ready?"

Estiel grimaced, taking care no one would see. "I'll never be ready." She cleared her throat, forcing her demeanor into a brightened one. "Maybe the news will sway the public into ignoring their woes for a week."

"One could hope."

They shared a laugh. The conversation died as they approached the center of the district. A large swath of the giant spiral cleared out to provide a rectangular market. Stalls lined the street on either side. Fresh bread scented the air, and bolts of cloth added color to the otherwise undecorated area. Semi-precious stones, incense, and clay pottery took up multiple vendors. The walls built behind them allowed a light breeze to filter down as they approached a raised stage. Soldiers took charge of their mounts, and the twins took their seats with Gaebrel and Alken on either side of them.

As the crowd gathered, Estiel watched Luka lean to the side, murmuring to Gaebrel. A smile was his only response. Luka hid his exasperation, standing to address the townspeople. His voice rang through the area and everyone fell silent.

"Good people of Djalen—before we begin, we have an announcement." Pausing, the people waited attentively as he turned. Estiel rose, followed by Alken. "In the king's infinite wisdom, two of our kingdom's greatest houses will be joined in the coming years. Princess Estiel and Alken Shol have been promised to one another through the bonds of matrimony."

Cheers sounded as the two stepped forward. They raised their linked hands high. When the noise died, they took their seats, and Luka continued.

"Your congratulations are much appreciated, beloved people of Shandjal. More news will be announced when the date draws near. For now, I am sure we have much to discuss." Reclaiming his seat, he sat tall and scanned the faces below. "As always, we will do our best to hear every concern. Please wait your turn to help keep this orderly and efficient. Will the first party approach?"

The first hour passed without incident. Luka listened to complaints and ruled, paying heed to his siblings' and Alken's advice. Halfway through the second hour, he stood, thanked the crowd, and bid them return the next week.

A high pitched, frantic voice reached his ears. "Wait, please! Prince Luka, what about the murders?"

Three voices from the crowd yelled for her to be silent, but he held up a hand. Silence descended. His eyes landed on the woman who spoke. Her red hair lay in a mess. Shadows claimed her green eyes, which sank into her skull. The other three nobles watched the woman closely. He spoke with a kind, firm voice.

"What murders?"

Relief swept across her dirty features. "There've been murders in the streets. My husband... No one will listen!" Her face disappeared behind her hands. Stepping down from the stage, Luka took her shoulders in his hands. Estiel stood behind him, compassion saturating her expression.

"What's your name?"

Slowly, she dropped her hands, disbelief warring with hope. "Jora, Your Highness."

His smile allowed her to relax a tiny amount. "Jora, I will listen." Glancing up, he searched the myriad of faces. "Perhaps in a more private location. A coach will bring you to the palace so we may speak."

"Thank you, Prince Luka. I didn't know what else to do, who else to..."

Tears welled up again. Estiel led her to a waiting coach. Settling her inside, she murmured encouraging words before retrieving her horse. For a brief second, her eyes connected with Gaebrel's, whose expression fell into a troubled mien. They looked away, mounting for the ride back to the palace. Alken rode beside her, though they did not speak.

To Estiel's relief, she was not included in the conversation with Jora after their return.

Three days passed without another word about the murders. By the second day, in the brief moments she spent with her twin, shadows dug beneath Luka's eyes. On the third, lines pinched his mouth and eyes.

She sought him out near the end of the third day. He stood in their father's office, leaning over the desk. His brow furrowed in concentration. Papers lay strewn about. With a light touch on his arm, she gazed at his haggard features when he blinked up at her.

"Esa, what are you doing here?"

Pursing her lips, she shook her head. "I worry about you, Luka. You need to rest. Eat something."

Without warning, his arms encircled her in a tight embrace. Her eyes widened and her lips parted as she blinked. "Luka? What's wrong?"

He did not respond. His arms tightened before he gave her enough room to breathe. Slowly, she returned the hug, closing her eyes. When Luka pulled away, reluctance and fatigue slowed his movements. She tried to catch his gaze, which swung back to the desk. His eyelids drooped, and he let out a heavy sigh.

"You should go, Esa."

Her arms crossed, her stance shifted, and she rolled her eyes. "Don't start that, 'This is no business for a woman,' nonsense.

You know me better than that." She softened her tone. "Besides, I might be able to help."

"Esa—"

Estiel waved her hand in the air. "Fine, I won't push you to share. I will push for you to take a break, though. I'm not moving until you agree."

Color returned to his face. He stifled a laugh, shaking his head. "I suppose a break wouldn't hurt. A short one." He peered at her through the corner of his eye. "What did you have in mind?"

She grinned. Winking, she made a shooing motion. "You'll see. Wash up a bit. Meet me at the stables when you're done."

Luka gave a sweeping bow and left the room. Estiel turned her attention to the desk. Two documents sat atop the rest. The contents of one made her core turn to ice. After reading it, her eyes closed, and she sank into the king's chair. Several breaths stuttered in her chest. One hand clutched the cloth between her breasts as the dread deepened.

"Father," she whispered. "You've betrothed me to one of the Sanguine Shadow. The earring was evidence enough, but... Why?"

After composing herself, she rose, smoothed her skirt, and left to change into riding leathers.

Despite her delay, Estiel arrived before Luka. Hopping to sit on a fence post, she kicked her feet as she waited. She grinned when he appeared. With a jump, she jogged toward him. Before he could speak, she grabbed his hand and went to retrieve their horses.

Neither bothered to saddle them. Mounting with ease, they rode past the obstacle course. She shushed him when he went to speak, offering a cheeky smile instead of words. Estiel took them around the side of the palace and weaved through a sudden wall of trees—a forest enclosed within the city walls. Deer and other wildlife lived within their limits. The further they went, the more energy she exuded, allowing her true spirit to break free.

When they stopped to dismount, she murmured and cooed to the horses. They were left to roam free. Turning to Luka, a mischievous smirk appeared. His lip quirked, and he studied her loose posture.

"What are you planning, twin of mine?"

Estiel raised her eyebrows at his exasperation. Without a word, she crouched, leaping to grab onto the lowest branch above them. Her muscles bunched while she pulled herself up, performing a lithe hop to the next branch.

"Come on, slowpoke." The skin beside her eyes wrinkled. "What are you doing down there?"

A sound, half laugh and half sigh, slipped from him. Luka lifted his palms, his voice vibrating with suppressed laughter. "This is a short break?"

She winked and jumped to catch the next branch. "You coming?"

He grinned, her mood infectious. "Okay, but if I catch you, you're in trouble for distracting me."

Laughing, she swung up and let her legs dangle. "Like I'm worried. I was always faster than you."

"That's not how I remember it." Raising his eyebrow, he followed her actions. Estiel gasped and scrambled to her feet by the time he reached the second branch.

He chased after her, further into the canopy, staying close behind until she disappeared around the trunk. When he reached the same spot, she flashed a catty grin. She felt her cheeks flush more at the laugh that burst from his lungs.

"Merciful Fates." Their feet rested upon a floor of wooden planks. She turned to gaze at their forgotten tree house, smiling at the memories it conjured. With a purposeful stride, she bent to avoid the top of the door frame and slipped inside.

Luka followed, sighing. "I forgot about this place. How did you find it?"

Shrugging, she plopped onto a pile of cushions. She closed

her eyes and reclined. "Mother reminded me. She thought it would do us some good to have our secret hideout again."

He dropped beside her. The barest hint of something dark entered his words. "She is wise, our mother."

She cracked one eye open. A pillow flew at his head. "No responsibility talk. That was our first rule, remember? 'No adult stuff.'"

After a small chortle, his expression sobered. "Esa..." When she looked at him, she flinched at his determined mien. He raised onto one elbow. "No matter what happens, I will always be here for you. You know that, right?"

Her eyes snapped to a spot on the floor. A breath parted her lips, and she shook her head. "You know the laws as well as I do, Luka. Once I'm married, we won't be family anymore."

"Laws be damned."

Wide eyed, she met his narrowed gaze. "What?"

"Don't. Not with me. Others might not have caught on to your schemes, but I'm your twin. You're smart, cunning, and lethal if you would choose to be." Leaning forward, his voice softened. "I know you want to change the laws we've held since our ancestors settled here. And I know why."

She ran her fingers through her hair. "Luka..."

"I want you to keep doing what you're good at. Find enough to blackmail the hell out of anyone that matters." He pursed his lips. "If something ever happens to me, promise me you'll do everything you can to keep Gaebrel off the throne. He would destroy our people, our family... our home."

She stared. Then, she giggled. "I should have known I wouldn't fool you." Her gaze dropped to her hands. With a slow blink, she sighed. "I have enough. Plus..." Shock halted her sentence.

Luka blinked. "What is it?"

"Mother knows."

Frowning, he rested his head on his arm. "Knows what?"

"She knows Alken is a member of the Sanguine Shadow, and I'm willing to bet she knows my plan."

His hand slapped against his face, sliding down. "You saw the letter."

The gentle wisp of her laugh preceded a sigh. "The letter only confirmed what I suspected. He's wearing their symbol; a blood-red diamond."

He flashed a sideways grin. "I don't know how you found out about it in the first place. Yes. Mother knows about them and the power they bring to the courts. The Sanguine Shadow serve the king alone. After twenty years of marriage, she was bound to learn about it."

Biting her lip, Estiel's brow furrowed. "She made a cryptic comment—something about my marriage to Alken being a hidden gem."

"Think about it, Esa. If something happens to me and you go through with your plan, Alken would be your consort, and male. They will instinctively turn their focus to him. He was brought up in the Sanguine Shadow... that means he's capable of a good deal of necessary evils."

Estiel could not stop her eyes from rolling. "That might be true." She paused to catch her breath, slowing her frantic heart. "He's as cold-hearted as he is gorgeous. He used to torture and taunt me."

Sadness melted all other emotions from his face. "That was years ago."

"No. He threatened me after our betrothal. He hasn't changed." She cleared her throat. "We can talk about this later. I have food waiting."

He burst into laughter. "You never have listened to rules or demands. This is not a short rest, Esa. All right, but I need to get back soon." Sobering, he sighed. "Promise me you'll do everything you can to force the change. Having a queen reign instead of a king is unimaginable to most."

Biting her lip again, her gaze locked on the door. "I promise, Luka." A long, drawn out stretch lifted her onto her toes. She grabbed a basket and sat with him.

After ten minutes, they put the leftovers away.

He spoke first. "Thank you."

"For what? Making you eat?"

Luka chuckled, sighed, and relaxed against the cushions. "Well, yes. And no. Thank you for being you—my bright, fiery, manipulative twin. It gives me relief to know you stand behind me."

His words froze her in place. Her eyelids drooped. "I won't be able to much longer."

A light laugh, not quite a chuckle, drew her gaze back. His eyes gleamed. He sat up, draping one arm across his knee. "You don't see it, do you?"

"See what?"

"Father betrothed you to a member of the Sanguine Shadow. One day, I will rule. They couldn't deny me access to my twin without disobeying." Pausing, he let a wry smile slip across his lips. "Besides, you're too intelligent to be delegated to running a household. In truth, you are more suited to rule than I."

"I doubt that. You were groomed to take over Father's position. I was groomed to be a good wife."

"But you are so much more."

When silence fell around them, they let it rest. Then, he sighed. "I really do need to get back."

Standing, they exited to descend. As they reached the bottom and whistled for their mounts, Luka turned to Estiel. His smile pulled one from her, as well.

"Don't worry about the marriage, or who you are to marry." He drew her into a hug. "Mother is right. Father's choice might seem like an unfair sentence—Alken's an unrepentant scoundrel, but he isn't an idiot."

She frowned and leaned back to search his eyes. "What does that mean?"

"It means eventually, he'll recognize your worth, and then... Well, the two of you together will be a nearly unstoppable force."

Her lips wilted. "A very pragmatic relationship."

"Show him, if you doubt it."

The serious tone produced a weary, sad frown. She petted her horse's flank as the mare appeared. "Let's get back."

The next day, Estiel moved about the bedecked throne room, her countenance hidden behind an amiable mask. Inside, she wished to escape the gathered nobles and their inane prattle.

As if drawn by an invisible line, her gaze wandered toward Alken. His eyes locked with hers. Somehow, she knew the thoughts running behind them held nothing akin to fondness. Nothing showed on the surface. It did not need to.

The moment passed when another couple approached. A gracious demeanor left none of her true mood on her face.

"Duke Croal, Lady Croal, what a pleasure it is to see you." The couple dipped in slight bows. "I hope your son is doing well. Is he still sickly?"

Kailah Croal sighed, her arm linked with her husband's. Her unremarkable features took on a saddened quality. "I'm afraid so, my dear. Poor thing has another illness plaguing him."

Tulnem Croal twisted his long black mustache between his fingers. "We have done everything in our power to help Terra."

They spoke of inconsequential topics long enough for Estiel to wonder why they lingered. Kailah sighed soon after the thought.

"I suppose we should get to the point."

The duke continued. "We had hoped you might be able to help our son."

All warmth faded from her eyes. "I'm not sure what you think I'll be able to do."

His lips pressed together in a light frown, then parted as he continued to twist his mustache. "You have access to the greatest sorcerer in the kingdom, as well as physicians and supplies. And..." He lowered his voice, his icy grey gaze unwavering. "I know you are privy to well-guarded secrets. Surely there must be something."

"With all due respect, I'm hardly in a position to hold such confidence."

"Perhaps I misspoke. Not privy, then, but cunning enough to have uncovered them."

Her gaze swept to the side, seeing Alken watching her. Her voice dropped further. "I sympathize, but I have no authority in anything that would be useful to you."

"You are aware of the Sanguine Shadow."

Air caught in her chest. "You cannot speak of that here. Nor am I who you should discuss this with. I have no influence in their inner circles."

Before he could protest, she caught sight of her betrothed weaving through the throng. She muttered a hasty farewell and disengaged at his approach. His arm threaded through hers as her face returned to a blank mask. Leading her away, they passed through a door and onto a raised balcony. One other couple spoke quietly. When they noticed Alken and Estiel, they went inside.

She pulled away and moved to the raised railing. Leaning, she stared out across the massive palace garden. He rested against his arms and observed her through the corner of his eye.

"What were you and Duke Croal speaking about?"

Not responding to his mild words at first, her voice emerged in a murmur. "They were just being polite."

"Polite enough to speak for twenty minutes?"

Her hands relaxed their grip on the rail. "They like to hear their own voices."

His far hand snaked over, snaring one of her wrists in a firm grasp. She stared at it, then raised her gaze. "They do not dawdle over nonsense for that length of time. Don't lie to me, Estiel."

"I don't need to repeat every conversation I have, Alken."

He stared until she averted her eyes. His tone dropped. "We will speak of this later." Again, he slipped his elbow through hers and returned to the gathering.

The rest of the night passed uneventfully, and she took her leave before the majority filtered out.

◆ ◆ ◆

Estiel retired to her rooms. Exhaustion pulled her posture forward. She made her way to her washroom, where a steaming bath waited. With a sigh, she took advantage of the luxury.

When she finished, she slipped into an elegant nightgown. A knock sounded as she toweled her hair. Crossing the room, she pulled the door open. Her expression soured before she managed to let it slip into a mask.

"What is it, Gaebrel?"

He ignored her hostile tone, holding his hands out. "I didn't come to harass you. Mother requests you join her in her rooms."

She examined his expression, allowing the silence to draw thin. "Why?"

Gaebrel's shoulders lifted. "She didn't say." The glimmer in his eyes darkened as he held her gaze. "By the way, how's your betrothal going? Alken seems like a nice guy."

Her hand tightened around the door handle. "I thought you didn't come here to harass me."

An amiable grin shifted his features. No hint of darkness remained. "I didn't. It's just a bonus." Turning, he sauntered away.

Pain blossomed in her palm from her tight grasp on the handle, and she closed the door. Purple indentations creased the inside of her hand when she inspected it. A low, grating sound emerged from her throat. She glided toward her room to change.

Within ten minutes, the guards opened the door to the king and queen's chambers. As it shut, her steps faltered. Remnants of a magical field hit her in fading waves. Her chest inflated with stuttered breath. No one sat within the greeting room, nor were they visible through the doorway across from her. Something felt wrong, off, leaving her out of breath. One foot moved, and then the other, until she found a stilted rhythm. Her hand grasped the door frame before she stepped into it.

A strong sense of relief hit at the sight of Istrella standing beside her bed. Only her back showed from her position, but

Estiel could see someone standing past her. Moving closer, she smiled when she saw Luka. His attention was stuck to an object in his hand.

"You wanted to see me, Mother?"

Neither reacted to her presence. Stepping closer, fear sparked inside her chest, anchoring to fester within her heart.

"Luka? Mother?"

Nothing. She hesitated, but forced her feet to walk around them. Her eyes widened. A hand flew to her throat as she took a step back. The other clamped over her mouth, stifling the cry of horror trying to escape.

Alabaster skin shone with a subtle aura. Soulless sclera overtook their eyes, leaving the irises and pupils sickeningly absent. The polished metal disk Luka held had barely left the table. Her attention slid to the side, caught by the gleam of a tiny red gem.

Snatching the diamond from the table, she deposited it in her cleavage. With one deep breath, she pinned her gaze to the oval disk and reached for it. Nothing happened when skin touched metal. Still, she flinched when it slipped into her hand. It fit in her palm, its weight that of solid gold, and left her skin tingling with residual power. A wave of nausea nearly rushed into her mouth when her fingers brushed the skin beneath it. Soft, and so cold. Her twin's flesh gave the right amount of resistance, but the chill spread up her arm. She took a hasty step back. The centimeter-thick disk vanished beneath her breasts.

Without wasting more time, she let loose a horrific shriek. She let the waiting tremors manifest. Both hands covered her mouth while she backed away. Mere moments passed before the guards appeared. One snapped an order to the other, who approached Estiel. His fingertips rested upon her shoulder. She jumped, turning a wild-eyed gaze to him. His hands grasped her shoulders to keep her from fleeing.

"Princess," he said, his eyes boring into hers. "It's all right. You're safe. Let's get you sitting down."

Her eyelids flickered, her gaze snapping to the frozen figures.

The guard grabbed her chin and forced her to look back at him.

"Stop looking. I'm sorry, but you have to leave this room." He turned her, ushering her to a seat in the sitting room.

"But, my brother... my mother! I can't leave them like that." Hysteria bubbled into her voice, though her consciousness watched with a keen eye. One thought, one image, had frozen in her thoughts; the blood-red diamond sitting within her cupped hand. "What happened to them? What's going on?"

The guard's eyes widened. He placed a single finger against her lips. "You mustn't yell. We need to inform the king before others hear of this."

Estiel collapsed in on herself, covering her face with her hands. Part of her became numb, hiding behind her analytical mind. She cried for five minutes as the guards moved around, and she let the noise taper off.

Her thoughts centered around the presence of the gem. This doesn't make sense. The Sanguine Shadow obeys the king. They have no reason to kill the queen or the heir. Nothing could come from that but conflict. And to leave a sign of their involvement in plain sight... They aren't that sloppy.

A slight tingle beneath her breast froze her in place. Her eyes lifted to peek above her fingertips. No one watched her. No one stood in the sitting room. Quietly, she slipped over to the door, wiped her eyes, and escaped into the hall. She drew her spine straight and strode with none of her chaotic emotions revealed.

As she walked the halls, Estiel kept her pace to a respectable stroll. Her hands stayed at her sides, though the urge to check if the disk remained hidden pulled at her arms. She drew a deep breath when her steps slowed to ascend a set of stairs. It wound up, floor after floor, until it leveled onto a stone surface. No door stood in the way, and she crossed the threshold.

For a moment, she gazed up. The roof vanished to reveal the cloud ridden sky, cutting off the light of the moon. Rain escaped while her eyes wandered. It did not reach her, but bounced and slid from an invisible barrier. A soothing, abstract rhythm echoed in her ears. Closing her eyes, she took a moment to listen, to take another breath.

She scanned the room. No airflow moved between the tables and shelves despite the appearance of being outdoors. The moisture remained locked outside, keeping the papers and scrolls strewn about safe from damage.

A noise from across the room drew her attention. Muttered words filtered around the organized chaos. She blinked when a broken piece of wood flew through the air. Another went in the opposite direction. Estiel took one cautious step.

"Haithen." She raised her voice. By some miracle, she kept the tremors from her words. "I need to speak with you."

The muttering popped up behind her, and she spun. Haithen rummaged through the contents of a table as he sighed, shaking his head.

"I know it's here somewhere. Oh, bother. What did I do with that?"

"Haithen..."

He waved one hand in the air. "Yes, yes... What is it, Estiel?" Despite acknowledging her, he continued searching and let loose a string of mumbled curses.

With careful movements, she drew the oval disk from its hiding place. "Can you tell me what this is?"

His eyes snapped to it. A grin split his dry lips. "There it is! You found it!"

Not resisting when he grabbed it, she examined his expression. It transformed from one of joy to a perturbed frown. "What was this for, Haithen?"

"It's been used." Annoyance entered his tone. Skinny fingers brushed the surface, though no debris sat upon it. "This wasn't for you. Why did you use it?"

"Someone else did. Can you tell me what it was for? Were you supposed to give it to the Sanguine Shadow?"

A distracted nod confirmed her suspicion. She could feel her

43

skin paling.

"I didn't have a chance to give it to them." His words emerged quickly in his distracted state. "Now I'll have to make another one."

Relief stole her breath. So, it wasn't Alken. I knew this didn't make sense.

Haithen shuffled his feet and deposited the disk onto a shelf. Estiel followed. "Who could have used this?"

"Oh, anyone, so long as they knew how. It requires a piece of someone—hair, skin, what have you. Once it has that, it rips the soul of one or two close relatives from their bodies. It leaves them empty, cold, when one touches it."

One hand clutched the base of her throat. She gasped, the quiet sound barely audible. "Luka and Mother..."

Again, his expression brightened. "Will Istrella be joining us? Oh, it's such a mess. Come, child, help me tidy up. She always says I'm a messy person. Or was that just a mess? No matter."

She did not argue, stacking papers and placing items on shelves. "Haithen, is there a way to reverse what the disk does?"

"No, no. It's made to rend soul from flesh, but it doesn't store them. They can't return without a sorcerer's focus stone, and by the time one could get there—"

Her tone became urgent, making him pause. "How long would be too long?"

The frown etched beside his mouth made her step back and bite her lip. "It would be too late if the bodies had chilled, child. Now, no more chatter. I need to prepare if Istrella is coming." All annoyance melted away as joy replaced it.

Estiel's eyelids drooped. "Haithen, she isn't coming."

He stopped, not meeting her gaze, and became animated again. Words fell from his lips in a more hurried pace. "It's the king, isn't it?"

"What?"

"The king doesn't like when we spend time together. Not since their betrothal. Jealous man, the king."

It took a few seconds to process his words. Istrella's saddened face flashed through her mind as she remembered their conversation in the obstacle course.

'Our egos clashed immediately. And... Oh, no matter. The rest is in the past.'

A new pang struck her heart. She glanced away, unable to prevent the tremble in her reply. "It isn't the king. She... isn't feeling well."

"Pity." He abandoned his effort to organize. Instead, he pulled a box out from under a pile of random objects. "Look, Estiel. This is my latest experiment!"

About to refuse, she pursed her lips when he brought it closer. The top held a large metal plate, inscribed with numbers and lines at regular intervals. Two thin metal pieces moved at different rates around the circular surface.

"What is it?"

"It's a time keeper!"

"A what?"

"Here, look!" Excitement brightened his eyes. He moved a latch, swinging the top open to lay the insides bare. Clear crystals sat opposite shorter amber crystals. Currents of visible power ran between them. Estiel's eyes widened. The energy brought a gentle glow to the clear, flawless cylinders, arcing to connect each of the same color.

"The magic never runs out with how this is set up. Well, I shouldn't say never. It hasn't run out yet. The bigger ones run the part that gauges single minutes, and the shorter ones gauge the hour. Just think of the good this discovery could do! And not just with telling time. I can see so much more..."

"Haithen." Estiel sighed. "I'd love to listen more, and I will soon. I promise. I have some things I need to take care of."

With a wink, he replaced the box. The jovial words he sang tore a hole through her. "So considerate, indulging a madman and his whims... just like your mother. Tell her I miss her."

She choked on emotion as he disappeared behind a set of shelves. Before she descended the stairs, she retrieved the disk, tucking it beneath her breast.

◆ ◆ ◆

Estiel reached her room and slid to the floor against the door. Not caring how her dress lifted and skewed, she braced her elbows on her knees. Her fingers threaded through her hair as her hands covered her face.

"Luka." She smothered a sob with her arms.

"Where have you been?"

A gasp escaped her lungs. Dropping her arms, she stared up at Alken. He stood ten feet from her. His loose stature matched the unfeeling mien he donned. In a single instant, her body folded back against the door. One hand covered her eyes as she drew in a tremulous breath.

"What are you doing here, Alken?"

"Your father sent me to speak with you."

The tips of his fingers appeared below her hand. She stiffened, pinning his gaze with her own as she slipped her hand into his. With a gentle, guiding motion, he brought her to her feet. Estiel's eyes narrowed before she glanced away.

"What did he send you to say?"

"Estiel." He brushed his fingers beneath her chin, prompting her to turn back toward him. She flinched when she met his piercing eyes. "What did you find?"

"What do you mean?"

Pursing his lips, he let his features relax. "There was magic in that room, and you disappeared the first chance you found." Alken paused. He stepped back, gesturing toward cushioned seats beside a round table.

Surprise made her stare. Still, she followed his silent request. She would not meet his eyes when he took the chair opposite hers. As he leaned his forearms against the table, his hands folded.

"Few would be able to sense the leftover magic. What did you find?"

"I just wanted out of there." She forced her hands to remain in her lap.

"Don't lie to me, Estiel."

46

The slight warning in his words dragged a harsh laugh from her. It turned into a rampant giggle. "Or what? The queen and heir were murdered. Are you going to torture the princess?"

Silence met her question. Without making a sound, he knelt in front of her, and she jumped. Wide eyed, she pressed one hand against her chest.

A sigh slipped from his lips, though no reaction reached his gaze. "I'm not here to hurt you. The king wants to keep the situation quiet. I need to know what you know." He paused. "Unless your father is wrong, and you truly are as foolish as the rest of the women in the court."

Fire sparked in her eyes. Her voice lowered, holding a rough note. "I don't care what you think of me. My brother and mother are dead, and Haithen can't fix what was done." Tears sprang to her eyes, and she blinked them away. "The murderer used something he made for the Sanguine Shadow, and tried to lay the blame on you and yours."

For the first time, she saw shock register in his expression. A hint of darkness flickered in his gaze as he spoke in a low, rolling purr. "How do you know of the Sanguine Shadow?"

"Oh, please." Estiel let her head fall back. "Spare me your derisive views on women. I've been part of the court since I was twelve, and had reason enough to learn what I could about those around me." Stopping, she let her lungs fill with air. Luka's image surfaced behind her falling eyelids.

'...eventually, he'll recognize your worth, and then... Well, the two of you together will be a nearly unstoppable force. Show him, if you doubt it.'

She stood, moving past him. Her feet carried her into her room, where she knelt beside the bed. The hanging blanket flew onto the mattress. Bending down, she reached across the floor, her fingers running over the wooden planks. Estiel pried one of the boards up and grabbed something from the hole beneath it. Rising, she ignored the dirt on her skin, gazing at the ordinary journal in her hands.

Gradually, she held it out to him with a tight smile. His eyes settled on it before they flashed back to hers, accepting it. It closed seconds after opening to a random page.

"This is—"

"It's yours." Estiel sighed. She caught herself rubbing her arm, and she looked away. "I found it when I was fourteen. During one of your visits, you left your belongings unattended while you participated in sword training." Silence followed, and she turned narrowed eyes toward him. "You wanted to know. Now you know."

"Tell me what you meant by, 'They tried to lay the blame' on us.'"

Her shoulders slumped as her anger deflated. One hand pressed against her forehead. Fatigue threatened to drag her to the floor, tears brimming and waiting to fall. She wavered on her feet, but steadied, feeling his hands close around her shoulders. Vaguely, she realized he guided her to the bed. He knelt in front of her.

"What did you find?"

Her hands slipped into the front of her dress, removing the metal disk and tiny red diamond. Tears ran down her cheeks, her pupils constricting as the sight of the items sent a stabbing pain through her chest. Soft, trembling words fell from her lips.

"Luka was holding the disk. The diamond was on the table."

Another moment of silence passed before his hands covered hers. "What did Haithen say?"

Each word she forced out ripped the hole in her chest wider, until she gasped through the explanation. He put the objects in the inside pocket of his jacket, nodded, and stared at the wall.

His next words stopped her rapid breathing.

"I cannot fix the damage, Estiel. They are gone. What I can do..." He waited until her gaze lifted, hesitant and wounded. "I can help you and your father find out who did this."

For a second, her eyes softened. She snapped her chin to the side, allowing her hair to form a curtain between them. "Don't pretend to do this for me. Your loyalties are to the king. You have never hesitated to let me know your true feelings."

"No, I haven't. What makes you think I would care to start now?"

"Because you're a manipulative bastard."

The laugh he emitted made her stiffen, though it held more amusement than malice. "Yes. And, as the king commands, you are to be treated with the respect of your mother before you." He leaned in toward her ear, lowering his voice. "That is nothing to snub your nose at, future wife. Though, I still question your ability to hold such reverence in the eyes of the Sanguine Shadow."

Her hands shot up and shoved his chest without giving herself the chance to think. She put all the force of her upper body into it, leaning her shoulder toward him. Within seconds, they both had risen with his arms wrapped around her. Estiel inhaled a sharp breath and stopped breathing, feeling his breath on her neck.

"Get away from me," she hissed.

Alken said nothing, loosening his arms when she did not resist. He spoke, the murmured words spreading goosebumps down her arms.

"I'm not here to fight with you, Estiel. I'm not a man that will bestow endearments or comfort, but I will not look past what you have shown me this night. To think I underestimated you for so many years..." He pulled back to meet her conflicted eyes. "It will not happen again."

Hushed words met his slow smile. "Why does that sound like a threat?"

"Because you're not as stupid as you make yourself appear."

She stepped back, feeling his arms fall away. The sudden chill nearly brought her arms up around herself. Instead, she steeled her posture and met his unwavering regard. "A very pragmatic relationship, then."

Before responding, he studied her. "An apt description."

With a nod, she turned. "What does Father want to do?"

"He doesn't want the news to spread. Not yet."

Her hands shook, and they balled into fists. "I'm to pretend this hasn't happened?"

"Precisely."

"Is that all?"

"He won't be informing anyone outside of this small group."

Estiel bit her lip, releasing it to glance over her shoulder. "Not even Gaebrel?"

A single blink did not hide the flicker of a reaction. "He believes it's for the best for now."

"By the Fates." Sinking to the bed, her skin drained of color. "Gaebrel is to be heir? No. He can't be."

"I must go. Remember what we spoke of stays between us."

As he left, she stared at his back. The door closed. Her face fell into her palms, and Estiel allowed tears to flood from her eyes.

The next day, she stood in front of her father's office. Stepping past the guards, she shut the door with one hand behind her back. King Gaebrel Evantriel lifted his head. The hollows beneath his eyes matched her own. Slowly, she crossed to lower herself into a chair. Neither spoke, their expressions falling with each passing second.

Finally, she cracked a weak smile. Her voice held a thready quality. "Has there been any news?"

His forehead fell to rest on his hands. Fatigue weathered his words. "No. Still, we must keep up appearances."

"I understand, Father." Pausing, she filled her lungs. "What of the next open court?"

"I need you and Alken to take care of them."

Surprise made her lean forward. "But, won't that have people talking? If Gaebrel—"

"No." His hardened eyes appeared over his hands. "I will not debate this with you, Daughter."

Estiel sat back and straightened her spine. Murmuring, she glanced at the wall. "I wasn't trying to argue. If you wish to keep up appearances, why have me and Alken take those over?"

Covering his eyes with his palms, he sighed. "If we have Gaebrel take over, they will wonder more. No. You have yet to be wed to the Shol family. We will tell any who ask that Luka and Istrella are ill, and physicians have ordered they not be disturbed. Gaebrel will be given other duties."

Silence surrounded them. Allowing her posture to relax, she bit her lip. "Gaebrel will be proclaimed heir, then?"

He did not respond. She risked a glance to see he watched her with keen eyes. Hers widened when he pushed his chair back and rounded the desk.

"Stand, Estiel."

Hesitant, she obeyed, a crease forming along her brow. In one hand, he grasped hers, and ran the thumb of the other across her forehead. Exhaustion kept his features still, his words almost inaudible above her increased heartbeat.

"Listen closely. I had more than the obvious reasons for your betrothal to Alken, my beautiful gem." He continued with a sorrowful gaze. "I know you are aware of the Sanguine Shadow. I've seen you watch those members you know of over the years. I wish you hadn't needed to be as perceptive as you did growing up in the royal court." Leaning his forehead against hers, the warmth of his skin instantly spread to her own. "I should have brought you into this much sooner. Perhaps then we wouldn't be standing here, mourning our loved ones. You saw this coming... you and Luka both."

She raised her free hand to touch the side of his face. Heat radiated from him. "Father, you're burning up. You need to be resting. I'll—"

"Estiel." Commanding words silenced her. "My namesake cannot sit atop the throne. He lacks the traits necessary to rule, let alone the capacity to care about the people. I had hoped for more time to find a solution..."

A hard, stubborn expression slid across her features. She moved her father behind her. "You need to sit."

He did not argue, sinking into the chair as she knelt. Their gazes connected, his lacking energy while hers filled with worry.

"We must move quickly. Simply proclaiming you heir will have consequences. There will be naysayers throughout the country. Luka tells me you have ways to sway the proper people, but that might not be enough either."

Incredulity replaced concern. "You want me to rule?"

The king laughed, the sound hiding some of his vulnerable state. "Those of the inner court would not be surprised, my dear. Your mother often took care of matters I had no time for... on occasion, ruling in my stead."

"Alken said she was revered by the Sanguine Shadow."

"They obeyed her as they did me. It's unfortunate the rest of the kingdom did not see her the same way. It would have made matters easier. With our ways, for them to truly accept my decree, the circumstances would have to be severe."

"More severe than two deaths in the royal family?" Her beading tears blurred her vision.

"We must prove Gaebrel would not be fit to hold the country together. His age is one factor, but that is easily fixed by appointing someone to rule by proxy until he turns eighteen. No." As his voice softened, quiet regret drew her attention to him. "There must be undeniable proof he cannot handle what he must."

Understanding flickered across her face. Her lips parted, and she blinked several times. "You want me to find that proof."

A simple nod left her sighing. She stood. "I'll try my best, Father."

Grasping her wrist, he held her in place. "You and Alken will need to marry sooner than anticipated... by your birthday in two weeks, at the latest." She stiffened, and he closed his eyes. "I'm dying, Estiel. None of this will matter if you marry after I am gone."

Her muscles seized, and she choked while her chest refused to rise. "Father..."

Neither spoke after she threw her arms around him. When her quiet sobs lessened, he pressed one hand to the back of her head. "Considering the situation, no one will be surprised there wasn't a public ceremony. Normally, I would perform it, but... with my health, I believe you should be joined at the hands of the Sanguine Shadow."

Estiel sat up. "Why them?"

The barest smile preceded his response. "Because you must join their ranks for any of my plans to unfold, and their ceremony of joining is powerful. It involves magic, blessings, and will strengthen any bonds between you and Alken."

All color vanished from her cheeks. A fine tremble ran through her. "If this is what you need, what we need, I will do as you ask."

Relief relaxed his muscles. "Thank you, Esa. I know this is sudden, and a lot to put on anyone's shoulders, but I believe in you... just like Istrella and Luka had. I must return to work. Alken will be able to tell you more of what I need from you." Pulling himself to his feet, he returned to his desk. Estiel performed a low curtsy before retreating.

A few hours after sunset, she raised her hand to knock on the door before her. She hesitated, staring at the way her hand shook, and drew in a tremulous breath. Her nerves frayed further. Still, she pursed her lips and rapped against the wood. A voice called from beyond. Opening the door, she raised her gaze as it closed behind her.

Jensen Shol bore a great resemblance to Alken, down to the calculating expression he donned. One hand swept to the side as he bowed, and Estiel accepted the proffered chair. As she sat, so did he, a charming mien shifting his features into a less formidable one.

"Princess, to what do I owe this visit?"

Despite the etiquette driven into her from a young age, she fidgeted, shifting her seat. Her hands smoothed her skirt and rested on her abdomen. Wincing, she forced them into her lap.

"Pardon the intrusion, Duke Shol."

"Not at all. You're to join my family soon, after all."

Her eyes dropped. Again, she winced, meeting his with a wary gaze. "That's what I came to speak with you about."

His face smoothed into a friendly, comfortable mask. "Oh?"

"I..." She blew a breath through her lips as she swept her fingers through her hair. "Have you spoken to my father or Alken?"

He ran a single finger across his jawline, watching her gather her resolve. With a nod, he lowered his voice. "I am aware of the situation. Shouldn't you speak to Alken about these matters?"

She deadpanned. Her eyes held no warmth, though her tone did not change. "I had hoped to learn a little of what must happen before I speak with him. He's not the easiest person to talk to."

A tiny laugh escaped his chest. "No, he's not. He has much to learn about interacting with others. What did you wish to ask?"

"Is it safe to speak freely?" He nodded. "Father said a lot in a very short period. I'm having trouble processing it."

"I think I understand." Leaning forward, he propped his elbows on his knees. His fingers laced together. "You want to confirm the unbelievable course your life is taking, yes?"

Hesitant, she nodded. A wry, almost nonexistent humor crossed his lips.

"Let me see if I can simplify this. You are to be queen— married into the Sanguine Shadow, to keep Gaebrel from the throne in a land that will demand it. To do so, you need to keep your mother and brother's fate undiscovered, and manipulate the court, town, and kingdom into believing they would be better off following a woman."

Swallowing, her dry mouth gave the motion an odd, sticky sound. "I still don't quite believe it. I have no idea where to start. Everything has gotten so complex."

"There are simpler ways to deal with the situation."

Estiel blinked. Her jaw snapped shut. As her eyes narrowed, her fists clenched in her lap, and her voice forced its way through her lips. "I hope you aren't implying I kill my brother, Duke

Shol. We may not get along, but I've already lost two members of my family. And I will not sully my hands needlessly with blood."

His mouth quirked. "Not at all. Your father forbade it, at any rate."

The statement left her mouth agape. Jensen continued before she could recover.

"No, I merely suggest we set up a system of fail safes, in case the kingdom reacts adversely to your ascension."

Relaxing her hands, she inhaled a deep breath. "That would be a wise decision. Shandjal is steeped in its ways. It will be difficult enough to explain how I would be allowed to rule after marrying into another family."

Silence met her words. When she lifted her gaze, he watched her more intently.

"You are a wise woman, Estiel. I can see you take after Istrella, just as your father and brother have said." Rising, he offered a hand. He drew her to her feet, ignoring the wary glint in her eyes. "It is a sad truth that this kingdom suppresses those with spirits made of pure fire. You were not forged in it; no, you were born from it. That is what will make this work. Without you, Shandjal will destroy itself once your brother takes the throne."

"I'm afraid it'll destroy itself out of spite, faced with such a change."

"It will be difficult, no doubt. You have nothing to fear. The Shadow stands behind you, and the framework of the inner court. Alken will instruct you on the ceremony. We must hold it within the week." Pausing, he squeezed her hand when her eyes shifted. "Use this time to learn more about him, as he should with you. I believe you are a good match, despite past differences."

She offered a tired smile. "I'll keep that in mind. Thank you for taking the time to speak with me, Duke Shol."

"Of course. I would not dishonor your mother in such a way."

His words stopped her as she turned. Hesitant, she spoke in a quiet tone. "Was she truly revered?"

"More than revered. She was loved."

Tears welled in her eyes at the sorrow that slipped into his voice. Clearing her throat, she continued. "Thank you."

The tears came when she reached the sanctuary of her garden. Her body sank to the ground, and she wept.

Her lowered eyelids gazed at the tulips before her. They grew in a raised bed, and her fingers brushed a drop of dew from a petal. A sigh fell from her lips.

"Estiel?"

Spine stiffening, she lifted her chin. "Yes?"

Her personal maid hesitated. "Sorry to disturb you. You have a visitor."

"Who is it?"

"It's Alken."

Despite her tension, she forced her muscles to relax. "Show him in. Thank you, Sanja."

She smoothed her silken gown and returned her gaze to the flowers. Another voice sounded, flowing with a gentle, dry note. "You pay more attention to those plants than you do to me." Alken stepped close, his hands resting on her shoulders. "I may begin to harbor a dangerous jealousy."

"Hm," she replied, a tiny laugh stifled behind her lips. "I shall believe your words when they prove to be true." Estiel turned, her amused mask matching his own. It stayed in place until she heard her servant exit her rooms. "To what do I owe this visit?"

A small box appeared in his hand. The lid sat closed, held in place by a ribbon. Without lifting her head, she glanced at him. "What's this?"

"It's a present for my fiancé's nineteenth birthday." He took her hand, pressing it into her palm. "Happy birthday, Estiel."

Alken's words lacked warmth. She gave a polite smile,

speaking in a light voice. "My birthday is nearly two weeks away, but thank you. Will you stay a few moments?"

Silence followed her question. He gestured to the box. "Open it."

Blinking once, her expression smoothed. Her other hand unraveled the ribbon with a single tug. She lifted the lid, her heart racing in her chest. It almost stopped when her eyes beheld a bracelet sitting upon a bed of cloth. As she picked it up, her lips parted, and she let it dangle from two fingers. Small onyx pieces surrounded larger amethyst stones, spanning two-thirds of the silver band. A single blood-red diamond refracted the light in the center.

Words refused to form, her eyes flashing up to his and back again. She slipped it over her wrist and slid her finger across the top. Estiel let her features fall into a somber expression. "This is beautiful. Thank you."

Outwardly, she showed no sign of the chaos in her mind. Thoughts sped faster—screaming for the trees, the wind, anything but the confines of the castle. Images of her twin and mother stuck behind her eyes. Her chin lowered. She turned before her hands started to shake. One hand rose to clench between her breasts. The dread, fueled by the grief she fought to suppress, spiked until she hunched forward. It leaked into her words as she spoke.

"If there's nothing else, we can speak later."

Hm. I think not.

"What?"

His arm wrapped around her, forcing them closer. He rested his hand over the bracelet. With wide eyes, she did not move, staring at his larger hand.

"I need you to come with me."

Drawing in a slow stream of air, she muttered beneath her breath. "Where? What for?"

"Out of the castle, because we must speak. This bracelet is enhancing your innate abilities. It would be best to remove it for now."

What are you talking about?

With a sigh, he stepped around her, lifting her chin to reveal narrowed eyes. "I'm talking about how loud your thoughts are with it on."

As she glared into his neutral mien, panic transformed into fury. She kept still, suppressing the urge to shove him away. Gritted teeth made her angry words almost unrecognizable. "My father wouldn't allow me to leave. Besides, the last thing I want is to go somewhere alone with you."

Alken blinked, raising his eyebrows. "Your father doesn't have to know. Soon, you will reign in his place and make decisions accordingly. Now is not the time for petty grudges."

A single step back left a void between them. Her hand clutched tighter against her chest. She snapped her reply. "Petty grudges? This has nothing to do with a grudge. Along those same lines, I won't simply be your obedient wife. I will be your queen, Alken. Marriage or not, bonded by magic or not, I will not be treated like an errant, air-headed little girl. Your own father treats me with more respect."

"Estiel, the bracelet."

Frustration forced a growl to bubble up her throat. She removed it and thrust it toward him.

"You want to be free of these walls. I'm offering you the chance." He stepped around her. At the entrance to the garden, he glanced over his shoulder. "Come to the royal library in half an hour, if you wish."

When he left, her hands covered her eyes.

Traversing the halls, Estiel fought to keep her expression from betraying her inner turmoil. Despite her efforts, her pace slowed and her features fell.

Fingers slipped around her wrist. Within seconds, they tightened, and she glanced behind her. An automatic mask appeared when she met Gaebrel's gaze.

"Let go of me, Gaebrel." When he did, she turned. A bite slipped into her words. "What do you want?"

"Such hostility where others could see." He suppressed the laugh she saw in his eyes. "I just had a question."

Raising her eyebrows, she relaxed her stance. "What could you possibly want to ask?"

"I want to know what's going on with Luka and Mother."

Estiel froze. Her skin paled. She pursed her lips, crossed her arms, and shifted her weight. "They're ill."

Silence spanned the short distance while he searched her face. "That's what I was told. I don't believe it. You don't either. I can see it in your eyes."

Her eyes thinned to slits. "It doesn't matter."

"I don't believe for a second you'd let them separate you from your beloved twin... not without pushing further."

"This is not the place for this."

"Fine."

Grasping her wrist again, he tugged, tightening his hold as she tried to pull free. She winced, and he opened a door, swinging her through. He closed it behind them.

"What are you doing?"

He leaned against it. His arms and ankles crossed, his eyes pinning her with a chilly stare. "I'm making this more private."

"I don't have anything else I can tell you."

"Like hell you don't. I might not like you—"

"Likewise," she muttered.

"But I know you always have something up your sleeve. You wouldn't let anyone get between you and Luka, even if he had some sort of disease. Especially not then. What's going on?"

She straightened her posture. "It's such a shame. You have one of the most analytical minds I've ever seen, Brother, and you waste it on petty nonsense."

His eyebrow quirked and his lip stretched. The look faded as anger rose. "I see no reason to care enough to use it as you do."

"Not even for your love of our mother?" One hand encircled her wrist, rubbing to reduce the ache. "You care for her, if none of the rest of us. We both received our strengths from her. Does she not rank high enough on your list, either?"

The anger deepened, but his eyes closed. Gaebrel's words emerged slow and deliberate. "Stop dodging the subject. What happened to them?" Silence. He reopened his eyes. "Are they dead, Estiel?"

Her gaze widened. "Why would you think that? Father said they're ill."

With a frustrated sound, he pushed off the door and stalked forward. His face leaned mere inches from her own. "And you accuse me of nonsense. Don't treat me like I'm stupid. Everything stands to change with Luka out of the picture." Baring his teeth at her stony expression, he backed up one step. "I have no interest in becoming king."

At first, she gaped. Then she relaxed. "If that's true, you don't have to worry."

"What does that mean?"

She smiled, though it held little warmth. "It means things are changing. I don't have time to explain. I have a meeting to attend. Step aside."

As she stepped past him, his whispered words stopped her.

"I don't care what you think of me, Estiel. Don't leave me to wonder. They're my blood, too."

Grief shook her hands, and she cleared her throat as it tried to swell. "I'm not supposed to say anything."

"Then I'll ask again, and if it's true, don't answer. Are they dead, Estiel?"

Pain flared within her chest. Lowering her eyes, she reached for the door, exiting the small room without another word.

The encounter with Gaebrel left her breathless. Her pace quickened, and she almost stumbled when she closed the library door.

"Your Highness?"

She jumped, her gaze shooting up to see Sanja reaching toward her. The servant stopped, drawing her hand back.

"Sanja... I'm sorry. I didn't know you were here."

"I asked her here."

Glancing toward the voice, her eyes landed on Alken. He watched her, scanning her posture and expression.

"What for?"

"If you want out of the castle, you need to disguise yourself."

Sanja slipped one hand into hers, placing the other on her shoulder. "Come. It won't take long."

Exhaustion left her compliant. She sat in a cushioned chair for twenty minutes while Alken stepped from the room. Her brown-black hair, held up by a strip of cloth, lay beneath a wig of bright, curly blonde locks. What makeup she wore vanished under Sanja's sure hands. Powdered foundation paled her complexion. Vibrant shades of red and brown brightened her subdued style. When finished, Estiel changed into a simple skirt and blouse, switching her boots to slip-on shoes. A cloak covered it all, and she pulled the hood up around her ears.

Stepping back, Sanja nodded. "I think that'll do."

Estiel accepted a small mirror. Her eyes widened at her reflection. Tiny details made slight changes to her features. Murmuring, she handed the mirror back. "You did a marvelous job."

Sanja winked and ushered her toward the door.

"I'll clean up. Just go."

"Thank you, Sanja."

She stepped through the door. Alken nodded after a quick inspection and motioned for her to follow.

They moved at a decent pace, slow enough to not draw attention. Still, they halted as an older gentleman called out to Alken. Barlen Garol approached, relaxed lines creasing his features. Hints of red shone in his hair as he moved through the light in the hall. Hazel eyes cast a brief glance at Estiel, who lowered her gaze in the presence of the Duke of the Garoldrae estate.

"Alken, I had hoped to run into you. Do you happen to know where Princess Estiel is? I have reason to speak with her."

He spoke without hesitation, his steady words holding a spark of warmth. She knew it would show in his eyes, though it never did for her.

It's true, she thought. He's never hidden his feelings.

The thought did not bring comfort, nor unease. She folded her hands and listened to her fiancé's response.

"I'm afraid not. I was tasked with settling a servant's daughter in with the kitchen staff. What did you wish to speak with her about? Perhaps I can relay a message."

A slight noise within his throat almost drew her gaze, but she forced herself to be still.

"It is a rather... private matter, though I appreciate the offer. I will speak with her later."

Duke Garol bid him farewell. The tension in her muscles released at the narrow escape. Alken continued, leading her to the kitchens. They passed through another door on the far side of the room, descending a dimly lit staircase that exited into a deserted courtyard. Two readied horses awaited them. Mounting, he waited while she adjusted her clothes to work around the saddle. Her scowl warped her demeanor into one of utter discontent. She huffed and muttered.

"Saddles. Unnecessary pieces of junk."

Estiel ignored his stifled laugh. They urged their horses into a walk. The mare she rode was unfamiliar, but had a mild temperament. Nearly an hour passed before they reached the giant outer wall separating the wilderness from the royal forest. She pulled on the reins until the mare stopped. Alken ignored her confusion, dismounting to approach the stone structure.

His hands rose, pressing against the surface. Electricity wound its way through the air to shiver across her skin. Her eyes unfocused, and she saw auras of red light flash around his hands. The stone blocks wavered in her normal sight, then vanished completely. Eyes widening, lips parting, Estiel pulled the horse back. An opening spanned the entire width of the wall, giving a glimpse into the forest beyond.

Unaware he had moved, his voice startled her. Alken held a hand out to her, motioning for her to dismount. A curse fell from her as she struggled with the skirt. He lifted her by the waist to set her upon the forest floor.

Without a word, he secured the horses to a branch, leaving them to graze. She stepped into the tunnel after him, unconsciously holding her breath until they emerged on the far side.

A pair of trousers appeared in the lower corner of her vision. Blinking, she glanced at Alken, who raised an eyebrow. She changed clothes when he turned his back, staring at the way his shoulders bunched while he leaned against the wall, arms crossed in front of him.

"Thank you." She sighed and stretched skyward.

He regarded her as he turned around. "You're welcome."

The bit of relaxation the change had provided faded as he walked within three feet of her. Alken held her gaze, handing the bracelet to her. "You must get used to the effects of this bracelet."

Pausing as she went to put it on, she pursed her lips. "Why? I don't need whatever abilities this would give me. I do just fine on my own."

One eyebrow rose. "It isn't giving you anything, Estiel. It's merely enhancing abilities you already possess."

Estiel frowned, shook her head, and slipped it on. Her disbelief bled into her thoughts.

"You don't need to believe it for it to be true. The fact that you can sense magic is telling. You might not realize you're doing it. You've always been able to sense people's emotions and skim their unprotected thoughts." His grin revealed the rare, charming mien—the dangerous, coaxing smile. "How do you think you became so adept at ferreting out secrets? The Shadow Journal, for instance... It was constantly in my thoughts that day. I wasn't supposed to carry it with me. Projecting your thoughts is a less powerful ability I was unaware of, however."

"My point still stands."

"You need to wear it regardless."

"Why?"

The smile reappeared. Her feet shifted, a glint of wariness in her eyes. She could almost see his thoughts running behind his pupils. "Every member of the Sanguine Shadow must wear the symbol of our order. Each symbol is made to enhance any abilities we have."

She froze. "The symbol... should I be wearing this? The ceremony is still a week away."

"For all intents and purposes, you're already a member. The ceremony is merely a formality."

Suspicion crept into her thoughts. He blinked, but showed no other reaction. "You're being awfully helpful today. Why?"

His expression shifted. As he closed the distance, she took a step back. He purred, his gaze almost predatory. "Your mind is screaming right now. Do you ever wonder why you don't like me, Estiel?"

She grimaced, planting her feet. "Because you're an ass who likes to taunt me."

"No." His mood reverted, and she felt the same lack of emotion he expressed. "It's because of what you sense."

Estiel tensed and glanced away. "It's because you tortured me out of pure enjoyment."

"No," he repeated. "I paid no attention to you, until you reacted to me like a scared rabbit in the presence of a hawk."

Shuddering, her hands clenched. "What's your point?"

"You disliked me before we even spoke, because you sensed the differences between us." He reached up, tucking a stray hair of the wig behind her ear. "You're so full of emotion. You're driven by it, live your life by the code it instills upon you. Whereas I live by no code, and don't allow emotion to interfere with anything I do." Before he continued, he leaned closer. "But we are not as different as you think."

"Oh? Please, continue. This promises to be ridiculous."

"We both devote ourselves to what we hold dear. You, through subtle manipulation that springs a trap around your target, and I, by any means necessary. We gather information without allowing others to notice. We leave no trace of our activities. The only difference between us is I was brought up this way, while you developed it out of necessity. Still, here we are, in the same place."

With each word, her spirit deflated. She lowered her head, turning. "I hate you."

Behind the words, a memory swam. Luka's voice murmured through their minds.

'He was brought up in the Sanguine Shadow... that means he's capable of a good deal of necessary evils.'

'...the two of you together will be a nearly unstoppable force.'

"Your brother was wise."

Without warning, she strode toward the nearest tree, discarded the wig, and unbound her hair. The lowest branch sat within reach. His eyes bore through her as she grasped it, bent her knees, and hopped to pull herself up. Her blouse tore when her muscles moved in ways it was not meant to handle. She stood, ripping it more for ease of movement. Above her, the next branch barely hung low enough. An image lit behind her eyes, and she watched her muscles work to pull her up. It almost made her lose her balance.

Ignoring it, she climbed higher. He called to her, bemusement tinging his voice.

"Is there a reason you're climbing the tree?"

"I didn't come out here to stare at it, Alken."

Estiel ascended until the branches thinned, and she could see the palace rising against the evening sky. She breathed deeply, closing her eyes. A sigh slipped out before she let her knees grip the bark, falling backward to hang upside down. Surprise reverberated from Alken when she grasped another, using it to swing down. Her legs grasped onto a branch not far below, and she rolled sideways. The process continued until she found herself at the bottom.

Her eyes remained closed while she stretched, opening halfway as he spoke.

"I believe we understand a bit more about one another." A

satisfied glimmer filled his gaze. "The free spirit matched with the calculating assassin."

She sighed. "Have you come any closer to finding out who—"

"Not for certain. Your brother stood to gain the most."

"I don't believe it was him."

Estiel explained what happened before they met in the library.

"If he truly doesn't wish to be king, perhaps we can use that to our advantage. For now, we need to discuss the ceremony."

They spoke until the sun began to set before heading back to the palace. At the stables, they parted ways.

Before she had the chance to wash her face, a knock came at her door. All but her makeup had returned to normal. She called out, and turned to see Barlen Garol standing inside her receiving room. Estiel could not find her voice as his eyes widened.

"It appears I found you and hadn't realized." His flowing tone did not waver.

Blinking, she cleared her throat. "Is there something I can do for you, Duke Garol?"

Curiosity shone in his gaze, but he let the topic lie. "I've been trying to see your mother, but have been refused. I hoped you could get a message to her." Dark thoughts floated on the surface as he spoke, filled with a growing unease.

"I haven't been able to see her either, but I'll do what I can."

"Her sister, Idjora, has been missing for two weeks. I received word from her husband, Duke Janor, whom she lives with on their estate. I hoped your mother might know her whereabouts."

Her hand settled over the bracelet, willing it not to amplify her thoughts. The pit of grief bubbled and boiled to life. "I... If I can help in any way, I will."

Barlen slumped, but regained his composure, turning toward the door. "Thank you. Idjora hasn't been well, and being gone so long..."

Murmuring a vague response, she watched him exit the room.

The rest of the week passed without shedding light on the events that had occurred. Standing beside Alken, Estiel took a deep breath.

"Are you ready?"

Her gaze tore away from the wooden doors. She realized she had forgotten to breathe. Gasping, her eyelids flickered, and she met his eyes. For once, she wished they would show the remotest glimmer of compassion. "Yes."

Blinking, one hand grasped her wrist, pulling her toward him while the other brushed against her chin. "I told you not to lie to me, Estiel." His voice lowered. "This must be done, for Shandjal, and for us."

She gave a weak smile. "I know."

He returned it for a second. "It's time."

One hand grasped the metal ring bolted to the door. Hesitant, her heartbeat thrummed in her ears. She tugged, and it swung open. Candles lit the long stone hallway. The ominous atmosphere set her heart racing, and she stepped inside.

Behind her, Alken shut the door. They walked to the large, square room at the end. The center received almost no light from the candles. Taking her elbow, he led her to the middle, stepping in front of her. His mouth stretched in a genuine yet cold smile.

"I must stand with the others for now."

"I know." Despite the tremble in her words, her lips curled upward. He moved to join robed figures appearing from the shadows. She forced herself to be still, standing tall and folding her hands against her dress.

One figure stopped three feet from her. Dark eyes glittered in the candlelight. Estiel could not see his lips move when low, gravelly words surrounded them. She recognized his voice, however, feeling a bit of fear release at the presence of Duke

Jensen Shol.

"Princess Estiel Evantriel, second born to King Gaebrel Evantriel I, you are here of your own free will. Your will is the foundation of your destiny. Will you flee, Child of Fate, or stand firm with the knowledge that you are where you are meant to be?"

She could not help how her eyes widened, nor the way her lips trembled. The fear filtered into her reply, peeking through a firm resolve while she recited practiced words. "I stand firm in the shadows, ever shifting with the world's radiance. Their light shall not be my guide, for the darkness beckons."

He moved closer, murmuring. "It embraces you with open arms." His hand raised and she watched him cut the pad of his thumb with his teeth. It took great effort to stay still when he reached up, smearing blood from the corner of her eye to the edge of her chin. "Blood shall be your bond—a reminder that the Shadow cannot fear Death, for She is the portal to Death's door. When two shadows merge, the depth of darkness between them becomes their connection to the Final Lover."

Stepping back, his voice magnified without raising in volume. Alken joined her. "Do you accept the merging of your shadow with that of Alken Shol, son of Duke Jensen Shol, to open your connection to Lover Death?"

"I accept." Her whispered response echoed around them. She turned, and Alken caught her gaze. The same dark glimmer swam in his eyes. Her breath caught. In that moment, her heart fluttered. His smile at her reaction began to melt the hardened ice between them.

Jagged flashes of light encircled them, ceasing within seconds. Energy followed in their wake to wrap around their chests and limbs. She gasped, her heart rate accelerating. The robed figure beside them backed away, bowing his head to stand just within the weak light. Alken's hands rested on her waist and drew her to him. She did not resist. Estiel could not break away from the confident possession in his stare.

Soft notes weaved through his speech, his hands moving to

her shoulders. "With my bond, I vow to share my Fate with you, Estiel Evantriel. May our shadows entangle no matter the cost—through illness, wellness, prosperity, or poverty. We shall reach toward Death's door together when our path's end looms."

He accepted an object without shifting his eyes, and she forgot to breathe as he pressed it into her hands. Lifting the tiny, long handled blade, her grip tightened. She drew it across the curve where his neck met his shoulder. It proved difficult to speak, her shaking voice forcing her to focus. "I accept your bond."

Alken's hand slid up, resting on the back of her head. He guided her lips against his skin. Crackling light flew around them, spontaneous, numerous, and beautiful. Her eyelids fluttered, her arms encircled his ribs, and her hands grasped his shirt to bring herself closer. The sweet, coppery taste flooding her mouth made all thought flee her mind. When she pulled away, she let him support her weight.

With her voice barely above a whisper, she repeated the ceremonial vows. Bringing one hand around, she felt him remove the tiny blade from her fingers. The pleasure her body experienced dulled the pain as it parted her skin.

"I accept."

Those two words fell upon her ears in a satisfied purr. Her head fell back when his arms enclosed her in his embrace. The sensation of his mouth around her shallow wound felt unlike any she could compare it to. Overwhelming heat spread over her skin, crackling with the energy binding them—but within her body, her core began to cool. They grew in intensity, the blazing fire spreading to her veins. Yet, the heat could not thaw the glacial temperatures encroaching upon it.

Darkness closed in around her consciousness. Her features slackened, and she felt herself lifted into Alken's arms. The shadows howled in her mind, running irrelevant thoughts off to let her drift into a dreamless sleep.

Estiel awoke in her room the next morning. Staring at the ceiling, she blinked, raising her hand to touch the tiny cut at the base of her neck. Her eyes closed. She swallowed as the memory of the ceremony flooded her thoughts.

The heat... and the icy chill.

Remnants of the sensation tingled across her skin. With a sigh, she sat up. The covers fell to reveal a simple nightgown in place of the dress from before. Again, she blinked, filled her lungs with air, and rose.

Twenty minutes passed, and she had washed and dressed. She stared at her reflection, touching her pale cheek. A sound from the doorway alerted her to someone's presence.

"You're awake."

"Yes."

Alken crossed the room to stand beside her. Their eyes met in the mirror. "How do you feel?"

Hesitant, she glanced away. "I feel the same, but not at all."

"Estiel."

She allowed him to turn her toward him, locking their gazes. His searching eyes held the barest hint of... something. It was not as cold as she was accustomed to.

"Alken?"

He placed his hand on her cheek, where hers had laid, and raised hers to rest against his own. Her breath stuttered at the strange reaction flying through her—reminiscent of the previous night, but entirely different. An unmovable resolve settled within her, easing the ache of loss she had carried since the deaths of her mother and twin.

"What... is this?"

"It is the bond the Shadow provides." His expression thawed as he murmured, just enough to be noticeable. "It allows us to give a different kind of support when needed."

Her father's voice filtered through her mind, making her close her eyes.

'...their ceremony of joining is powerful. It involves magic, blessings, and will strengthen any bonds between you and Alken.'

Alken's voice brought her attention back to him. "We need to move quickly now."

A tiny smile appeared. "I will speak with Gaebrel."

He emitted a stifled noise from his throat. "It's a shame he isn't the one responsible."

Wincing, Estiel stepped back, turning to stride away. Her anger vibrated through her, and her hand slapped across the bracelet. It halted the thoughts from reaching him, but not before the first few escaped.

"Estiel..."

She snapped her response. "I know what you meant. It would have been the easy solution." Taking a breath, she forced her voice into a less hostile tone. "Try to find out who it was. I'll find a reason he shouldn't be given the crown."

The warmth from his hand seeped into the back of her neck. None appeared in his words. "I did not mean to upset you. Eat something. Your body is adjusting after the bonding."

Estiel did not move until she heard the door click shut. Her fists clenched and released. A minute later, she pursed her lips and left the room.

She stared at her empty plate. Replacing her spoon, she closed her eyes and expelled a long, slow breath. A knock sounded at the door. As it closed, it drew her attention, and she watched Gaebrel approach.

"I didn't think you would have the nerve to summon me, Sister." Deep lines creased beside his eyes and mouth. "There better be—"

She stood, speaking with a harsh voice. "I have neither the time nor the patience for your attitude, Brother. I told you we would speak. Now we will speak. Do you have a problem with that?" Her lips pursed and her eyes narrowed.

His sneer nearly undid the careful control she held on her anger. Estiel smoothed her skirt before crossing her arms. Lowering her voice, she stepped away from the table. She cast a glance at the single guard in the room. He left without a word.

"Are the guards taking commands from you now—a princess soon to be wed to another family?"

"Oh, stuff your derisive opinion down your own throat, later, on your own time. You said you weren't interested in the crown. Are you going to listen, or stand there pretending you're superior?"

Gaebrel's head snapped back. He stared, his dislike clear in the dark glimmer of his eyes. "You said things are changing. I have a hard time believing you would have a hand in that."

The smile she gave lowered her chin. Estiel motioned toward the chairs. "Sit, and I'll explain."

As he complied, she took her seat. She spoke without interruption for ten minutes. Her brother's gaze grew from incredulous to angry, and from angry to a deep, dark fury.

Shoving his chair back, Gaebrel slammed his hands on the table. "And you haven't found the party responsible?"

Estiel stood and leaned her weight on her hands. A hint of strain entered her words. "Don't assume to judge me when you've spent the last week doing nothing, even after confirming your suspicions." She pushed the chair away. Her teeth bared, her hands clenched, and her eyes narrowed. "How dare you—"

Mid-sentence, the door opened. A man she did not recognize entered the room. The siblings stared. Clearing his throat, he shifted his weight, performing a deep bow. Estiel's eyes flicked to a singular red diamond hanging from his ear.

"Speak." Her voice echoed around the room.

He cleared his throat again, not meeting her gaze. "Pardon the intrusion. Duke Shol wishes to see you at your earliest convenience, Your Highness."

She nodded. "I'll be there shortly."

When he retreated, her gaze returned to Gaebrel. His eyes held a curious glint.

"You truly are maneuvering to take the crown. Do you really think it will work?"

The emptiness in his eyes made her blink, with memories of

cruelty flashing behind hers. "I have the counsel, the Sanguine Shadow, and the king behind me. It won't be easy, but it will work."

"All this to keep me from the throne?"

"Yes."

"Why?"

Her eyes narrowed. "You don't want it, Gaebrel."

"There was no way for you to know that. Why?"

Gritting her teeth, Estiel's hip jutted to the side. "It isn't hard to see you're a threat if you sit atop the throne. You haven't tried to hide your nature from any of your family." She held one hand up when he went to speak, resting her elbow on her other arm. "Until our last talk, I assumed you killed them, Gaebrel."

Gaebrel's smirk left her breathless and staring. "I wouldn't be standing here if I had wanted them dead."

Her expression wilted, though her stare remained. "Father is dying. We don't have time to bicker or profess our dislike for each other."

His eyes narrowed, a shadowed glint swimming within. "I will not bow to any woman, let alone you, Estiel."

"You won't have a choice. Everything is already in motion... or would you have me killed instead?"

Her words made him take half a step back. "I will not."

"Then the point is moot." Estiel turned her back on him. Her eyes closed and she sighed. She could see the sneer he would be wearing behind her eyelids. Fatigue tugged at her, though it was only a few hours after sunrise. His reply made her spin around, standing sideways.

"You want me to kill you, don't you?" The sneer had never formed, the introspective gleam reappearing. Nothing but a serious demeanor sat upon his features. "I felt it, if only for a moment. You're tired and scared, no matter what front you put up. You want to die."

Her eyelids drooped, and she gazed at the floor. "Yes, I want to give up. I would like nothing more than to allow someone to relieve my burden." Eyes hardened, her sorrow turned into a bitter determination as she glanced up. One fist clenched at her side. Her words seethed with anger. "But I am no coward. I wouldn't dishonor Luka's wishes merely because I would rather someone else carry this weight. Too much rides on my choices from now on. Will you help me? Or will you act the petty fool as you always have?"

"Slinging insults isn't the way to gain my aid." Annoyance tinged his voice, but disappeared. "I'll go along with this, if only to see how it turns out. If I do, you have to keep me informed."

She frowned. "Why do you want to be part of it?"

His eyebrows rose, and the corner of his mouth quirked. "I may not want the crown, but I won't allow you to decide my fate entirely. I'll be a part of it, or you will truly see how much trouble I can stir up."

A minute passed while she inspected his expression. Her voice lowered. "Fine. Come with me." She paused. "Know this, Gaebrel—if you start causing trouble, I will have you locked up."

With that, she spun on her heel, her skirt swishing with her movement. Estiel ignored the furious thoughts weaving through her mind, placing her palm over the bracelet to silence them. She heard his hesitant footsteps, and she left the dining hall.

The royal siblings arrived at the duke's door. They stepped into the room to find Jensen murmuring to his son. Alken looked at her brother, then her. Estiel blinked twice, but strode over to them confidently. An odd sensation at the back of her mind let her know Gaebrel followed.

To Jensen, she nodded and spoke in a clear, level voice. "Duke Shol, you needed to speak with me?" When his eyebrows rose and he sent a pointed glance toward Gaebrel, she shook her head. "I need you to worry about the problems at hand. Have you any news?"

"Yes. We have someone who," he paused, "has information on the night of their deaths."

Alken stepped up to her, murmuring in her ear. "This is not a matter he should be present for. I—"

Muttering, she turned her head toward him. "I've already said not to worry about it, Alken. We will speak later." Raising her voice, she cleared her throat. "Who?"

When neither spoke, her chest rose and fell. Their hesitation, their uncertainty in her, flooded through her. She speared Alken with a furious glare. Letting her body loosen, she turned toward him. The strength of her emotions and determination spread from within her mind. Estiel could feel their surprise at the ferocity within her low, deep words.

"How dare you question my competence?" One hip shifted, balancing her weight. Her hands remained at her sides. "I did not come here to deal with your ridiculous doubts. If you've forgotten, I've dealt with difficult decisions for a long while. In essence, I'm already queen. I asked you a question. My patience isn't endless."

Alken's irises darkened, but held a glint of satisfaction. His hair shifted with a slight tilt of his head.

A few seconds passed before she heard Jensen mutter, "You should have been born a Shol." Louder, he continued. "Apologies, Your Majesty. Nellen."

From the garden door, a young man no older than Estiel appeared. His downcast gaze never lifted as he knelt between them. A pendent swung against his skin, the light catching the blood-red diamond set within.

"Tell her what you told me."

Nellen winced. "Forgive me, Your Highness. The king ordered my silence."

No sound rose. Estiel's voice held no inflection while her gaze pinned him in place. "What do you mean?"

His voice emerged level, if high pitched. "The king ordered me to obtain the disk. He didn't tell me why. I left it in his quarters with the diamond to identify it."

Tension built in the air around them. Behind her, Gaebrel stepped forward. "What does that mean, Estiel?"

75

She reanimated, turning from the kneeling man. He stared at her pale features. Her fingers refused to move. A fine tremble ran through her.

Luka. Their mother.

Neither moved, nor spoke. And their faces... their cold skin. The suffocating haze of invisible power.

A note of warmth cut through the images. It spread into her arms and chest, igniting the strange combination of icy core and heated flesh. Estiel gasped, a long, drawn out stutter, and blinked. When her eyes focused, she found herself within Alken's arms. He held her close. His face rested in the curve of her neck, his breath tickling her skin.

Alken's thoughts skimmed the surface of her own, sending a shiver through her. Your memories hit everyone, Estiel. Calm.

Though she felt no true concern for her wellbeing, she could follow each calculation his mind made in those moments. In an odd way, the unemotional, levelheaded mindset soothed her.

This feeling, she murmured in her thoughts. Ice and fire...

It is Death meeting Life, the foundation of our bond. The thought sighed through her head.

Gradually, they pulled away. Mere seconds passed between the young man's confession and Estiel returning to herself. When her eyes fell upon her brother, his face twisted in a savage expression. A single, brutal thought hit her, and she moved toward him with a speed she did not know she possessed. Her hand clasped around his wrist, her shoulder bracing against his chest when he moved to launch himself across the room. Light from the windows caught the sharpened edge of a blade. It sat inches from the bare skin of her upper arm.

She grunted at the impact. "Gaebrel!"

His growl reverberated through her, vibrating his chest. "He killed them!"

"No," she shouted. "It wasn't him. Father told him to retrieve it, that's all."

From their proximity, the hate in his eyes seemed deeper than she had ever seen. Their gazes locked. She could sense the others in the room moving closer, and she ignored them.

"Put it away."

In the same instant, they bared their teeth.

The standoff ended with a knock at the door. They disconnected with unnecessary force and stepped away. Her eyes stayed on him until the knife vanished. Smoothing her skirt, she straightened, crossing the room to answer the door. A frown creased her forehead when it opened to reveal a middle-aged woman. She looked familiar, but before she could place her, Estiel froze. The woman's eyes held no pupil or stable color, the hue a milky blue. Faded, messy red hair fell around her head. Recognition hit her, the memory of a crying woman at the open court surfacing.

"Jora? What are you doing here?"

Her smile, as absent as her gaze, formed and faded in three seconds. "I can explain what happened."

The muscles along Estiel's spine clenched to suppress a shudder at the woman's empty stare. Still, she stepped aside. "How could you possibly—"

"My name is Idjora."

Jensen's grunt of surprise drew their gazes, save for Idjora's. He spoke in the same level voice he often did. "Idjora Janor. I did not recognize you."

Estiel's lips parted with an inhaled breath. Her eyes widened. "Mother's sister?" Unconsciously, she covered the diamond in the bracelet. Her thoughts flashed to the short encounter with Duke Garol—her mother's father from before her marriage. "I don't understand."

The smile appeared and vanished again. "I had to get into the castle undetected, so I found a way. It was difficult getting the charm to keep you from reading me, but..."

Staring in shock, she shook her head to dispel the fog in her mind. Her voice rose in pitch. "Explain." Alken wrapped one arm around her, letting their skin come into contact.

"I came to speak with your father. The Azure showed me so many things."

"The what?"

Alken spoke. "The Azure is the sacred sight, gifted to very few by the Shadow's counterpart and consort, the Radiance. It is said to show visions of the future."

A derisive noise drew their attention to Gaebrel. "You speak these names as if they're gods. The Fates are the only gods recognized in Shandjal."

Alken's unwavering eyes landed upon him. "They do not wish to be known."

Idjora continued, staring at Estiel as if the others did not exist. "I saw your father's death." She paused. "And I saw Luka's death." Another pause. "Gaebrel took the throne, and the kingdom fell apart." Her gaze tore away, and her eyes closed. "I saw such horrors."

Blinking, Estiel's eyes narrowed in thought. "Duke Garol said you went missing. Why didn't you come directly to my father, instead of making up murders?"

A poignant silence spread through the room. Then, "I saw that future, too. It took me longer to set things in motion, and it happened the same way. There was only one way to get to the king in time. When Luka took me to your father, the king dismissed him. He recognized me, as I knew he would."

The revelation that they met in private sank in as Jensen Shol spoke. "The king didn't inform anyone of her presence."

Idjora lifted one hand to stare listlessly at it. "When I told him what I saw, he wept. He said he would rather die and take his namesake with him than let his beloved people suffer."

Despite Alken's aid, Estiel bent forward, one hand clutching the cloth above her abdomen. The air left her, rushing out in one breath. "He what?"

"He planned to use the magical disk to save Shandjal from destruction."

Estiel's eyes flashed to Gaebrel. He stood still, showing no reaction. When his eyes met hers, he smiled, and she felt a chill. Her words emerged breathless. "You stand there and smile after hearing our father meant to kill you."

"Oh, I'm sure you'll like the rest."

"What did you do?"

The sighing of Idjora's voice interrupted them. Her hand turned to show her palm. "He overheard our conversation. The king didn't realize he has an ability much like your own, Estiel. After learning the king's plan, it wasn't difficult to follow Nellen and know when to set his trap."

All ability to speak left Estiel. Alken's hold tightened, his eyes narrowing as his voice gained a dangerous note. "You murdered your mother and brother?"

Gaebrel scoffed, but Estiel interrupted. Standing in one smooth motion, she locked her gaze on his. A quiet tone flowed through her speech. "No, he meant to murder me. He told me Mother wanted to see me."

Her brother sneered. "Luka wasn't supposed to be there. Neither was Mother. I meant for you and Father, that pathetic excuse for a man, to be the victims of that wretched spell."

The way he stood, his muscles loose, with nothing but contempt on his face, sparked a boiling fury within her. "Why, Gaebrel? Why do you hate me so much?"

His smirk accentuated his reply. "Because I could never read you."

"What?"

"Don't tell me you didn't notice the same thing. You can't read me, either, can you?" He did not let her respond. "Others are so easy to manipulate. They have so many thoughts and emotions. But you..."

Estiel's hands clenched. "You can feel and hear it all, and you're still a heartless monster. It's no wonder I never understood you." Her hands relaxed, and she sneered, narrowing her eyes. "Well, Brother, you solved two of my problems."

"What's that?"

"I know what to do with you now, and I have the proof I need that you're unfit for the throne."

The smirk vanished, caution warring with his hatred. "What do you mean?"

Ignoring him, she looked to Idjora. "As for you." The emotions within her had her shaking. "You saw all other outcomes. But now... Father is still dying, Luka is dead, and Mother... She was your sister. How could you—"

With the barest hint of laughter, Idjora moved within touching distance. The humor faded. "A wielder of the Azure cannot hold such relationships in the same regard as others."

"I don't understand. If the goal was to keep Gaebrel off the throne—"

"That was never my goal."

"You mean you meant for all this to happen?" Jensen's surprise shifted his normal tone.

Her reply was aimed at Estiel. She sounded almost apologetic. "I meant for you to seize the throne. It was the only way."

"You soulless..."

A sharp jab of anger made her blink, but she stood still. The moment passed, and every eye lay upon Gaebrel as he shoved his blade through Idjora's back. Rage etched his face. Blood gurgled in her lung while he pulled her back against him.

"Worthless whore," he spat. "Manipulating me to put that woman on the throne."

Before he shoved her to the floor, Estiel saw a tiny smirk on her face. Her gaze turned to her brother. His chest heaved as his fury hit her, and she bared her teeth. "I never said I couldn't read you, Brother. I've always been able to read your emotions. We are complete opposites, you and I, no matter what talents we share."

Estiel glanced at Jensen. "Summon the guards, and have the council convened." He gave a crisp nod. Within moments, guards grabbed Gaebrel's arms. Her sibling said nothing, his blank expression locked on her until he stepped past the doorway.

With a sigh, she knelt beside Idjora, whose struggle to breathe echoed through the room. Tears beaded in Estiel's eyes. Anger seeped into her words. "Was it worth it? All this death— all the sorrow—was it worth it?"

Idjora responded with a smile. "Yes." She reached up to place her hand across her forehead. "I wish it could have been different.

It was the only way. The king has passed, and you bear the burden of the crown. You will understand soon, Queen of the Radiant Shadow."

A shock went through Estiel as the woman's eyes closed. New energy met the Shadow's bond within her. It swept through, changing it while allowing it to remain the same. The complex feeling left her gasping, and she fell. Staring at the ceiling, she blinked, catching the slightest hint of images beyond her normal sight. Alken helped her sit upright.

"Are you all right?"

She nodded.

He drew her to her feet and murmured in her ear. "We must go. If the king has passed, we're out of time."

With purposeful steps, they headed toward King Gaebrel Evantriel's office.

Though not in his office, they found the king in his receiving room. He lay upon the couch, unmoving. Estiel nearly collapsed, stifled a wail, and ran from the room. Alken shook his head when he emerged. They continued to the council's chamber, him leading her as she regained control. His touch gave her the strength she needed, though it left a bitter taste of resentment in her mouth.

When they entered the council's chamber, the four dukes stood from their appointed chairs. Duke Croal scowled.

"Where is the king? Or the queen, even?"

Estiel met each of their gazes, taking her place in the largest chair at the circular table. Only a hint of a tremor crept into her reply. "They're both dead."

Barlen Garol paled to a deathly hue, his hands leaning against the table. "Istrella is dead?"

Nothing but a silent stare came from Raegin Janor, the Duke of the Janordrae estate. His tousled, greying hair covered half of one blue-grey iris. Tulnem Croal, however, slammed his hands on the table.

"I demand an explanation."

"And you will have it." She raised her voice to quiet the cacophony. "Please, sit."

They did, though with reluctance, and the details were laid out before them. Estiel, Alken, and Duke Shol reiterated the events of the previous few weeks. The other council members remained silent when the tale had ended.

When no one spoke, she stood and leaned toward them. "This will not be an easy transition. I need the full support of the council to avoid unnecessary bloodshed."

Tulnem Croal sneered, waving a hand in the air. "I will not agree to a woman, no matter who she is, ruling the entirety of Shandjal."

"It is... was, the king's will." Alken pinned him with his eerie, dissecting gaze.

"The king is dead and cannot speak for himself. How are we to know you did not kill him yourselves?"

Jensen stood, removing a scroll from inside his jacket. "This is signed and sealed by His Majesty. It contains his last proclamation. To disobey this order will be considered an act of treason."

Estiel watched the duke's face as he received it and cracked the seal. He paled as he read the contents. "Does anyone else have any objections?"

Slowly, Barlen slid one hand through his hair as he lowered his eyes. He stared with a blank expression, shaking his head.

Her gaze transferred to Raegin Janor, whose eyes held nothing but an introspective glimmer. His rolling words bore a lilt, gained from the dialect particular to his vast estate. "I've no objections."

"Duke Croal." She waited for his full attention. "There is still the matter of your son to discuss, is there not?"

His eyes widened. She could not hide the bitter, satisfied smile. Tulnem set the scroll down, moving in a slow, gradual way, while never breaking eye contact. "I suppose there is. I would be indebted to you, my queen."

Every eye swung to her. Nodding, she stood tall. A smile crossed Jensen Shol's lips and he folded his hands to hide it. "Duke Shol has set fail safes in place for the inevitable backlash. Here's what we're going to do."

They held the crowning ceremony in private the next day. Queen Estiel and King Alken stood before the council. Their queen hid her fatigue behind a smile.

"Duke Croal, are the members of the court gathered?"

"Yes, Your Majesty."

"Duke Shol, I assume everything's in place?"

"Almost, Your Majesty. A few more hours, and we'll be able to contain any unfortunate reactions."

Pausing as she turned, she met his eyes. "The people are not to be harmed." She held up a hand. "I understand incidents can happen. I hope your people can keep it from escalating to the point of violence; but if violence arises, tell them to have some restraint."

He nodded and bowed. The crown, bedecked in tiny blood-red and azure diamonds, sat heavily on her head as she left the chamber with Alken by her side.

They stood within her father's office. Estiel's gaze lay beyond the bay window, her eyes clouded with thought. The sun beamed down on Djalen, casting odd shadows through the spiraled streets.

Alken glanced at her from where he leaned against the desk. He crossed the distance to stand behind her.

"It's almost time for the announcement."

A single blink preceded her murmured response. "I know."

Neither spoke while they waited. Mere minutes later, a guard informed them the announcement had gone out. They acknowledged him and returned their attention to the city. Another half hour passed before any effects of the news showed among the populace. Though they were too high above the streets to see individual incidents, the evidence became plentiful.

One by one, fires took hold of four places throughout the city. When the first spread, Alken turned to leave.

"Will you not stay with me?"

He stopped. She felt his thoughts stir, and she nodded.

Still, he spoke. "I will help where I can."

The door closed and she pressed one hand against her chest. Queen Estiel Evantriel, ruler of the kingdom of Shandjal, watched Djalen burn.

"This is only just beginning."

CUTHBURT AND CROWE

DREW CARMODY

"Come on, Crowe! What the hell is your problem, man?" Cuthbert asked, nudging his cousin who was sitting at their table in the café, brooding into his mug of coffee.

"My problem, Cuth, is that this idea is absolutely, mind shatteringly insane!"

"Oh come ON! It'll be a great adventure. Plus, think of the rewards and the reputation!"

"First off, the reputation won't do us a damn bit of good if we end up dead. Plus, since the main reward is the hand of the Princess Magdalena, it's unlikely to split two ways. I mean what, are you going to be married to her every other day, and I'll be married to her on the others? Use your head, Cuth."

"Oh, don't be such a damn stick in the bog, Crowe." Cuthbert said with a grin, "Yeah, I'd get the princess, but I'm sure that you'd be able to negotiate some kind of reward with the King. A title, maybe some land. A great whacking pile of gold at the very least, I should think."

Crowe took an irritable sip, and went back to glaring at his cousin. He sighed and shook his head, realizing that no matter what he said, the Bravo was NOT going to let this idea go. Still, for form's sake, the rogue needed to make his feelings known. "Again, Cuth," he said, "Can't spend a reward if I'm dead."

"You're always such a Negative Norbert, Crowe. I mean,

yeah, it'll be difficult, but I'm a hell of a fighter, and you're a hell of a stealthy bastard. If we get a few more people to join us on this quest, what could possibly go wrong?"

"Oh, for the Night Sister's sake, Cuth, don't start out saying that. We might as well stab each other in the face right now if that's the way you're going to be talking."

"I'm serious, cuz," Cuthbert said, grasping Crowe's hand and looking earnest, "If we're prepared, which we will be, and we're skilled, which we are, what could we possibly have to worry about?"

"What is there to worry about," Crowe said, staring at his cousin, "Well, let's run the list, shall we? For one thing, we're definitely going to need a few more on this insane adventure that you've got in mind. Second, I'm assuming that you're going to want to get this thing going quickly, since the King made it pretty much an open call, meaning whoever gets there and back first with the proof wins. That means starting out right as we're going to be going into whirlstorm season out on the Sea of Shattered Hopes, which is treacherous at the best of times."

"Oh, we can get Rex to take us across." Cuthbert said, waving his hand dismissively.

"Oh sure, at a hugely inflated rate!" Crowe shot back. "Rex may be a bit crazy, cuz, but he's NOT an idiot, and he's greedy as the day is long. In order to do this he's going to squeeze the hells out of our coin purses."

"We'll have enough when we get back." Cuthbert said.

"Again, IF we get back. I haven't even gotten to the real difficulties yet. Assuming we can get across the sea without getting the ship smashed out from under us or eaten by Sea Basilisks, we land on The Shadowed Shore and have to go directly through The Forest of Restless Haints."

"You can't tell me that a thief like you is honestly afraid of a scary forest, can you?" Cuthbert said, laughing.

"Shut up, the Forest has its reputation for a reason. How many parties have gone in there in the last couple of years and never come back?"

"Uh, I think it was about three." Cuthbert said with a guilty look on his face, gesturing for the serving girl to bring him another mug.

"Seven. It was seven." Crowe said, holding up two fingers of his own and looking around the nearly empty café and shooting a glare at a man sitting a couple of tables over and making an ill-concealed attempt to listen in.

"Well..." Cuthbert began.

"AND," Crowe said, cutting him off, "Assuming we get through that, we have to get up into the Serpent's Spine Mountains. Then, assuming we're able to climb them and not die, we've got to scale the Dragon's Crown, the tallest and most treacherous mountain in all the world and somehow either sneak or talk our way past The Order of the Draconic Blade."

"Oh, I'm sure they're not so bad. I'll bet you anything that their rep is exaggerated and they can be dealt with." Cuthbert said, not meeting Crowe's irritated glare.

"Oh yes," Crowe snapped. "I'm sure it's all been bad rumors, and they're actually one of the rational societies of isolationist, celibate warrior monks dedicated to making sure that Noxxramus, the Father of All Dragons doesn't escape his prison and descend to ravage the kingdoms of men."

"Well..."

"And THEN, as if all that wasn't enough, we have to actually get into the prison of the aforementioned Father of All Dragons, probably find a way to kill him, even though no one's managed to even come close to doing that in the five centuries the big cranky lizard has been alive, and we have to find and take the crown jewel of his treasure horde, the Eye of Eternity, and somehow get all the way back here, through all of that again, just so you can get yourself a royal piece of ass." Crowe fell silent, took another angry swig of coffee and glared at Cuthbert, daring his cousin to say something stupid. He didn't have long to wait.

"True love isn't about a piece of ass, Crowe. That's not what I'm after."

Crowe lurched forward and spit his sip of coffee out on the

table, noting with some satisfaction that some of it splattered on Cuthbert's bracers. "True love? How in the seven bloody hells could it be true love, Cuth? You barely know the woman. I grant you that she's attractive and all, but attractive ain't everything. If all you want is attractive, I'll take you down to Madame Bratavka's in the Dregs and you can work this out of your system."

"That's NOT all it's about, Crowe. Magdalena is beautiful, yes. But not just on the outside." Cuthbert said, a sulky expression creeping onto his face.

"Alright, fine, I'll take your word for it for now. You're not just looking for a piece of ass, you actually have feelings for this woman you don't know and you want to risk all to win the maiden fair. So where did you want to start looking for other lunatics to come on this insane quest?"

"I was thinking we head down to the Gilded Wildebeest in the center of the dock district. Usually a ton of adventurers looking for work down there."

"You're probably right. But if we make a few fliers and spread a little coin around to the criers, we might get a better turnout. Worth a shot, anyway. Let's go." Crowe said, draining the last swallows out of his mug and standing up. "Let's just hope that we can find some people that will help keep us alive on this wild Wyrm-chase of yours."

Two days later, Cuthbert and Crowe sat in the back room they'd rented at The Gilded Wildebeest, waiting to see if any of the more insane adventurers currently residing in Fairport's docks would show up to find out about the mission, and then be convinced to abandon any pretense of good judgement and sign up to come along. They'd spent most of the previous day spreading some coin around to the criers and hanging up the fliers they'd had made advertising for adventurers. They'd been sitting there for two hours and no one had shown up yet. Crowe wasn't particularly surprised, as he'd figured that it would probably be a futile gesture, but one never knew. Cuthbert, on the other hand, wasn't taking the uncertainty well at all. As the minutes ticked past, he got more and more irritable and sulky. Something inside him couldn't believe that there wasn't a stream of adventurers beating down the Wildebeest's door trying to get a spot on the expedition. For the last 20 minutes, Cuthbert had been pacing restlessly around the room muttering to himself.

Crowe looked up from his seat, where he was idly fiddling with one of his throwing knives and reading a battered copy of Hallbred's "The Golddiggers of Westreach" that he'd bought at the scribe's when they were having the fliers made and said, "For crying out loud, Cuth. Sit on your hands or something. Wearing a trench in the floor isn't going to bring anyone in any faster. Calm down, if anyone's going to show up, they'll show up."

"But what if no one comes? What if we can't get anyone?" Cuthbert asked plaintively.

"Well, then I'm afraid that if that ends up being the case, you're going to have to find some other way to win the hand of the Princess Magdalena, because there's absolutely no way in the heavens or the hells that just you and I are going to be able to survive the trip, let alone bring Noxxramus down. Or, we could go completely barking mad, still go on the expedition by ourselves and most likely end up as small piles of dragon dung somewhere on the highest peak of The Dragon's Crown. Hey, maybe if we're lucky, one of the members of the Draconic Blade will use us for furnace fuel. That'd be a worthy way to end our existence, yes?" Crowe chuckled softly, then went back to fiddling with his knife and reading.

"How can you be so damned calm about this?" Cuthbert spluttered, "I mean, I mean..."

"Calm yourself, cuz." Crowe said, "Look, either we'll find some people, or we won't. Getting ourselves all worked up about it isn't going to change anything. So why don't you sit down, try to relax, and see if you can figure out what to tell anyone that does show up that will make them want to go on this insane quest of yours."

Cuthbert had opened his mouth to say something scathing when there was a tap at the door, which then opened to admit a giant of a man. Nearly seven feet tall and clad in loose trousers and a white tunic emblazoned with the flaming seven-pointed star of Brahg, the man ran his hands through his long blonde hair, smiled uncertainly and said, "Yes, pardon me, but are you the two gentlemen looking for volunteers to accompany you on your worthy mission to slay the foul beast Noxxramus, the Father of All Dragons?"

"It is that indeed, my friend!" Cuthbert said, winking at Crowe, who just sighed and rubbed the bridge of his nose.

After leaving the Wildebeest, Cuthbert and Crowe headed back to the nearest coffee shop and sat down to discuss their options. Out of the people they had seen, Wilfred the paladin, Verminaar a rather oily, yet obviously competent necromancer, Clarell, an exotic, ebony-skinned battlemage from the Southwark Islands and Magus, a female Shi' ahran monk were the only ones that they felt would be worth bringing along on the expedition to the Dragon's Crown. And Crowe was still expressing concerns about Wilfred.

"It's just that I don't trust him to not be corrupted into absolute insanity." He was saying, as Cuthbert sipped at his mug and idly watched a few passersby in the street.

"Well, if we bring the necromancer along, perhaps we could avoid that fate for him. I mean, he is able to control demons and spirits, isn't he?"

"True, he is, at least he is if the tales I've heard about necros are true at all," Crowe replied, "But I don't know that I fully trust him either. I mean, I know that not a lot of people really know what's what about necromancers, but they don't exactly have the world's strongest reputation for trustworthiness and plain dealing. This Verminaar character seems like he's dealing straight with us, but again, we don't really know him." Crowe shrugged and added another spoonful of sugar to his coffee.

"Might be best to see if Clarell would be willing to keep an eye on him. I'd think that if anyone could counter anything he might do to betray us, it would be another magic user."

"Sound in theory, but not necessarily in actual practice. They're of two entirely different schools of thought about magic. Clarell might not be able to actually check him in any way. But it won't hurt to ask, I suppose."

"So, then I guess we've settled on our group?" Cuthbert said with a grin.

"Yes, I'd say we have. We'll see if they all still agree to come with us, and we make sure that they understand that this could be a complete suicide mission, but I think that the group we've seen should at least stand a decent chance of getting there an back again,"

"So what's our next order of business?" Cuthbert asked.

"Now," said Crowe, "Comes what will most likely be one of the more unpleasant, and certainly more costly parts of this whole enterprise. We'll have to go and try to convince Rex to agree to sail us across to the Shadowed Shore. We should probably go to the counting house first and get out most of our money. Because Rex may be greedy, but he's not stupid. He's obviouslly going to soak us for as much coin as he possibly can, if he even agrees to set out onto the sea that this time of the year."

"And if he doesn't?" Cuthbert asked, looking uncomfortable.

"Well, we'll simply have to burn down that particular hay barn when we get to it. For now, let's go get some gold and go see Rex. Do you happen to know where he hangs out when he's in port?"

"I think he spends most of his time at the Drowned Rat. I heard he's sweet on one of the barmaids that works there. Let's go see him." Cuthbert said.

"Yeah, that'll be a hoot. I hate that place." Crowe said.

Cuthbert and Crowe walked into The Drowned Rat, looking for Rex. They found him with his feet up on the table, sipping a mug of ale. When he saw the two of them walk in, Rex sighed to himself, shook his head and set his mug down. "Whatever it is the two of you want," he said, pointing a finger at the cousins as they walked up to his table, "You can forget it. No, don't sit down, just turn back around and walk right back out of here. Whatever it is, I'm not interested, and there's no way in the hells I'm taking the two of you anywhere. So you might as well not even bother to ask, because I'm not doing it."

"Now, Rex," Cuthbert said with a disarming smile, "You haven't even heard what we're proposing."

"Shut yer damnable mouth, Cuthbert, I don't need to hear it. Every time, EVERY damned time I agree to do something for the two of you, it always ends in the same way. I end up with my ship damaged somehow, and most of the time, I get stabbed."

Rex never even saw Crowe move. Suddenly, the rogue was at his side, one of his daggers unsheathed and resting along the side of his neck. "You're right about that, Rexxie, old chum," Crowe said with a smirk, "And I can guarantee that you're going to get stabbed if you don't listen to our proposal. I'll do it just to relieve some of the irritation at the prospect of having to find another ship captain. We go through this every single time, Rex. We don't have a lot of time, so why don't you just quit foaming at the mouth, have another ale, and just listen. If you don't want to do the job, fine, we'll understand. But at least listen to what we've got to say. You owe us that much for the last time. Or did you forget about how Cuth and I dragged you screaming out of the mouth of a razorfish?" Crowe said.

Rex sighed and gave Crowe a half-hearted glare. "Somehow I KNEW you were going to bring that up. Fine, I'll listen. You want to relax the steel now?" Rex said with a gesture at the knife.

"My pleasure," said Crowe. He handed Rex his fresh ale after taking a long pull off of it before giving it up, earning him another half-hearted glare from the ship captain. Crowe shifted around the table and sat down in front of Rex, with Cuthbert snagging an unused chair from a nearby table and sitting down as well, "Now, I think that you're going to actually like this one. You see, what we've got in mind is..."

Rex sat back in his seat, looking off into space, with a completely stunned look on his face. "You can't be serious. Tell me that the two of you are not being serious about this insane idea. Because if you are even the slightest bit serious about this, then I'm going to have to discreetly slip away, summon the City Watch and have them take the two of you off to one of the King's gentle and humane asylums where the two of you can get the care that you obviously need, and need desperately."

"Sadly, no, we're not fooling around with you, Rex," Crowe said, giving a sideways glare to Cuthbert. "This mad scheme is coming to you straight from the brain of my worthy cousin here. And he is quite serious about it. And, as I made a promise to my Uncle, his father, on his deathbed to do whatever I can to keep his nincompoop son alive, I'm going to have to go with him just to make sure that the lackwit doesn't, in fact, get himself killed somewhere in the Serpent Spine Mountains, assuming he even gets that far."

"You're both mad. I mean, stark, barking, and raving mad. I've heard some mad things before, but seriously, hand on heart, that's madder than our current king's great grandfather who went so mad he talked to the doorways and tried to marry his daughter off to a wildebeest because he thought that somehow, that would secure an alliance with the Southern Island nations. Never mind the thought that they kept insisting that that wasn't how their marriage and sovereignty customs worked. What on the earth, in the Heavens or the Hells could possibly make the two of you crack brained enough to try something like this?"

"Like I said," Crowe replied, "Cuthbert's the cracked one. I'm just going along to try and make sure that he's not dead in addition to being cracked. And on a normal day, Rex, I'd say that your plan to summon the watch was a good one. Hell, I'd have been willing to keep the lummox distracted while you went for the purple coats. And I'd have made a point of visiting my poor, unfortunate cousin in the cuckoo's nest at least once a week, schedule permitting. But I'm afraid to say that the madness that has seized on Cuthbert's brain cannot be cured by any ken of modern medicine or psychological theory. No, dear Rex, I'm afraid that the fair Cuthbert has succumbed to that mad distemper that occasionally strikes down both emperor and beggar alike. He's fallen in love, and the way to win said fair lady's hand is to go and do this mad quest."

"Oh, in the name of all the gods at once." Rex said, putting his head in his hands. "Well, fine then, what is it that you want me to do, apart from ferry you across to the Shadowed Shore? Let's have it, there has to be something more. There's always something more with the two of you. So go on, hurry up and get it out, so I can further cement my firm belief that the two of you are starkers."

"Nothing," Cuthbert said, sulkily, "The only thing we want from you is to take us over there, then stay close to where we go ashore and wait for us for at least a week. Shouldn't take any longer than that to get to the Dragon' Crown and back."

"Actually, he should probably give us two weeks, just to be on the safe side," Crowe corrected. "Would that be acceptable to you?"

"Fine. So I need to lay in enough provisions for a party of six passengers, then be ready for a 2 week stay on the Shadowed shore. Oh, yes. My crew is going to LOVE this one. Now, I hate to ask this, because I think I already know what the answer's going to be, but what sort of payment are the two of you thinking of offering me?"

"Well, for starters," said Crowe, pulling out a heavy coin purse and thumping it on the table. "We thought that would be a good start. Cuthbert, anything to add to the negotiations?"

"As a matter of fact, cuz, yes, thank you." Cuthbert said with a smile before he pulled out an equally weighty coin purse and slapped it down onto the table next to Crowe's. "Is this starting to feel like a just compensation?"

Rex scowled as he considered the two purses. Then he leaned forward, pulled open one, then the other, and let the coins inside cascade over his fingers into his own purse, which he then hefted in his hand. "Hmmm. Yes, that's not a bad start," Rex said, "But I'm afraid that that's not going to square our account."

Crowe sighed theatrically and said, "I didn't think that it would. What else are you going to want as a just price, at least in your eyes, for a run across the sea and hanging around waiting for two weeks?"

"If it was that simple, I'd say we're quits," Rex said, shooting an annoyed glance Crowe's way. "But it's NOT that simple and you damned well know it. You're perfectly well aware what time of year this is, and how treacherous the Sea is going to be, which thank you so much for deciding to kill yourselves now and take me with you, really, it's an incredibly sweet gesture. No, even if we get there in one piece, I'm going to be twiddling my thumbs on the gods-damned Shadowed Shore. Who knows what unpleasantness we'll run into there? So, since it's not a simple sea voyage, yes, I'm going to require further compensation. Now, the two of you are heading to The Dragon's Crown, so it doesn't exactly take a genius to figure out what it is you're after. Couple that with Cuthbert's apparent love sickness, and the only logical, and I use the word loosely, conclusion to come to is that the two of you are going to try and take down The Father of All Dragons. Now, on the off chance that you SHOULD succeed and aren't eaten, the way that we're going to square the balance is a very simple one. Assuming you do take down the big lizard and manage to not die yourselves, you'll be there in the middle of a dragon's treasure horde. So what I want you to do is to take your practiced thief's eye, find the most valuable bits and bobs that giant flying iguana with bad breath has collected over the centuries, and use them to fill this." Rex reached down beside him, picked up an empty 50 pound flower sack and dropped it on the table in front of the cousins. "Do that, and we can consider ourselves square. Deal?" Rex held out his hand. Cuthbert and Crowe looked at each other, then shrugged and shook the sea captain's hand.

"Sounds fair to us, Rex." Cuthbert said with a grin.

"Only if the two of you survive to complete payment," Rex grumbled. "If you should even think about giving me the shaft by dying, then I swear by the Sacred Sister of the Shadowed Waters that I will seek you out in whatever afterlife you go to and sing sea chanties at you for all eternity. Or at least until I get bored. Shouldn't take more than a millennia or two."

"Well, here's hoping we don't have to enact that clause." Crowe said. "Oh, and speaking of sea chanties, Rex. On the voyage there..."

"Yes, I will be singing sea chanties. If you don't like it, Crowe you can go ahead and find yourself another captain. It's my damned boat, and I'll sing sea chanties if I want to. Consider it a preview of what happens to you if you don't pay." Rex fixed Crowe with a glare and started to hum "Pull the Porpoise to the Poop Deck, Me Boyos", wordlessly daring Crowe to say something else.

"Fine, fine," Crowe grumbled. "Now shut up and let's have another drink."

The next day, Cuthbert Crowe, and the rest of the group were assembled on the docks at Rex's ship's pier. Crowe had always liked Rex's old ship, the *Indignant Grizzly*. It hadn't been the most luxurious ship that he'd ever seen, but it had gotten him, Cuthbert and Rex through more than one hairy adventure on the Sea of Shattered Hopes. But he couldn't feel too bad for Rex, looking at the much smoother and more impressive lines of his new ship, the *Wild Rover*. Crowe just hoped that not only did he, Cuthbert and their whole team make it through this, he hoped that Rex's ship made it through this. Because if it didn't, they'd never hear the end of it from him. And if he went down with his ship, Crowe was more than certain that he'd make good on that promise to find them in the afterlife and sing sea shanties at them. Hell, someone as bloody minded as Rex might find a way to do it while they were still alive, and that would be something incredibly embarrassing to have to explain to a necromancer or a cleric. "Yeah, the ghost doesn't really do anything, but he won't leave me alone, and he's been singing sea shanties at me non-stop. Oh, Gods, there he goes again, that's the seventh time in a row he's started singing 'The Lusty Hagfish'. Please, for the love of the gods make him STOP!" Yeah, not the type of thing they would normally deal with, and not only would they charge him a ridiculous fee, but they'd make a mockery of him all over the kingdom. Well, best way to avoid that was by making sure that Rex and the *Rover* survived.

"Ok, everyone here?" he asked, looking over the group. Everyone was present and accounted for with all their baggage. Looks like just about everyone had decided to pack light, bringing with them no more than was essential. Of course, they were probably all thinking that that meant they'd have more space for plunder on the way back, assuming they managed to pull this off. "Good," said Crowe, "Let's get on board get all our gear stowed and get ready to get out of here. The sooner we head off on this wild goose chase, the quicker we can come back."

"Love the confidence, thief." Clarell said with a smirk as she shouldered her rucksack and headed for the *Rover's* boarding ramp.

"This is one hell of a group you guys have put together," Rex said, coming to stand beside Crowe. "Please tell the magic users to not blow up my ship. Also, if the monk could refrain from punching holes in things, especially the lower hull, I'd really appreciate it."

"I'll be sure to mention it," Crowe said, "You all ready?"

"Yeah, just waiting for your band of misfit toys to get their stuff stowed, then we can put out on the next tide."

"Well then, let's get to it," Crowe said, shouldering his own bag and heading for the ship. No going back now.

They managed to get through the first day of the sea journey to the Shadowed Shore without anything bad happening, which was honestly a day longer than Crowe thought they'd make it before the first catastrophe set in. They saw the distant funnel clouds of a couple of whirlstorms, but thanks to some superb seamanship on the part of Rex and his crew, all they encountered were a few light squalls of rain. While squalls made everything wet and miserable, they didn't do any damage to the ship or to the crew, only to their state of mind, and the most strenuous thing that Crowe had to deal with was straightening out a couple of petty squabbles between the group, mainly between Clarell and Verminaar, who'd been wrangling over the proper uses of magic for most of the day. "How can any self-respecting magic user sully themselves with the base activity of weaponcraft?" Verminaar said, looking with distaste at the slender scimitar Clarell habitually wore on her left hip.

"Because, Death Diddler," the battlemage replied with a chuckle, "No matter how powerful you are, at some point the Magikala's going to run out. When that happens, crack the basatard's skull, or jam three feet of steel through his guts. Makes the point just as well as a fireball or a shadow bolt."

The second day of the trip was a bit more pleasant, weather-wise. Not a pleasant day from a seafaring perspective, but at least there were no whirlstorms anywhere near the ship, and Clarell and Verminaar had called at least a temporary truce. The most exciting event of the day was the occasional schools of Daggerfish that swam alongside the boat for at least an hour at a time. Clarell was busying herself trying to snag one of the fish as they leapt out of the water near the ship. Whenever they leapt out of the water, it seemed that they stared directly into the eyes of whatever crew member was nearby. Rex assured them that it was just their imaginations, that it was just a strange quirk of Daggerfish that no one had been able to adequately explain, and that it was just something that happened all the time out on the Sea of Shattered Hopes. Rex looked over at Clarell, trying to catch one of the fish and reminded the mage that it wasn't a good idea to take

Daggerfish lightly. He reminded her not to jump in the water and go for a swim, since all they'd get back would be bits of her skeleton. And he told the mage that if one of the ravenous fish jumped out of the water and latched on to an arm, it would still gnaw at the limb with it's steel-trap jaws and keep going until either the fish was burned off, or the limb came away completely, not a desirable situation for a spellcaster who relied on complicated hand gestures to practice their art.

Instead of becoming abashed, Clarell simply nodded, grinned, then said to the Captain, "Well then, I guess I'd better go get my dragnscale gloves and a net," before heading below decks to retrieve the items.

Rex shook his head and chuckled, "Mages." He said.

It was early on day three of the voyage when one of the bigger threats on the Sea of Shattered Hopes finally reared its ugly head. Rex had been hoping that they that they'd be able avoid them, as he'd managed to do on several occasions, but it seemed that sailing in whirlstorm season, when most sane captains stayed in port, meant that there was less sea traffic to keep the Shattercoils' attention. Luckily, he'd come prepared for the situation.

One moment, everything was normal. The next, water spouts started erupting on all sides of the ship. Rex cursed quietly to himself, and then shouted, "Shattercoils! Everyone stand where you are and no matter what happens, stay still."

"What the hell is going on, Rex?" Crowe demanded.

"Just shut up and do as I say," Rex replied through gritted teeth, "We'll get through this fine, but I need you to just trust me." Rex raised his voice, "For those of you that haven't sailed this way before, you need to listen! We're about to be boarded by the Shattercoil Mermen. They won't attack unless their chief orders them to, and he won't give that order unless he's provoked. So let's make sure that no one does anything to provoke him. I've dealt with the Shattercoils before, and I know exactly how to deal with them. Just remain calm, don't do anything stupid, and this will just be an inconvenience." Rex turned to one of his crewmen and had a fast, hushed conversation. The crewman gestured to two others, and the three of them quickly headed quickly below deck into the lower hold, and each came back up a few moments later, each carrying a barrel. They quickly deposited the barrels in the center of the deck, then fell back and took up positions by the main mast.

With no further warning, the waterspouts around the ship started to pulse with energy, and began disgorging humanoid shapes that soared through the air and landed on the deck. Crowe took in the creature closest to him. Roughly seven feet tall, it looked mostly human, except for the green, scaly skin. The creatures had powerfully built arms and legs with large, flippered hands and feet. Each also had a crest in the shape of a huge dorsal fin running along the center of their heads down the middle of their backs. Each Merman was armed with either a pike, a trident, or a large, vicious-looking scimitar.

The one in the lead, the chief, was wearing an elaborate headdress made from what looked like seaweed and shells, towered over Rex and said, "Greetings, Captain Rex. It is odd to see you on the Great Above at this time of season."

"Well, needs must, Chief Shattercoil."

"Mmmm. I can understand that. Your business is, of course, no concern of ours. Do you have the standard toll?"

"Three barrels this time," said Rex, "One extra due to the unusual timing, and for making you come Above at this time of year."

"Fantastic. That will be much appreciated, Captain," the chief said, looking over the three barrels on the deck. He strode over to the nearest one and pulled the lid off.

"What in the hells are you smuggling to these creatures?" Cuthbert hissed at Rex.

"Be quiet, you idiot! The last thing you want to do is annoy Shattercoil! Trust me, you won't like what happens to you if you do that." But it was too late. The Mer Chieftain heard Cuthbert, looked up at him, and his eyes narrowed. Shattercoil scowled, then reached into the barrel and pulled out... a pear.

The Shattercoil chieftain aggressively took a bite out of the fruit, then stalked over to stand in front Cuthbert. Shattercoil stood there for several moments, chewing on his pear and regarding Cuthbert with an icy glare. Eventually, he swallowed the pear and said, "You are on this adventure for the sake of the love you feel for a woman. You are here to do what you must to win her heart and her hand. But the woman that you desire is the very woman you shall not have. You may complete this quest you have set for yourself, but you shall not have the woman for your wife." With that, he looked at Cuthbert for a few more moments, and then turne away and barked something in the Shattercoil tongue. He and his people started to leave the ship, jumping back off the ship and into the water spouts that sprung up around the ship again.

"What the hell was that?" Cuthbert asked as the last of the Shattercoil picked up the barrels and leapt back over the side of the ship.

"That was a prophecy. The Shattercoil chieftains have been making them for hundreds of years. They look into your deepest desires, find what you want the most, and then tell you why you won't get it."

"Are they ever right?" Cuthbert asked in a nervous voice.

"Often enough. Why do you think they call it the Sea of Shattered Hopes?" Rex replied.

"So you're telling me that these guys invade ships, then walk around make dire predictions about how your deepest desires aren't going to come to pass?"

"Yeah, that's what I said," Rex replied with a smirk. "Hey, just be glad that you didn't seriously offend the chief. Those pikes and things they carry aren't just for decoration. And the last thing you want to do is get into it with a Shattercoil raiding party. Just be glad you only got their fairly standard, downer prediction of disappointment."

"So," said Wilfred from where he was standing at the gangway to the lower decks, "You'd say that they aren't so much Mer-Men as they are BUM-Mer Men?"

Everyone on deck turned and stared at the paladin. "What?" Wilfred said, "Just trying to lighten the mood."

"Make a joke that terrible again and I'll toss you over the side, and you can find out first-hand what a bunch of bummers they are, clear?"

At the end of the third day, the team was on the beach at the Shadowed Shore. They stood there watching the *Rover* head off, Crowe realized that they were absolutely committed to this insane quest now. "Well, this is it, he said to Cuthbert, "No going back now."

"Why would we go back?" Cuthbert asked in surprise, "We've only just gotten started!"

"Yeah. Need I remind you that we've just gotten started and already you've been cursed?"

"I wasn't cursed, Crowe, the Shattercoil just said..."

"That your most heartfelt goal on this trip won't come to pass. I mean, that sounds like a curse to me."

"Well, Rex said that they're not always right, you were there."

"Yeah, he also said they're right often enough. Need I remind you what sea we just crossed?"

"Alright, fine. Well forgive me if I choose to maintain a positive outlook on things right now."

"Oh, that's rich," said Verminaar as he walked up to the cousins, "You're keeping a positive outlook on this suicide mission. Hysterical!" he started chuckling.

"If you're so sure that it's a suicide mission, then why did you come?" asked Crowe.

"Oh, I fully expect it to be a suicide mission for the rest of you, but you seem to forget that for a Necromancer like me, well, we don't look at suicide missions the same way that other people do."

"What in the bloody hells are you babbling about?" Cuthbert asked, "If you die, you're dead, aren't you?"

"Not necessarily," Clarell spoke up as she joined them, "Judging from the intolerable air of smugness our necro friend is generating right now, I'd be willing to bet all the gold I'll ever make in the rest of my life that he's got a soulstone somewhere."

"A what?" Cuthbert asked.

"A soulstone," Clarell said, "It's one of the necromaners' favorite tricks. They enchant their soul into a gem. That way, their soul doesn't reside in their body anymore, but it still exists. So that way, if the Necro is killed, the gem breaks open, and the soul shoots back into the body, where it wants to be anyway. That's why you hear all the stories about how necromancers can't be killed, but it's a load of goblin dung. All it really means is that you have to kill a necromancer twice."

"Scoff if you will," Verminaar said with a smug look on his face, "But if this dragon kills us all, you'll all be permanently dead, but I'll get the chance to live on. Perhaps I'll even get away with some valuable trinkets. So yes, I don't view this 'suicide mission' the same way the rest of you do. So sad. But if that's what happens, then I promise to honor your memories on the day of your deaths going forward."

"Don't be too smug about it, Death Diddler," Clarell said with an evil grin, "Fine, let's say that we all die on this trip. First off, how do you know that your soulstone even works? Have you tested it? Want to test it now?" Clarell drew her sword from her belt and waved it around under Verminaar's nose.

"Hey now, that's not-" Verminaar protested.

"And let's say that it does work. Let's say we all get snapped up for dinner by The Father of All Dragons, and we all die. Then, your soulstone fires off, and your soul jumps back into your body and Abra-kapocus, you're alive again! Huzzah! Only problem is, you're alive again, and on the wrong side of a dragon's throat. How do you imagine that that's going to work out for you? I imagine not too well, as I've heard that even though a soulstone can return you to life, when it does, you're as weak as a new born kitten and unable to even get up for several hours, and by that point, the dragon will have started digesting you. Now I don't know, since no one's ever come back from being eaten by a dragon, but I imagine swimming around in a dragon's digestive juices has got to be somewhat on the painful side, to say the least. Under those circumstances, all your much vaunted soulstone will give you will be a second, much slower and much more agonizing death. So if I were you, I'd think your best bet is to make sure that you don't die in the first place, and your best shot at that is helping to make sure that the rest of us don't die either. Wouldn't you say?" Clarell smirked, sheathed her sword and walked away, leaving both Cuthbert and Crowe fighting to keep from laughing, and Verminaar looking like someone had just stabbed him in the chest.

"By the gods, she's right. Why have we never thought of this before?" he wailed softly.

"Well, seems pretty simple to me, Verm," Crowe said, unable to contain the chuckling any longer, "You Necros got yourselves so convinced of your cleverness and your fantastically unexpected solution, that you bought into your own reputation, which is pretty much always a fatal mistake. I'd say that the battle-mage has a pretty damn good point, don't you?"

"I hate to admit it, but you're right," Verminaar said with a scowl.

"Oh, don't look so downcast," Cuthbert said clapping him on the back, "All this means is that you'll have to do your best to keep us all alive. And just think of the reward that's waiting for you if you do. Fame, and great wealth. And all you have to do is your best, and that's all anyone can ask of you." Cuthbert said with a sunny smile before he walked off to join Clarell around the campfire that Magus and Wilfred were making for the night.

"And just think," Crowe said in a softer voice as he pressed one of his daggers lightly against the necromancer's back, "If I think for even a second that you're not doing your damndest to keep us all alive and make sure you succeed, I'm going to help you test out that soulstone of yours. Might not help you when we get to the dragon, but hey, at least you'll know that you cast it properly in the first place. And if not, well then you won't be around to care. So I'd call that a win, win. Wouldn't you?" Crowe gave a much darker smile of his own and headed off to join the others.

Verminaar sighed to himself, shook his head and followed after the rogue. "I hate this job," he said to himself.

The group sat around the campfire, waiting for the next day to begin the trek to the beginnings of the Forest of Restless Haints. "So how are we going to get there in a reasonable amount of time?" Asked Magus in her oddly muffled voice, "We have brought no horses with us, and there are no settlements anywhere along the Shadowed Shore from which we might procure them."

"You're right, of course, monk." Crowe said with a nod, "We didn't bring horses with us. For one, Rex hates transporting horses on his ship. Something of a superstition with him. He had a bad experience once with a cargo of horses, and ever since then, he's vowed that he'd never haul them again."

"What happened," Wilfred asked, taking a bite of the dried apple he'd produced from his rucksack, "Horses seem a strange thing to be afraid of."

"Let's just say that the last thing you want to do before you transport a cargo of horses is to piss off a Greskellian Beastmaster," Cuthbert said. "They have ways of making even the most friendly of creatures into something... unpleasant."

"What do you mean?" asked Wilfred.

"Just trust me on this one, paladin. I really don't want to talk about it." Cuthbert said.

"The point is," Crowe said in a slightly annoyed tone, "We weren't able to bring horses with us, and we're not going to be able to find any to use anywhere around here. It would have been a bad idea anyway. Horses don't do well in the Forest of Restless Haints. Any sort of live animal is not going to do well in that cursed wood."

"So how are we getting from here, across the hundreds of miles to the Serpent's Spine?" asked Magus.

"Well, hopefully, Clarell has taken care of that for us if she managed to do what I asked her to do before we left Fairport. Clarrel?" Crowe asked.

"You're a lucky man. I managed to find Zobeskin in the mage's quarter of Fairport, and he was more than happy to make these for us. Gave him a chance to practice a skill he hasn't been able to use in quite a while. I think he rather enjoyed it, actually."

"What are you talking about," Verminaar asked, "You mean that old, doddering fool Zobeskin that sits on the Mage's Council? What in merry hells could he have possibly done for you? The man hasn't cast a decent spell in more than 10 years, I'd wager."

"That's another reason why you're a fool, Verminaar," Clarell said with one of her characteristic smirks. "Just because he's old and because he's not a necromancer like you, you assume that the man is a useless, senile waste of space. But the truth is that Zobeskin is as sharp today as he was when he was first inducted to the Mage's Council. He made us these." Clarell reached into her satchel and took out a bundle of miniature rugs. She handed one to each member of the party and kept one for herself.

"How does it work?" asked Wilfred, "I'm not a mage, and neither are most of the rest of us."

"We made it so that you don't have to be a mage to use them. You can talk, can't you?" Clarell said.

"Well, yeah," Wilfred replied.

"You use the same words you'd use to control a well-trained horse, actually." Clarell said, "Zobeskin and I thought that that would be easier. All you have to do is the following," Clarell set her rug on the ground, took a loop of fabric off the end of it and looped it around her right wrist. "You need to put the loop around your right wrist. That connects you to the rug. Then all you have to do is say, Ayup!" The rug expanded to a full size carpet, and Clarell moved to stand in the center of it. She then said, "Giddap!" and the rug began to hover a few feet off the ground. A further shout of "Hiyo!" and the rug began to move forward. She stomped her foot on the back and the rug picked up speed. She leaned to her left and her right to steer the carpet. She made a few fast circuits of the camp before swinging the rug around and said "Woah!" to bring it back to a hover. "Set down!" she said, and the rug settled back down to the ground. "So you see," she said, stepping off the rug and muttering "Sleep now," causing the rug to shrink back down to the size of a large napkin. Clarell folded it up and put it back in her satchel.

"Those are the only words that are necessary?" Magus asked.

"That's it," Clarell said with a smile. "Anyone can use one of them, as long as you have the loop around your wrist. We figured that it would be the easiest way to get to where we need to go, and these rugs have no minds, so there's no worry about them being broken when we get into the Forest of Restless Haints."

"How fast will they go?" asked Cuthbert.

"They'll run for a day as fast as horse, then they'll have to recharge overnight. The magical energy of the world feeds them, so there's no need for you to do anything. Again, we thought that it would be the easiest way to make sure that we could reach our destination quickly. And since we knew that there would be non-magic users in the party, something simple and easily controlled. We didn't want you all to have to worry too much about trying to control something that you didn't have any experience with. As long as you can stand on a rug and balance yourself, you'll be just fine using one of these. But I do recommend that you all get a bit of practice with it before we head out tomorrow."

Everyone else nodded, took their rugs and began to try them out. There were a few crashes and a couple of minor injuries, but nothing debilitating, and it wasn't long before the rest of the party seemed to have gotten the hang of the flying rugs. "One thing down," Crowe said to himself as he maneuvered his own rug in for a landing. "One day down, and who knows how many more before we get this damn thing done?"

That evening, as they all sat around the campfire, no one really had much to say until Wilfred suddenly piped up and said, "I'm curious about something, friends. I know why I've come on this expedition, I want to see Noxxramus destroyed for the greater glory of Brahg, but I'm curious about the rest of you. This is hardly a stroll in the park. Why are the rest of you here?"

"Well," Verminaar said, looking up from the hunk of bread he was eating, "I figure that a dragon as old as this one has to have a very impressive hoard of gold and other magical items as well. I'm here to look through those and see what items of interest there might be."

"I'm here for the same reason," Clarell said with a chuckle, "An untold hoard of magical items, and all I have to do to get to it is kill an overgrown salamander? I'm in!"

"That's all well and good," Crowe said, "But just remember that King Roderick has already demanded that we bring him the Eye of Eternity, anything else, sure, have at it."

Clarell shrugged and nodded, and Verminaar said, "That's fine. The Eye is useless for Necromancy anyway. Monk? Why are you here?"

"There is a dragon. It must be destroyed. I will help to do that." Magus said briefly before returning her attention to her water canteen and not saying anything else.

"Well, that's certainly admirable!" Wilfred said with a grin. "Cuthbert? Crowe? What possessed the two of you to put this all together?"

"Cuthbert's here because he can't afford a matchmaker and wants to find himself a wife. He figures the Princess Magdalena is worth the trouble," Crowe said, chuckling as Cuthbert threw a piece of bread at him, "I'm here to make sure that Cuthbert doesn't die in the attempt. And, of course, the notion of all the gold I can carry out of a dragon's hoard has a certain appeal to it."

"Hardly, a noble goal," Wilfred said looking at Crowe with a disapproving frown, "I would have thought you would at least see the wisdom in trying to help vanquish an ancient evil."

"I disagree, Will." Crowe said, brushing the last crumbs of his dinner from his hands and standing up. "Get some sleep everyone. Tomorrow, we really get going on all of this, and we're all going to need our rest."

The next day, the group headed off towards the Forest of Restless Haints. Crowe looked around him and he couldn't help but smile at the sight of six misfits cruising along the coastal region, each on their own personal flying carpet that had been provided for them by their battle mage. It looked like pretty much everyone was enjoying themselves, too. With the possible exceptions of Verminaar, and that only because the necromancer never seemed to look like he could enjoy anything except being creepy and off-putting, and doing something that was actually fun, even for him, caused a severe cognitive dissonance within the magic user that he couldn't just ignore or look scornfully at. The other one who was hard to read was Magus, and that was mainly because it was hard to read the monk's expression over the demon-mouth half mask that she wore. But looking closely, Crowe was fairly certain that her eyes were sparkling, so he was pretty sure that she was enjoying herself. Again, by their reputations, he wasn't sure if the Shi'arhan monks were allowed to, or even capable of enjoying things in the traditional sense, but he didn't want to unfairly prejudge an entire group of people that he knew practically nothing about.

As they all flew along, Crowe found himself looking at the monk more intensely. He found himself hoping that at some point before they reached the Dragon's Crown, he'd have an opportunity to watch her fight. The stories he'd heard about the Shi'ahran monks' fighting methods and abilities were fascinating.

Some of them were downright unbelievable, no doubt purposely exaggerated in order to give the group a certain reputation. Crowe knew first-hand the value of a good, scary reputation. But he assumed that even though some of the stories were no doubt gilded more than a bit, he was sure there was a nugget of truth in each and every one of them. He was hoping to see that nugget for himself at such a time where he could actually sit back and enjoy it, and not have to be worried about fighting for his own life at the same time.

Later on, he would wonder if he shouldn't have had that thought, because within less than an hour, they were attacked by a roving band of highwaymen. Apparently, whichever one of the many gods that exist in the universe was in charge of the region around the Shadowed Shore was in a rumbustious mood that day, and prepared to roll up his or her sleeves and really get up to some mischief. One moment, they were all travelling along having a good time, looking forward to the rest of the day. The next moment, the air was full of crossbow bolts and arrows. It was a more than minor miracle that no one in the party got hit directly. A few of their rugs and packs took some fire, but the closest thing to an actual injury was the arrow that flew just a little too close to Magus' head and ended up slicing a thin line across her left cheek. Uttering a curse in Shi'ahra, Magus brought her carpet to the ground and jumped off before it had come to a full stop, tucking and rolling on the ground before coming back up to her feet in a ready stance. She pulled her brass knuckles out of her pouch, slid them on, and then took a sip from one of the gourds she carried. She slammed her fists together, and a pale white aura surrounded her. Everyone else was bringing their rugs in for more traditional landings as the arrows and bolts continued to fly from in front of them. However, none of the projectiles got through. Magus started whipping her hands and arms around, and the aura that surrounded her seemed to expand. The energy followed her movements, intercepting the projectiles and smashing them, the monk's blindingly fast movements creating an unbreachable wall of protection in front of the rest of the party. Crowe whistled to himself as he hopped off his rug and unlimbered his own bow. He started firing arrows into the trees in front and to the side of them as Clarell and Verminaar started firing off magic projectiles of their own. Clarell's looked like bright white miniature comets, and Verminaar's looked like thin bolts of pure shadow. There were several shouts and screams from the tree line as several of the projectiles, both magical and mundane found their targets, and twelve bedraggled, dirty men with crude weapons and patchwork armor burst from the undergrowth.

The one in the lead, a lanky, evil-looking man with greasy black hair and a tangled black beard stepped to the front of the twelve remaining outlaws and said, "You have killed some of our brothers," the rest of the men grumbled and drew their weapons, "We will let you keep your lives if lay down your arms, give us any gold or magical items you may be carrying, as well as at least half of your provisions. If you do, you may leave. If you don't, then we will be forced to..." he never got to finish the sentence. From off to the side, a roiling mass of white energy in the shape of a snake's head came shooting in and sent the man flying backwards into a tree. The sound of the man's back snapping was audible to everyone in the clearing. At the back of the roiling mass was Magus, one leg tucked up, the other extended forward. She continued to soar through the air, sending two more outlaws flying before she landed and spun around to face the rest. It was the legendary Shi'arhan Flying Serpent Kick. Crowe stood and stared in open mouthed surprise. Well, he could check at least one story about the Shi'aharans off his list. That one was true. Everyone else seemed to be frozen in place after the display that they'd just witnessed, and the monk seemed to run out of patience. Her eyes narrowed above her demon mask and she reached out, grabbed one of the remaining outlaws by the shoulder, spun him around and landed a shattering punch to the man's jaw that sent him directly out of the fight. She stood there looking at the rest, raised her right hand and made a small "Come ahead" gesture. The remaining outlaws seemed to snap out of whatever spell had held them transfixed, and they all charged forward in a mass.

"They're going to overwhelm her!" Wilfred cried. He unsheathed his greatsword and started forward. Crowe reached out a hand and placed it against the paladin's chest.

"Just hang back a moment, I think that if she needs us, it's going to be very apparent." Crowe said. Clarell chuckled and nodded in agreement, reaching into her pocket and taking out a thin cigarra case.

"Yes, I think our fair monk is more than capable of handling this particular situation. We'll keep an eye, but I think she'll be fine." The mage smirked, placed one of the cigarras between her lips, and then conjured a small flame at the end of her fingertip to light it.

Clarell's words proved to be prophetic, as within a few minutes, Magus, moving like a whirlstorm made entirely of legs, arms, punches and kicks, had all of the remaining outlaws lying on the ground around her in varying states of consciousness. She place her right fist into her left palm, gave a curt bow, and went back over to where her flying carpet lay. She got back on, looked at her companions and quirked up her eyebrows. Everyone else shrugged and headed back to their own carpets and within another couple of minutes, the whole group was underway again.

"This is turning out to be more fun than I thought it would be," Clarell said, exhaling a thin blue line of smoke from next to Crowe. "I must commend you on your selection of Companions."

"Well, I'm here to entertain," Crowe said with a smirk of his own.

Later that night, they called a halt and made camp not far from the Forest of Restless Haints. They could see the trees of the forest over the next rise. It was making all of them a bit nervous, as every one of them had heard at least a few of the stories of adventurers who had ventured there and never come back. Supposedly, it was the souls of those slaughtered adventurers that made up the Haints that the forest was so infamous for. Verminaar was the most nervous looking out of all of them. Most likely, his ability to hear the dead was what was causing him difficulty. For the first hour after they'd stopped for the night and made camp, he'd sat on a stump muttering to himself and occasionally stealing glances in the direction of the forest. This was making Crowe nervous as well, since he hadn't bargained on the Necromancer going crazy in there. He was sure it was going to be Wilfred, if it was going to be anyone. And to be fair, Wilfred wasn't taking the proximity to the cursed forest much better than Verminaar was. He sat on another stump on the other side of the camp, fidgeting with his greatsword and staring out at the forest. "Oh, for the love of all the gods at once," Crowe muttered to himself, "Please let me be wrong and neither one of them go off their nut. Or if you absolutely HAVE to have one go bonkers, please let it be the paladin. I think we could handle him if it came down to it. The Necro isn't someone that I want to have to tangle with."

"That's awful! Are you actually praying for someone's madness?" Cuthbert said coming up behind Crowe and sitting down next to him.

"Not praying FOR it, cuz. I'm praying against it, and I'm bargaining. Everyone knows how the gods work, and what twisted senses of humor they have. They'd like nothing better than to see a necro go bonkers in the middle of the Forest of Restless Haints. But I think they'd find it even funnier to have a devoted paladin of Brahg be the one to go insane and try to kill us all. I'd hope that he'd not make us kill him. I'd much rather just incapacitate the big oaf, but again, the gods work in cruel and malicious ways, and I'm just trying to bargain. So think about it, Cuth. Who would you rather face off against if it came down to a knock-down, drag out? A necromancer who isn't all that principled to begin with, who's powered by who knows what kinds of unholy magic, or a straight up sword-hound, who though he may be empowered by the god of righteousness and war, is at the heart of things a good man who just might hesitate at the crucial moment and let us get the better of him."

"Well," Cuthbert mused.

"Yeah, it's a shitty choice, I recognize that. But take a look. Wilfred and Verminaar are the only two right now that look like something's getting to them. Ok, it could be Magus too, since I can't see most of her face, but look at her, she's over there meditating. Seems pretty serene to me."

"Well, if all your talk about the gods is right, then wouldn't that be the cruelest joke of all, for the danger to come from someone we're NOT expecting and from someone who, let's face it, none of us really know how to fight." Said Cuthbert.

"Well, let's just hope that the gods haven't thought of that, or that if they have, they aren't feeling like quite such a bunch of vindictive pricks today. Still, keep an eye out and stay on your guard. We're probably going to have to deal with one of them sooner or later, and I think it's going to be sooner. Just call it a gut feeling."

"This is one time when I hope that your gut is wrong, Crowe," Cuthbert said softly.

"Me too, cuz. Me too." Crowe said, stroking his chin.

The next day the group finally crossed into the Forest of Restless Haints. It was not a pleasant piece of land for anyone to travel through. The trees were really the only feature of the land, and they pressed in close to the few trails that managed to meander through the cursed wood. The woods pressed in so closely that the party was forced to get off their flying carpets and walk. The trees were all twisted with blackened trunks and ash grey leaves, as if some horrible apocalypse had occurred within the forest centuries ago, and the forest was still trying to recover from it. There was almost no animal life at all within the forest. They encountered no game at all. The only living thing the group came across the entire first day they were travelling through was a deformed, malnourished-looking raven that had three eyes on its head instead of two, the third one sitting right in the center of the bird's forehead. Most of the party didn't even want to look at it, except for Verminaar, who stared intently at the bird, as if afraid that it might launch itself off its perch and attempt to fly to him and claw his eyes out with its talons. He only looked away from it to shiver for a moment before he returned to staring at it. He seemed like he was going to be content to stare at the twisted bird all day.

There was a twang, a swish and a thunk, and an arrow buried itself in the center of the bird's chest. It gave an abbreviated squawk and tumbled off the bough, falling to the ground dead.

"What did you do that for? Waste of an arrow if you ask me. You're mad if you think I'm going to eat any of that horrid thing," said Clarell as Crowe walked up to the corpse of the bird and retrieved his arrow. As he did so, Verminaar seemed to come back to himself somewhat, shake himself as if he was coming up for air after being submerged in water, then continue forward through the trees.

Crowe fell into step beside Clarell as he cleaned his arrow before returning it to his quiver. "No, I don't expect you to eat it. Hell, I'm not going to eat the damned thing either. It's just that I wanted the thing out of the way. I've come across three-eyed ravens before and trust me, the damn things are a pain in the ass, and they always seem to be the harbingers of bad events. I figure this trip is dicey enough as it is without adding any more bad omens to it. Call it preemptive retribution. Also, the way Verminaar was looking at it? Well let's just say that I don't have the highest level of trust in him right now, and I wanted him to at least be thinking about other things."

"Ah," Clarell said with a nod, "So you think he's going to crack up, huh?"

"You figured that out too?" Crowe asked, lowering his voice.

Clarell gave Crowe a condescending look, "It's not my first trip around the block, Crowe. Yes, I know all about the reputation that this forest has. The nasty one, I mean. I've experienced it second hand, actually."

"What happened?" Crowe asked.

"Friend of mine signed on to an expedition that came through here. Let's just say, he doesn't seem to be much fun anymore."

"Dead?" Crowe asked with a grim look on his face.

"That'd be kinder," Clarell said, kicking a loose rock, "He's completely gone out of his gourd. Doesn't even know what century it is anymore. So, you think Verminaar is going to lose it?"

"I figure him or Wilfred." Crowe said, looking over at the paladin.

"Don't forget about me," Clarell said, "This place does seem to be particularly hard on magic users. Which probably means that Magus is struggling too."

"Yeah, I'd thought about that, too. I'm honestly hoping that if someone does lose it, it's Wilfred or Verminaar. Magus or you? Don't think we'd be able to handle that. So yeah, my head's on a swivel, keeping an eye on all of you." Crowe said bluntly.

"Smart," Clarell said with a grin, "I seem to be holding up pretty well so far, but there is this uncomfortable pressure at the back of my mind. I don't like it, and I'll be happy when we get back out of these damned woods again, but I think I'll be able to handle it. No desire to murder you in your sleep and drink your marrow if that's what you're worried about."

"Well, thank goodness for that." Crowe said with a smirk. "What about the others? How do you think we can go about dealing with it if things break badly for us and someone loses it?"

"Well, for one thing," Clarell said thoughtfully, "If you haven't already, you should start praying to whatever gods you believe in that if someone does go dotty, it's only one of them. I think we could handle one. Two or three? No chance."

"Good to know. You want to tell Cuthbert?" Crowe asked.

"No, I don't think he could keep it quiet. He's too earnest." Clarell said.

"You're right. He's always been annoyingly honest. Well, maybe we'll get lucky and none of them will lose it."

Clarell looked sideways at Crowe and said, "Yes, and maybe

the sky will cloud up and rain gold over us for a year and a day. And maybe you'll also suddenly receive a message telling you that you've been named Emperor of all Solandaar and get to wear a shiny hat, but I wouldn't bet on it."

Crowe nodded, "You're probably right. Well, then let's do what you suggested. Pray and hope."

"Yeah" Clarell snorted, "And keep your sword arm limber and your eyes open."

"Oh thank you, that's a great comfort." Crowe said scowling.

By the time night was falling, Crowe figured that they were almost through the forest, and about to cross over into the foothills around the Serpent's Spine Mountains, where the Dragon's Crown was waiting for them. Looking around at the group, he could see that everyone was tired, everyone was struggling to keep going. He knew that he felt almost ready to drop, but he felt that continuing on until they reached the foothills and were out of the cursed forest would be the best bet. So far, they'd been lucky. Apart from the near exhaustion, most of the party had seemed alright. He'd seen the strain and discomfort on Clarell's face all day, and Verminaar had been distracted and distant for the same amount of time, but he also looked like he was still fully in control of himself. Magus seemed like her usual, inscrutable self, regarding the wasted land they were travelling through with the same stoicism that she'd regarded every other aspect of the journey up to this point.

The one who was worrying him was Wilfred. The paladin seemed to be jumpy and even more distracted than the necromancer. If the forest was getting to the big warrior, it would definitely be to their benefit to keep going into the foothills and hope that whatever damage was occurring within Wilfred's mind would be reversed once they were out of the region. Crowe held up his hand and called a halt. Everyone settled to the ground and the rogue turned to look at everyone. "I know that you're all tired, I know that you all need rest. Hells, I need it too. But from what I can tell, we're less than half a night from the foothills of the Serpent's Spines. I think we should keep going and get the hell out of this forest, then we can have a good rest before we try to scale the Dragon's Crown. What do you guys all think?"

"Let's keep going," Cuthbert said, "I know that I'm ready to drop, but I know that I'll sure rest easier once we're out of this damned forest."

"I agree. I don't want to spend one second longer than we have to in these woods." Clarell said, massaging her temples with her fingers.

"Yeah, let's continue," Verminaar said, still looking around distractedly and also rubbing his head, "I hate this place. All I can do to keep the voices at bay. Let's go on."

Magus didn't say anything, but the monk just looked around briefly, narrowed her eyes and nodded, making a gesture towards the mountains.

"Ok, Wilfred, what about you?" Crowe asked, looking over to where the paladin had been standing just a few moments ago. The big man's carpet was empty. Crowe swore quietly to himself and started looking around. After a few moments, he saw the big paladin standing over by a particularly warped and twisted tree. He stepped towards Wilfred and repeated his question. "Wilfred, can you keep going? What do you think?" The big warrior turned around to look at Crowe, and what the rogue saw made a cold sweat break out at the base of his spine.

The vacant, far away expression that had been on Wilfred's face for pretty much the entire day was gone, and in its place was a cruel smile that reminded Crowe of a starving wolf. There was also an unnatural light in the paladin's eyes, they were almost glowing red. "I don't think so, rogue filth," Wilfred said in a voice that was both like and unlike the paladin's normal tones. The strange harmonics underlying the man's words set Crowe's teeth on edge as if he was listening to the sound of someone's fingernails being dragged down a slate tablet. "I think that we should stay right here. This mission of yours is utter foolishness, but this forest. It is lovely, is it not? A true monument to the glory of Brahg."

"How in the hells can you say that?" Cuthbert asked, the disbelief thick in his voice, "This place is a nightmare."

"Brahg has nothing to do with this forest, Wilfred," Crowe said, loosening his short swords in their sheathes, "And neither does whatever's happening to you right now." Crowe turned and said in a low hiss to Cuthbert, "You see? I TOLD you!"

"Nonsense," Wilfred interrupted, "This forest is where I wish to stay. How can you dislike it so much, Crowe? Why, I would think one that follows your wretched Night Sister would find it a wonderful spot. All the shadows, all the darkness. Why would you want to leave?"

"Oh, that's just about enough of that," came Clarell's voice. Crowe turned and looked to see the mage had taken the dagger from her pouch and was soaring through the air towards the paladin on her flying carpet. She was just about to bring the dagger down into the big man's leg when he gave a bellow like an enraged bear, dragged his sword, thankfully still in its scabbard from his back and whipped it sideways. The flat of the blade caught the mage across the face, sending her flying through the air to crash in a heap at the bottom of another of the forest's twisted trees.

"This is the way you want it?" the paladin bellowed, "Well that is just fine by me!" He tore his blade free of the scabbard and swung it again as if he was intending to disembowel both Crowe and Cuthbert in one swing. Thankfully for them, Cuthbert managed to get his shield up in time, and Crowe back flipped out of the path of the greatsword's blade. Still, the shattering impact drove Cuthbert sideways and knocked him to the ground. Wilfred was bringing his sword up to swing again when there was a glimmering light from the other side of the clearing and Magus came flying through the air towards the paladin, using the same Flying Serpent Kick she'd used to take out the bandits earlier. Unlike the bandits, however, the paladin had a defense against the monk's attack. Shouting a word in the battle-language of Brahg, Wilfred conjured a glimmering wall of energy that protected him from the front and the sides. He then just stood there, a self-satisfied smirk on his face. Magus' attack hit the glimmering wall of energy, and there was a bright flash. Her forward flight was stopped dead, and before she could adapt, the paladin stepped forward, jammed the hilt of his greatsword into her stomach, then backhanded her roughly across the small clearing they were standing in, where she fell near Clarell, also knocked senseless by the paladin's unnatural strength.

"Try to keep him busy!" Crowe shouted as he ran over to the mage to check and see if she was alright apart from being knocked unconscious. From a quick glance, she seemed to be fine, just knocked out. They could deal with that if they managed to subdue the paladin. As he was about to turn and go to check on Magus, Crowe saw the dagger that Clarell had tried to use against Wilfred. As he snatched up the dagger and turned to see what was happening, Verminaar and Cuthbert were barely managing to hold their own. Verminaar was firing shadow bolts at the paladin, but no one could penetrate the shield of energy the warrior had managed to erect. Cuthbert was trying to get around the paladin, but wasn't having any success, being held at bay by long, sweeping swings of Wilfred's greatsword. Crowe stood and watched for a few moments, and then an idea struck him. He shouted "Keep at it, Cuth!" and ran over to where the necromancer had just stopped firing shadow bolts. "Is there anything else you can do to distract him?"

"I might be able to conjure up a few skeletons. It takes a moment or two to summon them from the Beyond." The necromancer closed his eyes and started chanting. Within a few moments, three skeletons burst out of the ground and were standing in front of Verminaar as if awaiting orders. "What now?" he asked Crowe.

"Just keep Wilfred distracted," Crowe said, reaching into one of his own pouches and pulling out a vial of nightshade oil, which he poured over the blade of Clarell's dagger. Nightshade wasn't deadly, but it was extremely painful. Verminaar sighed and pointed at the paladin where he was battering Cuthbert's shield with a series of powerful overhand and side strikes that the bravo was just barely able to keep turning aside. A few minutes more, and Cuthbert would be completely overpowered by the larger and stronger paladin. Hopefully, Crowe thought to himself as he snuck as unobtrusively as possible through the trees, hoping that the paladin wouldn't notice him and that what he thought he'd observed about the man's magic shield was right, he'd be able to end this quickly. Also, he really hoped that the pain of the Nightshade oil would be distracting enough to break the paladin's concentration.

In a few moments, Crowe had managed to sneak around behind Wilfred, and thankfully the paladin hadn't seen him. He gripped Clarell's dagger in his hand and dashed forward. At the last moment, Wilfred must have heard him, and the paladin started to turn. But it was too late. Crowe darted in low, sank the dagger into the back of Wilfred's right leg, and rolled away. The paladin howled in pain, and reached down to pull out the dagger. But his attention was distracted when a blow from Cuthbert in front of him showed that the shield he'd conjured had disappeared. There was a look of disbelief on the paladin's face as he turned back to confront Cuthbert's attacks and Verminaar's skeletons. Not waiting for the temporary advantage to go away, Crowe darted forward again, taking a heavy lead-filled sap from another of his pouches. With the paladin's attention directed towards the front, it was doubtful that he ever heard Crowe coming this time, but it ceased to matter when Crowe leapt into the air and brought the sap crashing into the back of Wilfred's head, dropping the man to the ground like a sack full of iron ingots. "Get some rope, tie him up and gag him," Crowe said to Cuthbert and Verminaar,

"We'll get him onto his carpet and get it flying somehow. We'll leave him at the base of the Serpent Spines and come back for him when we're done. I'm going to go check on Clarell and Magus." A quick examination showed Crowe that Clarell was merely stunned. In fact, the mage was starting to come back to consciousness, groaning a bit and starting to shift around.

Confident that she'd be alright with a bit of rest, Crowe walked over to where Magus was lying face down on the ground. He saw her demon face half-mask lying on the ground so he picked it up, meaning to give it back to her when he woke up. He knelt down beside the unconscious monk and rolled her over to check if she had any injuries. He got a look at her face for the first time as she settled on her back and he gasped, not sure he was believing what he was seeing. On the ground in front of him was the unconscious face of Princess Magdalena.

By the middle of the next day, the remainder of the party was well into the Serpent's Spine Mountains and well on their way to the Dragon's Crown. The revelation of Magus' true identity had had a varied effect on the party. Verminaar didn't seem to care. Since leaving the Forest of Restless Haints, the necromancer had regained most of his surly and smug demeanor. He didn't have much to say to any of them, keeping his eyes on the trail ahead and occasionally muttering to himself about "damned paladins". Clarell seemed mostly amused at the revelation of the monk's true identity, being more focused on the task ahead of them. Crowe found himself feeling a great deal of respect for the princess. Not only had she elected to come on this insane mission, but she had obviously been training in secret for years, as he had never even heard a whisper that Magdalena was also a Shi'ahran monk. The one who was most effected by the revelation, though was Cuthbert. He seemed to be both more smitten with the princess than ever, and yet at the same time, having seen how skilled in combat she was, he was extremely intimidated as well.

"I just don't get it," he was saying for the third time in as many hours, trying once again to break through the stoic silence that Magdalena had maintained even after her identity was revealed, "How is it that you were able to spend years in training, become a Shi'ahran, and your father never even knew about it?"

Finally giving up, Magdalena sighed tiredly and said, "Who says that my father never knew? Who do you think it was that suggested I learn some form of combat? Who do you think paid for the tutors? My father, of course. He's always been of the mind that everyone should be able to defend themselves, even a princess."

"What made you decide to become a Shi'ahran?" asked Clarell, "Seems like an odd choice when there are several other skills you could learn to defend yourself that would have been far less difficult to learn."

"True, but my father brought in all kinds of tutors trying to find out what sort of martial skill I'd be best at. It turned out that I had an affinity for the Shi'ahran Way. And when it was explained to me, and the master gave me a taste of what I could learn, I knew it was a challenge I'd have to undertake. And besides, the notion of being able to beat most other warriors with my bare hands was more than a little appealing."

"Fair enough," said Crowe, "I respect that."

"It just doesn't really make sense to me." Cuthbert said.

"Well, it doesn't matter if it makes sense to you or not, does it?" Magdalena demanded, "When we get this task done, you'll still have the option to marry me, but if you think I'm going to settle down and be a proper, doting wife to you, then you're in for quite the shock."

"I honestly don't know what I think of all this," Cuthbert said, thoughtfully.

"Well, figure it out. But don't let it distract you from what you've got to do. We need to get moving." With that, Magdalena pushed past Cuthbert and took up a place at the front of the group, heading determinedly towards the Dragon's Crown looming before them.

"You're going to have your hands full if you end up marrying that one, cuz." Crowe said with a grin.

"Mmmm. Cuthbert said distractedly, staring after Magdalena.

"That's not going to be a problem for you, is it?" Clarell asked with a smirk of her own, "You're not the type that wants a shrinking violet for a wife, are you?"

"No, no, it's just," Cuthbert said before stopping and shaking his head, "I don't know. Let's keep going." He said before resettling his pack on his shoulders and striding off after Magdalena, leaving both Clarell and Crowe grinning behind him, a scowling Verminaar bringing up the rear.

Later that afternoon, they finally made it to the base of The Dragon's Crown. They found something they weren't expecting, a narrow path leading up towards the towering summit. The path obviously hadn't been maintained for some time, but there was no doubt about the fact that it wasn't a natural formation, it was man made. The stone dragon heads spaced several hundred yards apart proved that. Nervously, with everyone on their guard, the group started up towards the summit.

"I don't like it," Magdalena said, her brass knuckles back on her hands and a gourd of her elixir ready at her side, "Isn't this supposed to be where The Order of the Draconic Blade keeps an eternal watch over Noxxramus? Why the hell would they make a path? It's not like they're going to want people dropping by for a visit."

"Well," Cuthbert said, "It does stand to reason, they must have to leave every now and then for supplies and whatnot, and I'd imagine that a few of them have to leave now and again to find new people to join the Order."

"That's a good point," Said Clarell, looking around, "Still, we should probably be careful. Let's keep going and see if we come across any sentries or watch posts or anything like that."

After a few more hours, as night was falling again, they came across just such a post, carved from the stone of the mountain itself, but one look around the small structure showed that it had been abandoned for some time. "Well, at least we don't have to sleep out in the open tonight," Crowe said, looking around the room and laying his pack down."

"No," Verminaar said, doing the same, "Still, we should have a watch. It would be the height of foolishness to leave ourselves vulnerable at this point."

"I agree. Would you like to take the first watch?" Crowe asked.

"Fine. You all sleep, I'll wake one of you in a few hours. Sooner if something happens." Verminaar said, sitting down on a carved wooden stool near the door to the stone building.

"Good idea," Crowe said, starting to set up his sleeping roll,

The rest of the night passed quietly, with everyone taking turns keeping watch for a few hours. Nothing happened, no one came, and nothing disturbed the party all night. As they were all waking up, everyone seemed less comforted by that than they otherwise might have.

"I don't like this," Cuthbert said nervously as they set off up the path again, "This is just too easy."

"Don't worry," Crowe replied sourly, "I'm sure it'll get much more difficult later on. Like when we actually get to the top and are confronted with The Father of All Dragons. Let's not forget about that."

"Oh, right," Cuthbert shot back sarcastically, "I'd completely forgotten why we're here."

A few hours later, the group rounded the last corner of the trail, passed through what appeared to be a natural, narrow stone archway, and stepped into an entirely different world. The scene before them looked like someone have hollowed out half the peak of The Dragon's Crown and made an artificial clearing. Several buildings were carved out of stone that had been left behind obviously serving as living and working space for the Order of the Draconic Blade. A path snaked up the small hill that had been left behind to a massive cave opening into the remaining half of the summit. "Well," Cuthbert said, looking at the scene, "Looks like we've found what we're looking for."

"I still don't like the fact that we've gotten all the way here and no one has tried to stop us," Clarell said with a slight nervous tone, "The Order is supposed to be one of the most hardcore societies around, I mean, they're tasked with making sure that The Father of All Dragons doesn't bust loose and start wreaking havoc on the world again."

"Well, they seem to be doing their job," Magdalena said as she took an appraising look at the area, "I mean, it's been at least 500 years and Noxxramus hasn't attacked anything. Honestly, I'm not sure why my father wanted to send someone on this expedition anyway, doesn't look like there's any looming threat here."

"That's because every once in a while, some king or other gets it into his head that the horrible and terrifying Father of All Dragons is just days from escaping his mountain prison and going on a killing rampage throughout the land. Honestly, it's pretty damned predictable. I could almost set my planting schedule by it," said a voice from off to the side. They all spun around, raising weapons or readying spells, but only one man was standing there, leaning against the doorway of one of the stone outbuildings. The man looked like a ranger, carrying a bow and a quiver of arrows on his back, a sword on his hip, dressed in mostly brown and dark green leather armor with a dark green hood up hiding a good deal of his face. The man raised his hands and stepped forward slowly.

"Sorry to startle you. Don't get too many visitors up here, unless of course they're here to try and take out Noxxramus. Bad idea, by the way. Still, if you'd all like to come inside, I can make you some tea or maybe something to eat. I'm Daxos. Order of the Draconic Blade. If you could all relax that stuff and ease down on those spells, I'd appreciate it." Daxos stepped forward again, then raised his hands further and drew back his hood. It revealed a slightly older, yet kind-looking face, and even though the man's hair and well-trimmed beard were shot through with a good deal of grey, there was no sense of age or feebleness to him.

"So, what position do you hold in the Order?" asked Clarell, letting the fireball she'd conjured into her had dissipate.

"Well, I pretty much AM the order at this point," Daxos said, heading towards one of the larger buildings and beckoning the rest to follow him.

"Wait," Crowe said, "What are you talking about?"

"It's pretty much just me and the dragon up here these days. Well, except for the occasional idiots who come by to try and kill him."

"Is it really just you?" Cuthbert asked, a look of disbelief on his face.

"Yup. The leader of the Order always gets a sort of, agelessness I guess you could call it. It's part of the gig, to make sure there's always someone here. The wards that keep Noxxramus in place depend on that."

"But you're supposed to have a whole order of warriors here with you, I mean in case say, an army attacks the place trying to release the dragon for their own ends, stuff like that?"

"It's been a couple centuries since anyone tried anything that stupid," Said Daxos leading them into a barracks and heading over to busy himself at a small hearth in the corner. The warrior started making tea as he explained, "Yeah, that's happened before, but it seems like most people finally caught on to the fact that trying to use an ancient, all-powerful dragon to wipe out your enemies might seem like a good idea at first, but eventually, the dragon would get bored and probably turn on you, then you've got an all-powerful dragon decimating your army and there really ain't a hell of a lot you can do about that. Since then, it's pretty much just been the occasional group of adventurers who show up here, thinking that killing Noxxramus will make them famous, win them the hand of a princess, make them the heir to their kingdom, crap like that."

"But if that's the case, why don't you have others here anymore. I mean, if you're all ageless..." said Verminaar, sipping his tea and looking fascinated.

"The LEADER of the Order's the ageless one," Daxos said, putting a generous dollop of honey into his own tea, "The rest of the guys would just age like they normally would. So, old age, and the occasional skirmish with adventurers who were, let's say, less polite than others took a toll. And it's been pretty hard to recruit people. I mean, how do you sell sitting up on a mountain top making sure an ancient dragon doesn't bust loose for the rest of your life?"

"That does sound, problematic," Magdalena said, taking a thoughtful sip from her own mug of tea.

"So, we're here to try and..." Crowe began.

"Kill Noxxramus, I know." Daxos said with a nod, "Do you have any idea how many folks have tried to take out that big lizard over the last few hundred years? A lot. And, well," Daxos gestured to himself, then shrugged. "So you can go take a shot at if you want, and I'm certainly not going to try and stop you. Hell, it's not my job to talk people out of getting themselves killed."

After finishing their tea, the group set out for Noxxramus' cave. Even though he said he wouldn't stop wouldn't stop them, Daxos came along as well. "There's a lack of entertainment up here," he said. "It's been at least five years since someone came to take a shot. Plus, someone'll have to clean up the mess when it's all over."

"What will you do if we manage to take him out?" Crowe asked.

"Won't happen, but that's the spirit, kid." Daxos said with a chuckle.

"Humor me," Crowe said.

"Well, if you actually beat the odds and beat Noxxramus, then I guess that's it for the Order. I imagine I'll start aging normally again, and obviously, I won't hang around here anymore. I'm a well-trained fighter, so I guess I'd head back down into the kingdoms and try to find some mercenary or guard work. Or maybe I'll take some of the dragon's horde and build myself a tavern somewhere. That'd be nice. I don't know, I don't really think about it too much, since it's not going to happen."

"Well, we might surprise you." Cuthbert said with a smile.

"Yeah, I haven't heard that a thousand times. No offense, kid, but I'm not gonna hold my breath. Let's just go ahead and get this over with, huh?" As they finished the discussion, they arrived at the massive stone doors blocking the entrance to Noxxramus' cave. Daxos took a key from his pocket and stepped up to a much smaller, normal-sized secondary door cut into the massive stone, unlocked it, swung it open and gestured for everyone else to step inside. He followed them in, then turned, closed, and locked the door. They found themselves in a high-ceilinged stone corridor that lead to another opening. There was a faint glow coming from the opening, and they could hear what sounded like a massive blacksmith's bellows pumping.

"That's Noxxramus." Daxos said. No one else spoke as they walked down the corridor and walked through the doorway into a massive stone chamber. The sight before them was more than a bit imposing. At the back of the chamber were massive piles of gold, gems and other objects, some of it extending out to another massive pile that covered most of the chamber's floor. However, the most imposing sight was that of a huge black dragon laying curled up on the pile, managing to seem like he was filling the entire cavern. The dragon's massive wings were folded against its side, and glittering silver horns sprouted from the beast's huge head. A row of silver spines ran down the dragon's back, culminating in a cluster of spikes protruding from the end of the dragon's tail. One large eye was open, regarding the group with disinterest. The eye slowly shut, and the dragon gave a tired-sounding sigh before opening both eyes and raising his head.

"Daxos, what is this? Another group of doomed meat come to die?" the voice rumbled through the cavern like thunder capable of forming words.

"'Fraid so. They're here to try and take you out. But hey, at least it's been five years this time, huh? That's got to be something of a record."

"Yes, perhaps the little morsels are learning back there in whatever land it is that spawns them. Still, this is all incredibly tiresome. Oh well, I guess that I'll just have to kill and eat them all. But I won't enjoy it. I'm not even hungry right now. Maybe it would be more of a challenge if I faced them as a being of their size."

The dragon shut his eyes again and began to mutter a few words. Within moments, the creature had shrunk down to the size of a man of about Wilfred's height, but even more powerfully built. Long black hair flowed down Noxxramus' back, and the man seemed to be encased in glittering obsidian armor. The dragon eyed his human form critically, then nodded in seeming satisfaction. "Well, it's been awhile since I took this form," he said to himself in a deep, pleasant sounding baritone, "Glad I still know how to do it. If you would all just wait a moment, I'll go get a sword and we can do this properly." As Noxxramus turned to walk over to a rack of weaponry standing against the wall, Verminaar couldn't control himself. He shouted, then leapt forward, hurling a huge blast of shadow energy at the dragon's back. Noxxramus' shoulders slumped and he let out another sigh. "That was a very cheap shot," he said as the blast of energy struck his back and dissipated harmlessly into the air around him. "I said wait." The dragon made an almost off-handed gesture and a blast of force sent the necromancer flying backwards to crash into a heap at the base of a cavern wall before turning and heading back towards the rack of weapons, where he stood looking over the armaments for several minutes. While the dragon was preoccupied, Crowe looked all over the room, trying to see something that might give him an inspiration on how to get everyone out of this. The dragon had just shrugged off a blast of shadow magic that should have left him in a smoldering heap on the floor. Now that the dragon wasn't filling up most of the room with his bulk, Crowe could see what looked like another dragon's skeleton lying on the ground behind the dragon's horde. It gave him an idea. He beckoned to the others and as they stepped over to him he said, "Look, there's no way we're going to beat that thing in a straight up fight."

"You've got that right, did you see the spell Verminaar chucked at him? I don't have anything more powerful than that." Clarell said, "So what are we going to do? Pretty sure he's not just going to let us walk out of here, he probably considers himself honor-bound to destroy us or some crap like that."

"Probably, but I have a plan. Just follow my lead, ok?" Clarell, Magdalena and Cuthbert all nodded, and they turned to face Noxxramus, just as he had apparently decided on a huge double-bladed battle axe. Resting it on his shoulder, he turned and started walking back towards them.

"Ok, I feel sufficiently armed now. Shall we begin?" the dragon asked, stopping in the center of the cavern.

"I have a proposal to make to you first, and if you agree to it, I think we can all solve our problems without the need for violence." Crowe said, looking at both the dragon and Daxos.

"Very well, make your case, but be warned that if you fail to convince me, I will still kill you all. Nothing personal, you understand, but a Dragon does have a certain reputation to maintain, no matter how ridiculous I find it to be."

"Well, my proposal speaks directly to that point, actually, for both you and for Daxos over there. From what I can gather, the both of you are pretty damned sick of living here at the top of the world, all alone on the top of this mountain, am I correct?"

"Well, yes" Noxxramus said, looking over at Daxos, who shrugged and nodded.

"Ok, now a question, how long can you stay in that human shape?"

"I can maintain this as long as I choose," replied the dragon, "But I've never liked it that much, though it does possess certain advantages that my normal form does not."

"Ok, now," said Crowe, "That dragon's skeleton over behind your horde, what is that?"

"That is what remains of my brother." The dragon said, a note of contempt sliding into his tone. "He attempted to kill me, I resisted. As you can see, I triumphed."

"Ok," Crowe said turning to Daxos, "Are you willing to renounce the leadership of The Order? I mean can you even do that?"

"Oh there's a way, but it requires a drop of Noxxramus' blood, so I figured that was never an option."

"It might be," the dragon replied, "I believe I see where he is going with this, and I think I may approve, as might you."

"Ok," Crowe said, "If you were to ever get out of here, Noxxramus, what would you do? I mean, a dragon flying around would panic every single kingdom until eventually, they would unite and find a way to take you down. However, let's say a wealthy lord from some foreign land showed up somewhere, well that sort of thing happens all the time. And judging from the size of this horde, it's not like you'd be hurting for funds, would it?"

"You do indeed make an interesting point. What would it cost me for you to renounce your vow, Daxos, if you are, as I am tired of this existence?"

"Well," Daxos said, rubbing his chin, "I'd say that letting each of us poke through your horde a bit and taking what we can carry would be a fair price. Also, a vow from you to not terrorize the land, on your word of honor."

"I deem these conditions acceptable. The rest of you?"

Crowe turned to look at the others, receiving four sets of nods. "Looks like we have an accord."

"Now just a minute," Noxxramus said, eyeing the group, "How would you convince your king that you have supposedly killed me?"

"We wouldn't necessarily need to convince anyone that we had. No one has come up here in five years, you said, and as far as anyone knows, you've been here for centuries, and no one knows how long dragons live. So if you let us take your brother's skull with us, all we have to do is take it back to her father, tell him that when we got here there was nothing left of you except the skeleton. And if Daxos quits, and you go and live life as a human, at least for a while, there won't be anyone to say any different, will there? This way, you both get to leave here, and we

132

don't have to die in a pointless battle that we could never win."

"Hmmm," Noxxramus said in a thoughtful tone, "That is actually a fairly decent plan, human. My compliments. But what am I to do? Where shall I go?"

"Even after we pick through your horde, you'll have as much money as a medium sized kingdom, so it's not like you'll be starving. You could set yourself up anywhere, in any city, then just do what you will. I mean, you'll have to live as a human, but you said yourself that the human form has advantages over the dragon. Plus, whatever you do would have to be more interesting than just sitting around here on a pile of gold all day."

"That does get extremely boring. Very well, I agree. Daxos?" The leader of the Order nodded. "Very well," Noxxramus said, dropping his battle axe and rubbing his hands together, "We have some work yet to do. Let us get to it."

After striking their bargain with Noxxramus, it was relatively simple to finish their task. While Noxxramus gave Daxos a bit of his blood and the old warrior performed the necessary ritual, which merely consisted of ingesting the blood and for all intents and purposes saying, "I quit," the rest of the group poked around in the dragon's horde. Crowe found the Eye of Eternity and slipped into his bag after Noxxramus assured him that the stone was largely useless if you weren't at least part dragon. They even separated out a portion of gold for Wilfred, assuming he was still alive after two days on his own at the base of the Serpent's Spines.

With the wards that held him to the Dragon's Crown broken by Daxos' resignation, Noxxramus agreed to transport them all back to the Shadowed Shore, even though he felt it was beneath his dignity to be used as a transport, even stopping along the way to pick up a very hungry, very terrified, yet still very much alive Wilfred. After Noxxramus and Daxos had taken their leave, Clarell sent up a fireball, and in a few hours, the *Wild Rover* pulled into the Shadowed Shore, and they began the trip back to

Fairport. The trip back was uneventful, as no mermen made an appearance and they again managed to avoid any whirlstorms. Upon making landfall in Fariport, the group decided to forgo reporting in for at least a little while and headed straight for the nearest tavern, where they commandeered a table near the back and each ordered the largest ale the tavern could serve.

"So, what are we going to tell King Roderick?" Crowe asked after they had all gotten at least part way through their ales.

"We're going to tell him that the job's done, that Noxxramus is dead, and that he and the rest of the kingdom can sleep safely. At least until the next crisis comes up." Magdalena said before taking a long pull of her ale. "Oh, and one other thing, Cuthbert. If you think that I'm going to marry you, you've lost your mind."

Cuthbert chuckled as he sipped at his own ale, "Why, what's wrong with me?"

"Well, apart from the fact that I don't really know you, I don't particularly want to marry anyone. I'd much rather go on another journey and do something to help protect the kingdom."

"Sounds reasonable," Clarell said with a grin on her face, "And I'd like to make a further suggestion. After this nonsense we've been through, it's pretty obvious that we all work together pretty well as a team, I say that when the next threat to the kingdom arises, we all go and deal with it together."

"Sounds good to me," Wilfred said, taking a delicate sip of his own ale. "And here's hoping that this time, I don't get corrupted by foul evil, and I'm actually there for the whole thing."

"And next time, if you could NOT try and murder all of us, that would be great." Magdalena said.

Everyone else laughed. "Alright then," Crowe said, "Let's finish these drinks, head off to the castle, both relieve and infuriate King Roderick, see what we can wheedle out of his treasury, then get ready for the next time the kingdom is in terrible peril." The six all grinned their agreement and crashed their tankards together, holding them there for several moments before Verminaar said, "How long are we supposed to do this for?"

"It does look pretty ridiculous," Crowe said, pulling his tankard back and finishing his ale at a gulp. "Ok, let's go and get to work." Everyone else finished their ales, then they all stood up and headed for the door.

ONE LAST PAYDAY

BY P.A. CORNELL

Turns out sleeping in your piece-of-shit hovercar because you sold your apartment isn't as bad as they say it is. It's worse. As I rubbed the kink in my neck, I tried to remind myself that the credits I'd made from the sale, plus the few I'd managed to squirrel away, were worth it. A few more big scores and I might actually be able to leave this mud ball behind for a life off-world. I still couldn't afford the luxury resort stations where the richies liked to spend most of their time, but there was a chance I could at least start a life on one of the colony planets. Somewhere with a real future. I was sick of living hand-to-mouth on Earth, a planet full of people too poor to leave—who could barely afford the ridiculous taxes or the Platform access that let them pretend their lives didn't suck. But I was sick of pretending. That's why my Platform system had been the first thing I sold. What good was living the perfect virtual life when you always had to come back out to the real one and be reminded that you were going nowhere? Earth was for losers, and I was done being one of them.

I straightened in my seat and reached over to turn on the car's comm system. There were two messages. The first was from my sister, Arden. I was going to just delete it but it'd been a while since I'd heard her bullshit so I played it instead.

"Vega it's me again," she said. "Can't you just call me back? Look, I know we didn't exactly part on great terms last time but we're both living in the same city now, and whatever happened in the past...well, we should try to reconnect. We're all the family we've got, after all."

I stopped the playback and stared at her sanctimonious face frozen on the screen. Her perfect ponytail draped over her uniformed shoulder. She'd probably called during a break from busting criminals and saving the world. *Reconnect*, my ass. She'd been the one to turn her back on me, and now she had the nerve to talk about "family" as if I meant anything to her. Not a chance, I thought. We wouldn't be seeing each other any time soon unless I got myself arrested again and ran into her during processing. But it'd been a while since I'd gotten pinched. My skills were honed now and I didn't take the stupid risks I had as a kid. I'd built a solid reputation in the past few years, which was what I hoped would soon pay off in the form of passage off world.

I deleted the message without hearing the rest and skipped to the next one. It was from Jax, a friend I'd made growing up in the system after getting booted out of the academy.

"Vega, I got a job for you! Call me back."

I'll admit, I was intrigued. I didn't usually get my jobs from Jax. Sure, we ran in the same circles but his thing was digital theft, while I specialized in acquiring the rare items that couldn't be accessed digitally. That didn't leave much, these days, since even solid objects could be scanned and printed elsewhere, but for the more discerning customer only the original would do. That meant that while I didn't get as many jobs as Jax did, my clients were often willing to pay considerably more for what I could get them.

"Call Jax," I told the car.

He was up early, big smile and dark-framed digi-glasses as usual.

"Ah, there she is," he said. "You got my message, I take it?"

"Yeah. What's this about a job?"

"Came in last night," he said. "A pickup in High Town."

"Ooh, is someone stealing from the rich to give to the poor?" I asked. Knowing there were no Robin Hoods left on Earth, if there ever had been.

"Probably more like stealing from the rich to give to the equally rich. Client is unnamed, but the price is right."

I didn't like working for anonymous clients. I know how to keep my mouth shut, after all. But I liked them to give me something, so I knew who I was dealing with. Mostly so I could make sure they'd actually pay. Jax knew that, of course, so he cut me off before I could bitch about it.

"Ten thousand credits," he said. "And that's just the first half."

"Are you saying they're paying twenty for this job?"

Twenty thousand creds would be enough to get me out of here. I could leave Earth with just one more job. Jax knew about my plans, of course. No wonder he'd called me about this.

"This could be your last score," he said, knowing I was thinking it too. "All you need to do is pick up some data. Then you get the advance. You get the rest on delivery."

"Wait, data? Isn't that more your thing?"

Jax shrugged. "I guess they don't trust this getting moved online," he said. "They want someone to go in person and get it."

That was weird. I'd gotten all kinds of things for people over the years. Art, mostly. Once even a car. But data was something you called a hacker like Jax for, not me. It was no wonder he'd heard about this first.

"I'll pass you the details if you're interested. All I want is ten percent. Call it an agency fee."

He sat back and waited, blinking in that way that made it clear he was scrolling through stuff on his lenses while I thought about it. It seemed pretty straightforward though. The hard part would be getting in and out of the wealthy part of town without drawing attention, but it would hardly be the first time I'd done that. The rest was like any other job. Bring something to someone else, get paid.

"You have the pickup address?"

"Ha! I knew you'd go for it," Jax said, leaning forward again. "I'm sending it to you now. There's a contact that'll meet you there. The mark's girlfriend. Seems she's not as loyal as he thinks. Looks like she's been secretly working for the competition."

"So industrial espionage or something?"

"Looks like."

"Is there a name for this girlfriend?"

"They don't give one. Just says you get yourself to the apartment. She'll hand off the data and you get yourself out as fast as you can."

A readout on the comm showed me he'd sent the details. I touched my wrist to it and transferred it all to my wristcomp bracelet so I'd have it with me for reference. Sounded like an easy job, but the size of the payment made me wonder.

Contract acceptance got me access to High Town. All I had to do was let the eastern security gate scan the details off my wristcomp and, since it'd been an open call, none of my personal information was on record. No doubt my employer had covered their ass on their end too. There were no other checkpoints before I reached the neighborhood where I was to make the data pickup. I could see the building in the distance; one of those insanely-high skyscrapers that make you feel they're reaching out to space, as eager to get off this world as me. I decided to park about three blocks down. In High Town a beat-up old rust bucket like my hover would stick out like a dead body in a field of lilies. To make matters worse, it was still early enough in the evening that Earth's perpetual smog blanket would do little to block the sun or otherwise hide my car. At least the day was coming to a close and it would be dark soon. Hopefully before I got back to it.

I half-jogged to my destination, moving fast enough to get this job done as quickly as possible, but not so fast as to attract attention from the locals. High Town was covered in cameras, but Jax had made me a scrambler—a little gadget small enough to fit in my pocket, that when activated would ensure I'd look like nothing more than a blur to anything recording me. Sure, if anyone felt the need to check the security footage later, they might be able to guesstimate weight or determine my height, but that wouldn't help them much when they couldn't even say for sure if I was male or female.

I stopped just short of the building, taking a moment to see what kind of security it had. The first layer looked like your basic automated door scanner. Judging by the way the residents were looking up at it, it was an ocular scanner. That meant I'd need to borrow someone's eyes. No problem. I had that covered. Beyond the glass-enclosed entrance—bullet-proof I'd bet—was the main foyer with a security desk. An actual human rent-a-cop was sitting at it, but as I watched people coming and going I didn't see him look up once. He was wearing a set of glasses that could have been for fashion, though were more likely digi-lenses. Not surprising. With so much of the security being automated, this guy had to be bored as hell. He was probably watching sports, or porn, or God-only-knew-what to pass the time. He wouldn't be much of a concern.

Not far from the guard's desk was a set of elevators. People were scanning their eyes there too, then entering one at a time. Same security as the door, so I'd be ok there too. I smoothed out my clothes a bit and double checked my look as compared to what the people going in and out were wearing. I doubt I could have fooled any of them into thinking this was high fashion, but if no one looked too closely, it was enough to pass. They'd probably assume I was a nanny or some other paid help showing up for work. Hell, maybe a call girl. It didn't really matter to me. It was enough that my outfit didn't scream *Low Town*.

Paranoia made me check my scrambler one more time, then I put on one of Jax's other little presents: a modified set of digi-glasses. These ones had been made custom to help me bypass just this kind of security. All I needed now was someone to serve as my key. I spotted him within seconds.

The man was middle-aged and balding—a fashion affectation on trend with the elite these days, since no one actually went bald naturally anymore. Someone this vain was ideal. I watched as he exited the foyer then started walking right for him at a pace that would indicate I was in a rush. When I was close enough I bumped into him as if distracted. I grabbed his arm just shy of seductively and uttered some apologies. Smiling like a bimbo, I tossed the unshaved side of my teal bob with a flirtatious wink and scanned his eyes with my lenses as he took in my features. He looked like he wanted to continue the conversation, but I was done with him and moved toward the building entrance. Luckily he hadn't been enchanted enough with me to follow. As I approached the doors I glanced up at the scanner and my glasses replicated the scanned signature. The system was fooled and the door slid open.

"Welcome back Mr. Hardinger."

I ignored the automated greeting and made my way past the rent-a-cop. I'd have bet my scrambler that he was off-duty SecForce. Some colleague of my sister's looking to make some extra side cash. As expected, he didn't bother to look my way. His faith in the scanners was my ally.

The elevators didn't stop me either, scanning Hardinger's ocular signature and greeting me once more as I entered the cab. The door closed and an electronic voice told me we were going as high as the ninety-eighth floor, which I assumed was where Hardinger lived. This was my first glitch, but not something I couldn't deal with. My pickup was in the penthouse. It was an unspoken truth that the residents of High Town lived as high up as their wealth allowed. After all, you wouldn't want to live on the planet surface like the dregs of society—meaning me. This told me that whoever I was ripping off had to be a huge fish in the corporate pond. He probably only lived on Earth when he absolutely had to.

Lucky for me, all buildings still came standard with stairwells in case of emergency. I could hoof it the rest of the way. The question was whether opening the stairwell door would trigger the fire alarm. Some buildings had this feature so that a single person's escape would alert the entire building to the danger. As

I approached the door there was no signage telling me either way. The door appeared to be locked and there was only a palm scanner next to it. There was nothing to indicate whether anyone other than a resident could unlock it. Glitch number two.

If I tested it with my unregistered palm that might trigger an alarm too. I was still mulling over my options and running a mental inventory of the tech I had on me when the door opened and a haggard-looking girl not much younger than me came through, struggling with two full loads of laundry. She was muttering to herself about her employer who'd forgotten yet again to leave her the damn elevator guest pass. She gave me a quick 'thanks' as I held the door open for her, but with the baskets in the way she couldn't even see me.

Into the stairwell I went, my question about door alarms now answered. The only security on the stairs seemed to be cameras. I wondered if they were just recording or if the rent-a-cop could see me. My scrambler would keep me from being identified but I didn't need him coming after me because he'd seen a blur on his monitor. It was a bit of a risk but I didn't think he'd be worried about the cameras any more than he had been with the people coming in and out of the building. My employer hadn't been concerned enough to mention him in the job description either, which was a good sign.

I broke into a run, hoping to minimize my time in the stairwell. Because of the often physical demands of my profession I like to stay in decent shape, but with forty-seven flights to go I knew I'd be feeling this in my thighs tomorrow, especially after another night in the car.

When I finally reached the top I was surprised that I wasn't that out of breath. Hell, I was proud. I was almost looking forward to the run down, which would only be easier. Then back the way I came, right out the front door without anyone the wiser. I was all but humming as I made my way down the hall to the penthouse door.

I knocked and moments later the door slid open. A middle-aged Asian woman blocked my path and it occurred to me that I had no contact name to ask for. All I could do was assume this was the traitorous girlfriend—hell, not my place to judge. I'm sure she had her reasons.

"You here for the data?"

I nodded. She closed the door and I heard her talking to someone. The door then slid open again and next to her stood a young boy. Blond and maybe seven years old at most.

"Take him. Go quick," said the woman.

For a minute I just stood there, sure that English wasn't her first language.

"The data?" I asked again.

"Yes, yes," she said. "It's here. In the boy. You must go now!"

I looked at the kid and started shaking my head. No, this was not what I'd signed up for. I don't do kids, under the best of circumstances. What the hell was I supposed to do with him? But before I could argue she shoved him out into the hall. The boy winced but said nothing. He hadn't said a word during the entire exchange, in fact.

"I can't take this kid," I said. "I was told this was a data pickup. I figured it'd be something I could put in my pocket. I don't even have an apartme—"

There was a chime from inside.

"That's the front desk. They're back!" said the woman. "Go now!"

I gathered that time was nearly up for this job. I could get the hell out of here and be none the worse, but also none the richer, or I could take the kid, get my upfront payment and figure things out later. It seemed like a no-brainer, so I grabbed for his hand, and he pulled away and started screaming.

"He don't like to be touched," the woman said as the door closed behind her.

Great. I looked at the boy and wondered how long it would be before the elevator door opened and whoever was coming caught us.

"Look kid," I said. "You and me are leaving here together, got it? You can come with me and I promise not to touch you, or you can fight me and I'll have to grab you, and maybe even carry you. Choice is yours."

The kid did not appear to hear me. He didn't make eye contact. There was no evidence he even saw me. But he did start walking toward the stairs.

"Run," I told him. And he did.

The boy was slow on the stairs, but luckily none of the high-brows who lived here would be caught dead walking up and down them without a fire alarm as incentive. Maybe not even then. My original plan had been to take the elevator down from the ninety-eighth floor, then right out to the street, but with the kid in tow there was no way that was happening. People would notice. The security guy might even know him, or the kid might make a scene to try to get away. There was only one option. We'd have to run all the way down and use the emergency exit at the end of the stairwell.

Before we even made it halfway down, the boy started to slow even more, then finally sat on one of the steps and refused to move. Kids get tired so damn easily. I wanted to carry him the rest of the way but I knew he wouldn't react well, and the noise might attract unwanted attention. I had no choice but to let him rest for a bit, each second an agony. I'd never taken so long to get in and out on a job. For all I knew the kid's father had already called SecForce. I imagined opening the emergency exit door only to find my sister standing there with a smirk on her face, judgment dripping from her voice as she read me my rights—few though they were these days.

"Ok kid, break's over," I said. "You either move or I'll move you."

For a minute I didn't think he'd budge but after giving me a longer-than-average stare, he stood and started moving again at his slow pace. It wasn't ideal but it was better than sitting.

By the time we reached the bottom it felt like days had

passed. I braced myself as I pushed the emergency door open, thinking I might find SecForce or security there. But there was no one. I figured the girlfriend must have done something to buy us time. But opening this exterior door did trigger the fire alarm. It was loud and startled the boy who froze and covered his ears. I tried to get him moving again but all he did was scream, almost as loud as the alarm. I wasn't screwing around anymore. I grabbed him and lifted him over my shoulder and I ran like the devil himself—or worse, my sister—was after me. The kid screamed still louder, pounding and kicking against my body as he tried to get out of my grasp. *Christ was I gonna be sore tomorrow.* I held him tighter still. If I liked kids I might have worried that I was hurting him, but the kid was pissing me off, so I didn't think about it much.

When we finally reached my car I all but threw him in the back. Didn't bother to strap him or myself in, just drove as fast as I could—but not so fast as to attract SecForce attention—and got the hell out of High Town.

Back in my neck of the woods, when I was sure no one had followed, I stopped to take a breath. The kid was no longer screaming. He sat in the back breathing hard, his face wet with tears, but he said nothing.

"What's your name, kid?" I asked.

His eyes drifted toward mine, but he didn't speak.

"Fine. You don't have to tell me. We probably won't be together that long anyway. At least once I figure out what the hell to do with you."

I called up the job on my wristcomp again and found the contact number for the client. I keyed it into the car's computer and the call went through, but there was no visual. Whoever this was had blocked the camera. They said nothing; just waited for me to talk.

"I have the...data," I said. "Where do I take it?"

The reply came by text. An address and a time—tomorrow evening.

"No wait, you don't understand," I said. "I can't keep this

ki—this information on me! Not for that long!"

The only response was the transfer notice of ten thousand credits. The first half of my payment. Then communication was cut off.

"Dammit!" I said, pounding my fist against the dash.

What was I going to do with a kid for the next twenty-four hours? People would be looking for him. And my beat-up car didn't exactly qualify as a hideout. Besides, kids need to eat, pee, do kid shit I don't even know about. How the hell had I gotten myself into this mess? But then I remembered that I hadn't gotten myself into this mess alone. I headed to Jax's.

Jax had a place in The Mids. He didn't make any more money than I did—though his jobs were maybe more regular—but he'd gotten lucky when some fat cat client had paid him with a building rather than credits. Don't get me wrong, the place was a shithole; a three-floor walk-up in bad need of—well, every kind of repair you could make on a man-made structure. But it was in a better part of town than where his old place had been, though just barely. And he had the whole place to himself, which was just how Jax liked it. I'd tried to talk him into renting out some of the still-liveable apartments once, but he hadn't been interested, and anyway there weren't a lot of takers for a place that would have looked more at home in Low Town. He'd offered me a spot once but I'd passed when I saw a group of newborn rats huddled together in the bedroom closet. Earth made you tolerant to all kinds of stuff but I drew the line at sharing my home with anything that might start to chew on me while I slept. Jax didn't seem to mind the vermin though. He had laser traps set up all over his apartment, but I think they were mainly to keep the rodents from nibbling on his tech. Hacker priorities.

Since the place was just on the edge of The Mids, Jax was still close enough to Low Town to maintain the connections that brought him a lot of his business. Jax worked with criminals, but he was basically a decent guy. Like most people on Earth, he had payments to make and he had skills that lent themselves to this kind of work. Criminals just paid better than most legit employers. We all did what we had to to survive.

And to be fair, these days there was a fine line between legal and illegal employers. Ever since Earth had shifted from national governments to corporate control, competition had grown so fierce that basically anything was acceptable if it meant getting ahead. There was a sort of honor code among the wealthy companies that kept the off-world folk living in style, but lines were crossed all the time. They saw it as a gentleman's war and as the cliché goes, all's fair in love and...well, you get the picture. Sure, there were still some checks and balances to keep everyone in line. Like SecForce and what remained of old government bureaucracies like patents and copyrights, but even these were not what they had been in previous centuries. It was dog-eat-dog these days. Which was why a small fish in the pond like me didn't stand a chance of bettering her situation here.

Despite all that, Jax had no plans to leave Earth. A Terran born and bred, he'd never set foot off-planet and was terrified of space travel so his phobia kept him grounded. He seemed fine with it though. I knew I'd miss him when I was gone but as much as he meant to me, that wasn't reason enough to stay. Jax seemed to understand.

It was late when the kid and I showed up at Jax's place but I knew he'd be up. He'd never been one for sleep if he could avoid it. I palmed the sensor next to his apartment door and waited as the light turned green to let me know that Jax knew I was here. After a moment, the door unlocked and we stepped in. Jax was nowhere in sight, which was not unusual. He didn't like to leave his setup when he was working. If he was in the Platform, even more so.

"Hi," I said, my voice exaggerated cheer as I moved through the small apartment to the room that served as Jax's office. "How's your day been? Mine's been just peachy! You wouldn't believe it."

The kid entered the room behind me and began looking around.

"What the hell?" Jax said.

He must have been surprised because he actually removed his digi-glasses, which he almost never did. His eyes darted from the boy to me a few times, then his shoulders lifted, silently asking the question we both knew was on his mind.

"Oh this? This is just the data you sent me to pick up."

Jax leaned forward in his chair. "Who the hell is this kid, Vega?"

"The job, man! The girlfriend passed him on. Said the data is inside him or something. Didn't even explain what that meant!"

"Shiiiit!"

He put his lenses back on and started doing his blinking thing while looking at the kid. The boy imitated him for a bit before losing interest and resuming his exploration of Jax's shithole apartment.

"Got it," Jax said, after a while. "Kid's name is Cassius Lowell."

"Lowell? As in Damien Lowell, CEO of HabiTech? Practically the richest man in the system?"

Jax gave a single nod. We both looked at the kid who was playing with the headset from Jax's Platform system.

Damien Lowell was not a man you wanted to mess with. No wonder the job description had been so vague. If I'd known I'd been hired to kidnap the son of the man who owned the luxury residential space stations orbiting four of the planets in this system, I would never have taken it. No one would have. I had to sit down. There was no chair besides Jax's so I took a seat on the floor while Jax kept doing his thing with the lenses.

"Looks like Lowell's put the word out about his kid," Jax was saying. "Not long after you took him, I'm guessing."

"SecForce?" I imagined my sister hunting me as we spoke.

"Nah. He went through less *official* channels. He'll have some shady guys looking for you. Guess he figures they're more likely

148

to find him than the cops."

Even the upper crust knew how things got done on Earth. If this didn't mean Damien Lowell had put a hit on me I might have been amused. My only advantage right now was that no one knew who'd taken the kid, but Lowell would've hired the best. It was only a matter of time. And if the hired guns didn't get to me soon he'd send SecForce after me too. If I got lucky, they wouldn't track the kidnapping to me until I was long gone spending my credits in the colonies. Of course I'd never been lucky before, so there was no reason that would change now. And since Jax had got me the job in the first place, chances were this shitstorm would fall on him too. I was starting to wonder if even twenty-thousand creds was worth it.

"So what do you think the girlfriend meant when she told me the kid had the data inside him? Some sort of implant? Would even a credit-flush asshole like Lowell use his own kid as a data mule?"

Jax shrugged. "Hand me that scanner."

I wasn't sure what a scanner was but I followed the trail indicated by his index finger and tossed him a hand-held tool that looked as though he'd made it himself. Knowing Jax, he had. Taking it to the boy, he turned it on and passed it over the kid's body without touching him, which was good since I hadn't yet had a chance to tell him about the way the kid reacted to physical contact.

"I've never used this on a person before but it should still work," Jax said, staring at the instrument which was making a humming noise. "I'm not seeing anything though. I don't think this kid is chipped. Not even a tracker."

"Well thank God for that," I said. "Odd that a kid whose father is this rich wouldn't chip him with a tracker at birth."

"I'm not saying he didn't, just that the kid doesn't have one now," said Jax. "Trackers aren't easy to tamper with and they're near impossible to remove. I'm guessing if he had one she used a burner on it to basically melt the thing down to nothing. It's an extremely painful process." He looked at the kid as he said this.

"Might be why he doesn't like being touched. Speaking of which, you might want to back off. He's looking annoyed. Trust me, you don't want to set this kid off."

"Maybe he's hungry or something, you think?"

"How the hell should I know?"

"You hungry Cass?" Jax asked.

The kid looked at him but didn't react. Instead he put on the Platform headset and started turning his head as if it were on. Then he tried a few times to connect. It didn't seem to be working. Jax probably didn't have the credits to pay for this month's membership, and he sure as hell wasn't one of the lucky few to have Platform access provided by a legit employer.

"So if it's not an implant, then what...a memory? Can they even take that out of him?" I wanted to know why my clients even wanted this kid. Normally I did the job and asked only the necessary questions to get it done, but this was different. I was in a tight spot here. I wasn't sure if I should wait around for the other half of the money or cut and run while I still could.

Jax sat in his chair again. It shifted a bit under his weight. "It's possible," he said after a moment. "There are methods, though none of them pretty. Whoever wants him, if it's a memory they're after, the extraction process would likely kill the kid, or at least leave him with some brain damage. Especially if he resists."

"Any of your connections have the means to extract it?"

Jax leaned toward me and I could see by the expression on his face what he was going to say before he even opened his mouth.

"You're not serious. He's a kid, Vega!"

I shrugged, trying to make it look like it was nothing to me. "Look, the kid already seems to have brain damage. He's certainly not normal. Doesn't even talk, just screams when you touch him."

Jax looked at the boy. "Maybe it's autism?"

"Richies don't get that. They have vaccines for that shit, or something. Hell, this kid was probably genetically engineered."

"Well then, judging by the way his life seems to be going, my guess would be trauma," Jax said. "I mean, come on; you were a kid once. We weren't a hell of a lot older than him when we got shunted into the system. We're the last people who should be doing this."

He pleaded with his eyes and I admit I felt a twinge of something like conscience. But I couldn't very well call Damien Lowell up and say I accidentally took his kid—oops! Sorry. That was a good way to wind up dead. Even if Lowell took it well, my employer sure as hell wouldn't, and unlike Lowell they had better leads on how to track me down.

"It's too late," I told Jax. "The deed is done. Lowell won't let this slide. Besides, you know how bad I need this payday. All I have to do is hand the kid over tomorrow and I can get so far out of here, Earth won't even be a spot in the sky. You can use your cut to cover your tracks too."

"Aren't you even curious why they want him?" said Jax.

"Sure I am. But not curious enough to risk my life. I figure daddy must've given him some business secrets that the competition wants to use. Beat him to the patent finish line. Happens all the time. Not my problem."

"Well I'm glad you're so ok with this." Jax turned away from me and went back to watching the kid. I'd never seen him like this. We'd both done a lot of shady stuff to make it in this world but none of it had ever come between us.

The kid grunted and threw Jax's headset across the room. Jax had to roll out of his chair to avoid getting hit.

"Hey! Take it easy kid! I plan to get that running again next month. Or at least that'd been the plan for my cut of this job. Now I'm not so sure I want it." I pretended not to notice the glare he shot my way.

As expected, Cass said nothing. He sat on the floor, arms wrapped around his knees, staring at the Platform like the thing had betrayed him.

"Must be how he spends his time," I said. "His dad can probably afford the subscription every month. What do you think it's even like in there for him? The constructs his mind creates, I mean?"

Jax shrugged. "Who knows what's going on in his head. The constructs are built largely on imagination. I'd think the mind of any kid could come up with some pretty messed up shit. But that gives me an idea. Maybe we could use the Platform to find out what the kid knows—at least in general. We're gonna need a working system."

"Don't look at me," I said. "I don't even have my system anymore. Besides, that's insane. What's to stop him from contacting good old dad once he's in there?"

"He won't," said Jax. "I can lock him down so he's only able to talk to someone using the same system. All we need now is someone with access, but everyone I know is too broke these days to cover the fee."

I had a thought then. One that turned my stomach, but I couldn't find an option that was better. It was ludicrous to even consider it. The risk was enormous. But I knew Jax wasn't going to drop this and I had to admit I was curious too about what the kid knew. I could barely believe the words that came out of my mouth next.

"We could try Arden's."

Jax looked at me as if I'd gone insane. "Arden? Your sister Arden, who you hate? Who *are* you?"

"I know, I know. But Arden's SecForce. She'll have a working Platform—they get the membership free because they use it for training. And as far as we know SecForce hasn't yet been alerted about the kid."

"*As far as we know,*" said Jax.

"Well if you want to know what's in his head, Arden's our one shot. Otherwise I just hand the kid over blind."

"Don't you get it, maybe we can save him," said Jax. "If we find out what he knows we might be able to pass on the information without the kid."

There was no way it'd be that simple. No doubt taking his place would just get us killed instead, but I couldn't argue with him the way he was looking at me. I gave a half-hearted nod, but even as I did I knew I would finish the job no matter what. I had time to kill though, and if it made Jax feel better to go digging in the kid's head, then why not? I knew Arden. If SecForce had been alerted to the kidnapping I'd see it in her eyes the second she opened the door. It wouldn't be the first time we'd found ourselves on opposite sides of the law. I knew I could handle her.

"What will we tell her?" Jax asked.

"We can say he's ours. She hasn't seen me in years so for all she knows I have a kid," I said. "We'll work out the rest of the details on the way. I'll go into the Platform with the kid and your job will be to distract Arden while we do that."

"Ok," Jax said. "But promise me you'll at least consider leaving the kid with her. She's SecForce. She could protect him."

But where would that leave us? Ten-thousand credits wasn't enough to get me off-world. Especially not minus Jax's cut. Plus I'd still have Lowell coming after me. I didn't say any of these things to him though.

"I promise."

The thing about promising to consider something is that it doesn't mean you'll do it. It just means you'll think about it. And I did. I thought about how my sister had betrayed me when we were just kids and I was accused of tampering with the academy scores. I thought about how no one believed me but I was sure my big sister would have my back. But when she didn't, and I got shipped off the training station—sent back to Earth and a string of foster parents who were in it for the credits—I knew I couldn't trust her again. And I wasn't trusting her this time either. Not with this kid or this job or with me. We had to be ready to cut and run because if Arden did know this kid was missing, she would be the first to turn me in and earn herself a nice commendation. She wouldn't give a shit if I rotted in some SecForce prison. Hell, she might even visit from time to time to rub in the fact that she was so much better than me. To tell me how having been given the chance to enter the academy and join SecForce had been an incredible opportunity for a couple of war orphans. An opportunity I'd squandered and she'd risen to.

Bile rose in my throat as the three of us made our way back to my car. I hadn't seen my sister since I was nineteen. It hadn't been a happy reunion then either. I was dreading this.

As it turned out, Arden didn't live too far from Jax's. She was still technically in the Mids. SecForce cops weren't the poor lowlifes we were but they also weren't paid well enough to afford homes in High Town. But her neighborhood was a noticeable step up—or two or three steps up—from Jax's. As we pulled up in front of her apartment complex, I couldn't help but think that I could have had this life. I could have lived in a place like this, with walls that had actually seen paint in the last decade, trees (synthetic, but trees all the same), and neighbors you could trust not to steal your shit while you went to work. But I'd been screwed out of this life by my own flesh and blood. The only family I'd had left.

I felt stiff as I walked up to the building and while we stood in the elevator. I stared at my reflection on the door and felt myself moving toward her apartment as if on automatic. Like I was just along for the ride inside my own body. When Arden opened the door, she looked surprised to see me, especially as late as it was, but I don't think she felt the shock that I did seeing her face-to-face like this. Last time I'd been getting processed for something petty. She'd been helping the arresting officer with the data entry—a smile on her face the whole time.

"Vega," she said. Then she looked at Jax and down at Cassius. "I wasn't expecting you."

"You called me," I said, pushing past her and forcing my voice to sound neutral. "You said you wanted to reconnect, so here we are. This is my old man, Jax, and that's Cass, our kid."

Arden closed the door and took a longer look at Cassius, this time lingering and giving him a smile, as if to say, *I have a nephew.* It's stupid, but it made me angry. I thought, what right does she have to claim my kid as anything of hers? I know it makes no sense since Cass wasn't even my kid, but her smile always seemed to bring out the worst in me.

I swallowed my anger before speaking again. "Look, I hope you don't mind but I figured you'd want to meet the family. Plus Cass here's sick. Part of his treatment is on the Platform, but to be honest things are tight since Jax lost his job so I thought maybe you'd let us borrow yours. For Cass' sake."

I knew SecForce cops weren't really supposed to lend out their systems, but I could see her caving as she looked at Cass. She wouldn't have broken the rules for me, but for him, well that was a different story. It was a good thing the kid was kinda cute. Plus he didn't talk which made him all the more endearing, at least to me.

"You can use my system if that will help," she said. "What sort of medical condition is it?"

"Jax'll explain. Come on Cass." I made my way into the bedroom next door, where I assumed she kept her system, since I hadn't seen it in the main room. Arden called after me. Something about first talking a bit and catching up, but I said "later" without so much as turning her way. I heard Jax stammering as he began to give her the reason we'd come up with for Cass needing the Platform while I closed the bedroom door.

By the time I'd done that, the kid had already put one of the headsets on. Before he could connect, I ran over to plug in the program Jax had written to stop him from talking to anyone but me. I found a second headset next to the system. They came standard with two but it looked like it hadn't been used. The ice queen must not have anyone in her life to share it with, I figured. I put it on and connected to the Platform. Then the world vanished and I was in the non-descript entry portal that began each session. A prompt asked if I wanted to join the other person connected through this system. I said yes, bracing myself for what I'd find in this messed up kid's construct.

A boy appeared, but it wasn't Cass. At least not like I knew him. Rather than being seven he was about twelve years old. The same big eyes and sandy hair, but older. He stood with confidence in the middle of an enormous library—the kind they used to have back when there were still paper books. The shelves were lined with what looked like thousands of antique leather-bound books.

"Hi Vega," he said, greeting me as if we were old friends.

I hadn't told him my name but he must've picked it up when Arden said it. Who the hell was he gonna tell anyway?

"Cass...nice place," I said. "You're...different."

He gave a single nod. "I choose to project myself older here. My father tells me I'm an old soul. Maybe he's right."

Judging by the ancient look of the place he'd created for himself, I had to agree. It was strange hearing him speak. I realized I'd only ever heard him make grunting noises, or scream when he was touched.

"Yes, I can talk here," he said, as though reading my mind. "I can do all kinds of things on the Platform that I can't in the outside world. I often spend time with my father here and he tells me things."

"Things about his business," I said. "Company secrets."

"More like ideas he has," he said. "Improvements on what we already have. Or he shares problems he's trying to solve."

"You're his sounding board."

He gave another nod. "Yes. But I'm more than that."

I wasn't sure what he meant by that, but I let it go for now. I wanted to get right to the point before Arden figured out we were full of shit. She was probably grilling Jax as we spoke, poking holes in his lies.

"Do you know why my clients want you?"

"Yes," he said.

"Something your father told you? Something you overheard or he shared?"

He smiled. "That's what they think, at any rate."

"So you don't have the information they want?"

"I *am* the information they want," he replied.

I must've looked confused, even in avatar form, because he

156

continued to explain, speaking as if I were the kid here.

"My father's about to unveil a new design for his luxury habitats to the World Patent Committee. One that will outshine all the others he's put in orbit here and in other systems, but that will be a fraction of the cost to produce. This one is so cost-efficient he'll be able to launch multiple, even in deep space. It will be a luxury home unlike any before it. And it will make my father the most powerful man on Earth and in all our systems. But they don't know how he did it. They don't know what the plans consist of or how we managed to keep the costs low. They need that knowledge so they can beat him to the punch."

"So it is a patent race. I knew it."

I didn't know a lot about the corporate world, but I knew about patent races. Because tech had made it so easy to copy plans for virtually anything you could produce, or even the products themselves if they weren't too large in scale, it had made it near-impossible to determine who the original idea had come from. In the past, companies had tied up the courts for years trying to prove who had stolen from who. Once Earth became corporate-run, and the WPC was established, things had changed. Now it was a literal race to get a patent. Whoever presented the product schematics and plans first won the exclusive right to production. So it wasn't uncommon for a competitor to wait for you to do all the hard work then steal your ideas at the eleventh hour. Companies spent a lot of credits making damn sure their ideas couldn't be stolen, and guys like Jax made a good living finding ways around their security. Only HabiTech was known for being impossible to steal from, but somewhere along the line Damien Lowell had made a mistake and told his kid a little too much, and he was about to lose both his son and his new station because of it.

"Your father told you how to access his plans," I said. "Because you're his heir."

Cass laughed then. "Not exactly. See, there are no plans. No data to steal. No instructions for anyone to build with. There's nothing, except what's in my head and what I told my father during our planning sessions. And even with a memory extraction they won't get it without my help."

"What?"

The kid walked over to one of the stacks and removed a book. It looked like any average book I'd seen in historical archives. Yellowed paper bound between two hard sides that formed the cover. This one was a deep red color and had writing on it in gold. It seemed unremarkable though. I wasn't sure what he was doing.

Cass passed me the book and I looked at it. *Coriolis*, it said. I recognized it as the name of one of the luxury habitat stations. It was one of the early Earth ones that had come after the original—non luxury—space stations HabiTech had produced, including my home for over a year: SecForce Academy. Coriolis, I remembered, had been decommissioned a couple months ago. It had been all over the news because HabiTech had transported the entire population to a larger resort station orbiting Saturn.

I opened the book. Inside were detailed schematics of every part of the station, along with notes covering everything from the type of plumbing to the colour of the throw cushions.

"My first," he said. "My father's company had architects and engineers create the prototypes and the very basic stations that came before this one. But when my father took me to visit them I knew I could do better. I began to design them in my mind, dreaming of new and better habitats. And so I created Coriolis, the first of the true luxury stations."

He took the book back and flipped through the pages as if to reminisce. I glanced at the closest shelves and saw the books on them. Ideas of every kind from *What to Get Father for His Birthday* to *Plan for a Model Solar Sail Craft* were mixed together with no seeming order.

"The more I came up with ideas for my father's stations, the more I realized I could do it more efficiently than my father's employees could. Faster. Better. I could see things they couldn't and make sense of every last detail in my mind. And the Platform made it possible to organize my ideas into this library, within each and every book. I was able to compartmentalize the knowledge so that you need both my mind and the Platform to access the complete information. One or the other is not enough. You were right when you said I'd been genetically engineered. I was. To have an exceptional mind. That was my father's focus. Unfortunately, there were issues with my body that he did not anticipate, nor did those who engineered me, eager as they were to please him with my mind. They thought my father would not want me when I was born. They thought he would have them terminate me and begin again, but he didn't. And with the Platform, he got to know the real me. The 'me' who could take his business to a level he had not imagined."

"So you're the creator behind the stations?"

He didn't respond to that because we both knew that was what he was saying. This kid was the mastermind behind one of the richest companies known to humanity. He had used his imagination and the Platform to create the stations and had put the information here. I could see by the sheer number of books that even if you could hack your way in, it would be impossible for anyone—my clients included—to find the information they were looking for without Cass' help. At least as long as they didn't have years to search. And that's if it even occurred to them to look in the construct created by a mute, seven-year-old boy. No wonder HabiTech was impossible to hack.

"My one fault was that I initially lacked an understanding of the cost incurred in producing the stations," Cass continued. "I let my imagination run wild and left my father to control what could and couldn't be done. But I know better now and that's why this latest design is the best one yet. My *magnum opus* if you will."

"But as smart as you are, you must've known your father's girlfriend couldn't be trusted," I said. "You must've known something like this would happen to you. Why didn't you warn your father?"

"Ms. Lin is many things, but she's not stupid," said Cass. "She put on a convincing act, and I admit I was fooled, for a time. I knew she was planning something. I could see the interest she had in the private conversations my father and I had in the Platform. It did occur to me that she was working for someone who would want information about the new stations so they could produce them first and put my father out of business. But this was nothing new to my father. People were always trying to steal his secrets. By the time I realized she was dangerous it was too late. But I also realized that Ms. Lin thought only that my father had divulged secrets to me. I thought it was best to let them take me and attempt to extract those secrets. You see, HabiTech is about to file. All I have to do is buy them the time so they can get the patent before your client can. By the time the competitors realize I'm useless to them it will be too late and my father's company will be saved."

It took me a while to figure out what he meant. I'll admit, I wasn't the genius in the virtual room, but I did catch up eventually. The kid had known. He'd known that when they went in to get what he knew they'd kill him in the process—or at least damage him beyond repair. They'd get nothing out of him and they would not be able to use him to their own ends. His secrets would die with him. All the creativity. All that genius that had made HabiTech the empire it was today. But smart as he was, he must have given his father the information already—or somehow made it so that Damien Lowell, and only Damien Lowell, would be able to access it, even if Cass was killed. All he needed was the patent, and there were likely underlings getting the process started even as Lowell searched for his son.

"Jesus, kid. You sure must love your dad."

"He could have thrown me away," he said. "I was a flawed result to something he had spent a good deal of credits on. But he didn't. He took me home and he loved me and he made me his partner. He would have left me the business. Even if I die now, he will be set for the rest of his life with this new design. It'll allow him to launch resort stations in deep space. Far beyond this single solar system. And all previous designs will be rendered obsolete. HabiTech will no longer *have* competitors. They'll be driven out of business—at least until someone improves upon my design, which won't happen within my father's lifetime. I'll have given him something almost as valuable as what he gave me."

It made no real sense to me, but I guess this was where the seven-year-old came in. He loved his father *that* much. The way kids who have parents who love them do. I strained to remember having felt that once, before the war, when my parents were still among the living. But family had been a long time ago for me.

"Finish your job Vega," Cass said. "Hand me over. Get paid. And rest easy knowing it was for the best."

I disconnected rather than respond. A moment later the kid took his headset off too. We both stared at each other for a second. I could still hear Jax and Arden talking in the next room.

"You are one fucked up kid," I told Cass. I could swear I saw something almost like a smile form on his face.

We joined the others back in the main room. Jax and Arden were sipping tea like a couple of old ladies at bridge. Seeing them all chummy like that brought back the earlier emotions from when she'd smiled at Cass.

"We're done here," I told Jax. "Thanks Arden, but we gotta go now."

"What?" she said, putting down her teacup. *Real porcelain. Must be nice.* "You could at least stay for dinner. Give me a chance to get to know my nephew and for us to talk a while."

I mumbled something noncommittal and headed for the door. To his credit, Jax didn't try to stop me despite the fact that I knew he would rather I leave the kid there.

"Jesus, Vega! You're the one who showed up on my doorstep," Arden said.

I couldn't help myself. I stopped and turned, my body poised like I was going to hit her but I didn't. She'd probably charge me with assault. "Dinner?" I said. "Is this part of your happy reunion scenario? After what you did to me!"

"If you'll just give me a chance to explain," she said. "Christ, Vega! We were both kids, not just you!"

"Yeah, but we both didn't end up on a shuttle to Earth. We

both didn't end up living with strangers who didn't give a shit about us. With no education and no way to make a living. But you sleep easy. I survived. And I get it; you had to save yourself. No explanation required. That was my first lesson in looking out for number one and I guess I gotta thank you in that it served me well. Let's go Jax."

Jax muttered something to Arden while I turned to leave. I didn't care what it was. I just wanted to get away before the tears came. Tears I hadn't cried since I was eleven.

Just then her wristcomp went off and I could tell from her tone that it was official.

"Vega wait," she said in her cop voice.

I stopped then and turned to see her face so I could read her expression to be sure. But I didn't have to. Jax stood close enough to glance down at her wrist.

"She knows," he said.

We all ran. Even the kid didn't need to be told. Arden didn't immediately come after us and I suspected she'd turned back to get her stunner.

"Move!" I yelled back.

Jax picked up the kid and ran with him, Cass screaming and kicking like he had when I'd grabbed him. Poor kid. I actually felt bad for him. But I'd feel worse if SecForce caught up with us. Hell, Lowell would probably have enough connections to get us shanked while in holding.

I told my wristcomp to get the car unlocked and open so that by the time we exited the building all we had to do was jump in. I drove off fast enough that I could hear Jax and Cass toppling over in the back. It was pure inertia that kept me in *my* seat.

The comm chimed. I knew without looking who it was but for some reason I can't explain, I still answered.

"Vega, listen to me," Arden said. If I didn't know her so well I might have been fooled into reading her tone of voice as concerned. "You need to bring the boy back. If you turn him over to me I can tell SecForce you cooperated. I can get the charges reduced."

I laughed. "Hell no. I'm this close to getting off-world and I'm not about to let some misunderstanding ruin it for me."

"Misunderstanding? You kidnapped a child! What part of that is misunderstanding?"

"I might bother explaining it to you if I thought there was even the slimmest chance you'd believe me," I told her. "But we both know your track record for trusting what I say."

With that I shut the comm off, leaving her in the middle of a word. Whatever she was about to say, I wasn't in the mood to hear it. Instead, I pulled over and told Jax to get out.

"What do you mean?" he asked.

"Just go Jax. You're not part of this. Go ahead and throw me under the bus, I'm ok with it. If anyone's gonna get pinched for this it's gotta be me."

"And where exactly do you plan to go?" He was asking me but looking at Cass.

I let out a long sigh. "I'm taking the kid in," I said. "The sooner he's in the client's hands the sooner I can get off-world. Don't worry, I'll send you your cut."

He knew I was good for it but seemed conflicted anyway. He hadn't been in the Platform with Cass. He didn't know what I knew. He shook his head but got out of the car anyway. We were close enough to his place that he could walk. He'd be safer taking his chances on the streets than with me.

"You don't have to do this, Vega," I heard him say as I drove off. I watched him in my rear-view monitor. He stood there watching us drive away. I didn't like the way he looked. I knew what he was thinking—we'd been kids once too. But I didn't have time to explain to him that this kid wasn't really seven, at least not on the inside. And that he'd said it was ok. I'm not sure he would've understood if I *had* had time to explain. Besides, I could always make an anonymous call to SecForce after turning him over to the client. There was a slim chance the cops might find him before my clients tried the extraction.

"This is it," I told the kid. "I hope you're sure about this. We'll have to lay low until it's time to turn you over, but then you're out of my hands. You're probably exhausted anyway. You can get some sleep if you want."

He climbed into the front seat and sat next to me. Staring at me as I drove, in a way I couldn't really read. Not that this kid was ever easy to read. Then he put his arm out and I felt his hand on mine. A tiny little seven-year-old hand. Warm, and a little sweaty. He held it there for what seemed an eternity. I wondered if he'd ever willingly touched anyone before. If he touched his father.

"Thanks for making this easy on me kid," I said. "You probably wouldn't understand why this is so important to me because you've lived a privileged life. You've lived on those luxury stations you created and you've lived in High Town. You've never gone hungry or felt like you had no one to count on. Anyway, I'm done with all that. Your life may very well be coming to an end, but mine's finally about to start. I won't forget what you've done for me—even if you're really doing it for your father."

He stared at me a while longer, then took his hand back and closed his eyes. After barely a second he was softly snoring. Not even the jostle of the car seemed to matter. At least *someone* could sleep well in my cramped old hovercar.

It was after ten in the morning by the time the kid woke up. I saw him move from outside the car where I was sitting on the hood, nursing a cup of synthcaf—Low Town's answer to coffee—that I'd jacked from a now-broken vending machine. I pointed to the bag in my seat that held more goodies for the kid. He must've been hungry because he dug right in, predictably going for the snack cakes.

We were parked behind one of HabiTech's component plants. The plant was in shutdown for the moment, so no one else was around. The security systems wouldn't be triggered so long as we didn't try to break in. It was the perfect hideout since no one would think to look here of all places. Right in Damien Lowell's backyard.

We'd arrived about a half-hour ago. I'd spent most of the night just driving and making sure we weren't being followed. It was a good thing Arden had turned back for her weapon because if she'd had time to scan the car we would've had SecForce on us in seconds.

The synthcaf had helped clear my thoughts. And I *had* been thinking, a lot. About the conversation with the kid in the Platform. About what the money meant to me and what the future would bring. About Arden and Jax. About betrayal. And at long last I'd come to a decision.

I drained the cup and threw away the empty. HabiTech's sanitation bots would take care of it. Sliding off the hood I gave the kid an appreciative nod as he stuffed yet another snack cake in his mouth. Hell, if I thought I was going to be dead in a matter of hours I'd enjoy the little things too.

I got in next to him, handing him the bag so he could continue to help himself. He deserved it.

"Look Cass, I've been thinking," I said. "When I was a kid, a little older than you are, I was taken away from my home and my family, and it sucked. I didn't get killed, obviously, but there were times in my shitty life where that would've been a better option. I won't get into that now. Anyway, there was no one there to do right by me, growing up. Just Jax, but no adults. I swore I wouldn't be like those assholes. Maybe that's why I never wanted a kid. I didn't want to screw another person up the way I was. But here we are. Me with a kid that landed in my lap all the same. And I know what you told me in the Platform. I know you said it was ok, but how am I supposed to go live my life—live my dream—knowing what I did to you?"

He obviously did not respond, though his chewing slowed and his eyes shifted my way.

"A long time ago someone let me down," I continued. "She always said she had her reasons but I never wanted to hear them. I know I'm letting you down now, but maybe you'll consider what I just told you."

The kid yelled and threw the bag at me, then went for the door but I hit the locks before he could and without an override he wasn't going anywhere.

"I have a plan," I said. "One that I hope will keep you safe and still help your dad—even let you *keep* helping him in the future." This got his attention. "You're going to have to trust me." But I knew that if my plan was going to have a shot, the kid wasn't the only one who'd have to take a leap of faith.

Cass didn't look convinced and I could tell he was still mad, but I pretended not to notice. I turned on my comm and called my sister. She did a good job of hiding her surprise when she answered.

"Arden," I said. "I'm going to tell you where we are. I haven't trusted you since we were kids but I'm gonna trust you now. This really was a mistake. Jax can tell you, and believe me he had nothing to do with any of it. I'll give you the kid and then I'm gone. Out of your hair and your life for good. You have to give me your word you'll let me do that much."

"You have my word, so long as the boy is safe," she said.

I told her where she could find us and that all she had to do was keep the boy safe until HabiTech got patent approval from the WPC. Once that was done the boy would be useless to my clients. She agreed to keep Jax out of it. No one besides Arden, Cass and me had any idea he'd been involved anyway. I was the one who'd actually committed the kidnapping.

I knew the risk I was taking in trusting her. She could show up with backup, or with the kid's own father for all I knew. But what choice did I have?

Next I called Jax. I told him what I was doing and sent him ten percent of my advance. Unfortunately we wouldn't be getting the rest of the credits, but what remained would be enough to get me out of the city before my angry former client came after me. Maybe even out of the country. Unfortunately, not off-world. But I could find some place to start fresh and no one would have to die for it.

"You sure you want to risk this? Trusting your sister?"

"I'm sure. Whatever happens, at least the kid gets to live."

"When did you go and grow a conscience?" he asked.

"Maybe I just stole yours."

"Yeah, that sounds like something you'd do," he laughed. "I'm gonna miss you Vega. Take care of yourself. And if you can, let me know how I can get in touch with you."

"I will."

I had to end the conversation there before I started to get all emotional. I didn't know why this was so hard when I'd been preparing myself to leave Jax for years. I guess I'd let him get under my skin.

It wasn't long after that that Arden showed up in her squad car. I waited for a beat to see if any more would join her, but they didn't. She'd started walking toward my car so I got out to meet her. Cass got out too. We walked to where she stood and I gestured toward the boy.

"He doesn't like to be touched. He does, however, like snack cakes. The cheap ones with the pink jelly filling."

She smiled, of all things. For once it didn't piss me off.

"Where will you go?" she asked, then raised a hand as if to stop herself. "Of course you can't tell *me* that."

"You're really not going to turn me over to SecForce?"

"I gave you my word. But it was also the conversation I had with Jax. He gave me something while you were in the Platform. Records he'd dug up—I don't even want to know how. I looked at them after you left. They showed what happened at the academy when the grades got altered. They showed who did it. Julia Greyson. Daughter of Maxwell Greyson, one of SecForce's highest ranking officers at the time. So they covered it up and used you as a scapegoat. And I let them. I swear I didn't know Vega, but I was a scared kid. I was afraid they'd kick us both out if I didn't back them up. And I—I wasn't sure you *hadn't* done it."

I exhaled. Of course, I thought. They picked one of the orphans—one of the kids with no connections—and just pinned it on her. They could just as easily have picked Arden, but for

167

some reason they happened to pick me. Probably because even then I'd been a bit of a handful. Two birds with one stone. Jax must've dug all that up with his digi-glasses on the way to Arden's. *He hadn't said a thing about it to me.*

"I'm not going to tell you that I approve of your life choices since then," Arden continued. "You took this kid, whatever the misunderstanding, and you knew that was wrong. But maybe if I'd been a better sister to you none of this would have happened. We'd both be SecForce officers and working together."

I laughed.

"I guess I owe you this much," she said. "Maybe I can still do right by you."

At this moment she wasn't the Arden I thought I knew. Maybe if we'd had more time things could have been different between us. Not like they once were but...something.

"We should both go."

"You can still turn yourself in. It would mean some prison time but I could keep the charges down. You wouldn't have to go on the run."

"Thanks, but no thanks."

"Be careful, Vega."

"Hey, I learned a long time ago how to take care of myself," I said. "I'll be fine. I'm like a cat, always landing on my feet."

"That's a myth. About cats, I mean."

"Well, even if I land on my back I know how to roll," I told her. "Keep an eye on Jax for me."

"I will."

I walked away without looking back. At least not until I was in the car. She was putting Cass into her cruiser, making sure he was safely buckled in. So responsible. So Arden. I couldn't help it, I suddenly felt afraid that I might have put her in danger. But something told me she'd learned to take care of herself too.

FROM LOVE TO HATRED TURNED
BY ISA MCLAREN

Jules Brand watched the woman move across the room the way a cat watches a mouse, heedless to all but the prey. She was dressed to match the season in rich chestnut silk, her wrap in golds and reds playing against auburn hair. Other than a gaudy diamond on her left hand, she wore only simple gold jewelry. Curious, but more interesting was the way she flinched whenever the man next to her moved.

Brand smelled the expensive perfume before the familiar voice spoke over his shoulder. "She is beautiful, is she not?"

"She is but a candle next to your starlight, *mio tesora*."

The woman laughed, a deep throaty sound that always made Brand smile. "I did not bring you here for your flattery, Jules." Nevertheless, she was obviously pleased when Brand turned his attention to her.

"You have but to crook your smallest finger and I am here." Brand lifted her hand to his lips and kissed her knuckles three times. "I need no more reason than to see you."

"You are incorrigible." Contessa Mirella di Fiori was used to such treatment. It took more than simple hand-kissing and flattery to sway her. Artfully applied cosmetics and judicious plastic surgery only enhanced the woman's already considerable beauty. She aged with grace and charm and a very large bank account.

Brand offered his arm to escort her around the penthouse high above Park Avenue. A waiter offered a tray of champagne flutes and Brand gave one to Mirella before taking another for himself. He knew his role at these functions. He was an exotic pet, brought out only for special occasions like these, meant to show off young lovers and recent conquests. In exchange, Mirella introduced him to potential clients.

"There. You see?" Mirella gestured with her glass at a man frowning into his canape. "William Wendon." Her voice lowered to a purr. She loved gossip as much as Brand, although for different reasons. "He has a pair of Cezannes he needs to sell. His mistress found out he was cheating on her and told his wife."

Brand guided them to the patio where elegant chimineas warmed the cool night air. It wasn't enough for one young woman and she pouted. Her escort removed his dinner jacket, wrapping it around her shoulders. Brand wondered if her fingers twitched at the weight of the wallet now laying against her breast.

Probably not, as Mirella explained: "She collects Baccarat crystal." And men, obviously.

Brand gave a small shake of his head. He wanted no introduction. That wasn't his area of expertise.

Mirella's face widened into a grimacing smile as she returned a wave from a shriveled man tottering toward them. She spoke through her teeth quietly. "*Attento.*"

Every nerve tingled with that warning. The tiny man didn't appear dangerous but Brand knew just how deceiving looks could be. He shifted to offer the contessa a discreet distance only to find her fingers clamping around his arm.

The man bowed his head in greeting. "Your Grace, how lovely to see you again." Suddenly Brand understood. The stench of raisins and fish spilled forth with his breath, lingering on the palate, underscored by the disconcerting way his teeth shifted back into position with a click of his tongue.

"And you, *Professore.*" Mirella kept her face tilted upwards where the air was fresher. "May I present my guest, Mr. Jules Brand. He is a dealer in fine art. Jules, this is Xavier Powell. He is a professor of theology." She paused, turning to Brand, the smile revealing something he wasn't sure he liked. "He is looking for ... *Come dice?* Pictures of God."

Brand may be a pet, but the leash was diamond-studded and his owner, very benevolent. He perked up, moving his glass to the other hand so he could reach into his pocket. "Religious icons?" He offered his card. "I deal in quite a few of those, Professor. My specialty, as a matter of fact."

"My collection is rather modest, I'm afraid." People were always saying that. Brand knew when not to take the sentiment at face value.

"If ever you wish to share those glories with a fellow admirer, I would be honored." Brand fingered the pendant at his throat. Even faded and worn, it was clearly a saint's medallion. "My mother instilled me with a great love for the beauty of such images."

Powell registered the significance of the gesture and he beamed magnanimously. "Of course! Iconography should not be hidden away, but offered in communion."

Another wave of rotten fruit clenched Mirella's hand and she lifted her glass in defense. "*Mi scusi, Professore*, but I must introduce Jules to someone."

They both took deep breaths once they were safely out of range. Mirella giggled, putting her head close to Brand's. "May you grow fat with his purse."

"It better be worth it. I'll use a fortune in cologne when I see the collection, just so I can breathe." Brand procured fresh glasses of champagne and scanned the room. He saw the woman in the chestnut dress again. Her eyes were rimmed with red, her mascara smudged. There was no sign of her hulking escort. "Who is she?"

"These others," Mirella flicked her fingers dismissively. "They are not why you are here, *bambino cattivo*."

Brand tensed at the nickname: bad boy. Mirella was one of the few people who knew about his sideline. She tolerated his indiscretions as long as he didn't target one of her friends again.

171

"Who is she, Mirella?"

Mirella frowned, a far more effective expression than a socialite's pout. Brand would do almost anything to avoid seeing it. "Katarina Shelton." She kept her voice pitched low. "Her husband is Rutherford Shelton. He is a brute." She didn't have to go into detail. Her tone spoke volumes, as did the heavy makeup on Katarina's cheek. "I want you to do something about him."

Brand chuckled stiffly. "I doubt he's in the market for icons." He deserved the dark look she shot at him. "*Mi scusi, tesora.*" Brand shrugged. "But what do you want me to do?"

"You know people. I want him —" Mirella drew a manicured finger across her throat in a gesture that was at once clear and menacing.

Brand's eyes widened and he grasped her hand, looking around furtively. "My God, Mirella. You can't be serious."

She shrugged and frowned again. "He is horrible. And she is a friend."

"It's not really my area." Brand's head was spinning. Refusing to help wasn't in his best interest. But neither was wet work. He looked around the party and found the walking corpse in question. "Tell me about him." That was a bespoke suit, accented by a watch worth more than most cars.

"Oh, horrible." Mirella shuddered. "Jealous. Rude." Her nose wrinkled. "He is in investments."

That put him just one rung above lawyers on the slime ladder. Or lower, depending on the state of one's own accounts. "What else?"

"I do not know." Mirella shrugged, this time in apology. "I only know what she says."

Brand sighed. "Fine. I'll help. But not like that," he added quickly. "There are far better ways to hurt a man." He gave her a mischievous grin. "As you well know."

Mirella favored him with a kiss on his cheek, a genuine kiss that left behind lipstick. She wiped it with her thumb, her eyes hooded.

If she was willing to tempt him like that, this must be very important to her. "I'll need information. Obviously, we can't talk here. Set something up, something private." Brand took her hand once more and kissed it. "And you still haven't told me who she is."

Mirella's face closed off. "I am tired. Take me home."

"Of course, *mio tesora*. But first, I should set things in motion." Mirella must not have been that tired, since she looked at him with open curiosity. Brand grinned. "I need to ask you to ring for the car yourself and when it gets here, give me a wave."

"Where will you be?" She didn't look terribly happy with that demand but Brand needed only her cooperation.

"Next to my new best friend, of course."

Brand found Shelton talking to one of the party girls always adorning these events. He picked up a pair of champagne flutes and made his approach. "Say, I know you. You're that model." As the pair turned attention to him, he held out a glass to the woman. "I saw you at the car show, right?"

The woman giggled and blushed. It hadn't been difficult to guess; he knew the life all too well. She took the glass, posture shifting with pride. "I was on the Lamborghini."

"I knew it. I'd be amazed if anyone even saw the car." He took her hand and kissed it.

"The lady and I were having a private conversation."

Brand could feel the irritation coming off Shelton in waves. He kept hold of the woman's hand and turned his head, looking Shelton up and down. He met the hard stare with a blank look before turning back to the blonde. "Jules Brand. You, my darling, are the finest beauty in the room. I should know: I'm an art dealer."

"I said, it's a private conversation." Shelton reached out and yanked Brand's hand away from her.

"Hey, now." Brand backed up a step. "I don't want any trouble." He had to work quickly before private security intervened. He offered the blonde a business card. "Call me when Pops here gets old." He shot a glance at Shelton, adding pointedly. "Well, older." And there was Mirella's wave, just in time.

Brand stood in front of his mirror making minute adjustments to his attire. Whoever this woman was to Mirella, she mattered greatly. Helping her would help himself. More to the point, failing to help would be ruinous. Too many of his contacts were tied to the contessa. Rule 2: Don't bite the hand that feeds you.

He fingered his pale jade cuff links, the ones that matched his eyes. Would she be dressed in rich tones again? He added a pocket square of brilliant scarlet, pulling the corners into points. How had he never met her before? Why had Mirella never even mentioned Katarina? He gave his reflection a sly grin, certain they would have hit it off. Then again, perhaps that was why Mirella had kept him away from the woman.

The high-rise apartment building didn't have a doorman to avoid and the pretense of studying a newspaper kept Brand's face turned away from surveillance cameras. He checked his reflection again in the elevator. Confident that he looked his best, he raised his hand to knock on the apartment door. She must have been watching for him since it opened immediately.

"How lovely to see you again, Mrs. Shelton."

A scowl darkened the lovely features. "Please, just Katarina." She stepped back and gestured him inside. The bruise on her cheek was yellowing and she hadn't bothered with cosmetics.

The apartment was meant to impress. A narrow Turkish rug led into the living room where leather furniture dominated. Another hand-knotted rug covered the floor. The dark red walls were the perfect backdrop for the gilded frames of Rutherford Shelton's art collection. Centered over the fireplace, a large abstract of a car race demanded attention. He did a swift appraisal. All this and Katarina, too. Brand's fingers twitched.

"May I offer you some coffee, Mr. Brand?" Katarina headed

to the kitchen and he followed, trying not to grin like an eager puppy.

"Call me Brand. And don't go to any trouble." The kitchen had granite counters and stainless steel appliances. There were a few homier touches. A colorful dishtowel hung from the oven. A vase of daisies brightened the small table, laid with a vintage tablecloth, the kind picked up as a souvenir, depicting a travel destination. Brand didn't wait for further invitation and seated himself. Ah. France. This fanciful map was far better than the real country.

"I thought Mirella would be with you." Katarina glanced in his direction.

Brand brushed some dust from his trousers and folded his hands on his knee. "Did she tell you why I'm here?"

The pretty brow furrowed as she assembled mugs for coffee. "She says you can help me with —" She closed the cabinet door firmly and looked him in the eye, a defiant tilt to her chin. "Marital problems."

She was beautiful. And not just in that superficial salon-tended, well-dressed way. Her skin, where it wasn't bruised, was rich cream. Her eyes, as Brand had suspected, were brilliant green, flecked with gold in the diffused natural light. The curve of her breasts shaped the simple blouse and fitted jeans accentuated long legs. Bare feet were rebellious and vulnerable at the same time.

Brand held her gaze, gauging her resolve. He'd never get anywhere if she was skittish. He broke the standoff with a rakish smile. "I'm neither a marriage counselor nor a lawyer, darling. And just so we're clear, I'm not a hitman, either."

Those broad shoulders slumped for a moment. She put the coffee and accoutrements on the table silently. An unsteady sigh slipped out as she sat and she used her hands to push back her hair. "I don't know what to do. I was stupid enough to sign a pre-nip. I get nothing in a divorce. No alimony, no settlement."

He waited for her to look up at him. "Well, now. That is something I can help you with." He investigated the pitcher and

175

found the white liquid too thin to bother with. Not cream. And with no saucer to hold a spoon, no sugar, either. He stifled his irritation and picked up the artfully glazed mug. "Tell me everything about him."

"What do you want to know?" She cradled her mug in both hands, knuckles white.

Brand hooked one arm over the back of the chair, the other hand on the table, his legs uncrossed. Open and vulnerable to relax her. He studied the ceiling as if gathering his thoughts. "Let's start with something simple. How did you meet?"

"At one of Mirella's parties." She let go of the mug with one hand and tucked hair behind her ear. "He came up to me and said he thought he'd died and gone to heaven." She snorted softly. "He used to be so charming. I was young. I was in love."

No wonder Mirella was so insistent. She felt guilty over introducing them. "But that changed. Mirella says he's in investments?"

She nodded, both hands back on her cup. "He's very secretive about it. Says I wouldn't understand. I suspect some of his dealings are illegal but I don't have proof. He's just so... smug sometimes."

Brand had heard of brokers who were entirely honest but believed them to be as mythical as unicorns. "What does he do for fun?"

"Other than hit me, you mean?"

Brand's stomach clenched. Not all wife-beaters were sadists and he'd been hoping this one was the garden-variety barbarian. His thumb scratched at a faded stain on the tablecloth. It kept the worry from creasing his forehead. "Why haven't you left him?"

There was a long pause. Brand looked up from his musings to see her hunched in the chair. Heels on the seat, hugging her knees, every muscle tense. "Katarina, I am going to help you. Mirella trusts me and I need you to, as well."

She sniffed and Brand offered over a paper napkin. She blew her nose and dabbed carefully at her eyes. Her voice was shaky when she found it. "It's amazing, really, what you can get used

to. I told myself it was my fault, that I shouldn't make him angry."
She took a sip of coffee and paused. The defiant set to her jaw
returned. "It was the disrespect more than anything. We were at
a party last week and he humiliated me in front of his friends,
treated me like a child.

"Mirella is helping me with arrangements. As soon as I find
a place to live, I'm leaving."

He knew he was going to regret this and his hand went to
his pendant to rub. Brand added several spoons of sugar to his
coffee. The tablecloth could survive another small coffee stain
and he needed the fortification. "How do you know Mirella?"

Katarina let out a small laugh and the tension went out of her
feet. "When I was little, I called her Auntie Rella. She and my
mother were close. Neither one would talk about it, but I've
known her practically my whole life. She used to let me try on
her jewelry."

Images of a cozy domestic scene were at odds with Brand's
perceptions of the statuesque, formidable doyenne.

He checked his watch. Katarina must have felt the pull of
time as well. "What else do you need to know?"

"I can probably answer my own questions if you don't mind
me looking around." Brand stood and extracted a pair of grey silk
gloves from his pocket.

"I ... suppose."

Brand looked up and smiled at the concern on her face. "Just
a precaution, darling. I'm not a common thief."

An embarrassed laugh colored her cheeks prettily. "Yes, of
course. Whatever you need."

He stepped closer and took her hand in both of his. He could
feel the chill of her skin through the gloves. "Why don't you
clean up in here? No need to advertise you had a visitor."

Her eyes went to the pair of coffee cups. "Right."

"Good girl. I won't be long." Brand gave her hand a pat and
left the cozy kitchen. He started in the bedroom and worked
quickly. He found nothing helpful in any of the suit pockets,
although one had a blonde hair on the shoulder and smelled of

perfume that wasn't Katarina's. Nothing in his nightstand, dresser or watch case, other than confirmation the man spent money to impress others.

He found Katarina's jewelry case tucked into a corner of the closet. Much like the simple pieces she'd worn to the party, the jewelry was practically worthless. Her clothing was equally plain. Quality pieces meant to last but lacking the infinite variety and trendiness of most vain women. Her clothes took up less than a quarter of the shared closet space.

A thorough search of the office would take more time than he had so other than a glance at the art work and a quick check of unlocked desk drawers, he left it alone.

He headed back to the kitchen to find Katarina straightening the hang of a dishtowel. He cleared his throat, offering an apologetic smile when she started. "I just have one question." He nodded at the small painting hung over the breakfast table. A recent addition, based on its placement, not quite centered between the decorative plates on the wall. It was a tasteful nude, the model's hair a golden bronze. Visible in the background were the brightly colored trees of a Fall landscape. The piece wasn't bad but clearly an amateur's work. Far different from the rest of Rutherford's collection. "Where did you get that painting?"

"It was my mother's." A fond smile was accompanied by that pretty blush again. "It's not worth anything, just sentimental value. My grandfather painted it. That's my grandmother."

Brand took her hand again, his thumb stroking the skin on her wrist. "I can see where you get your beauty."

"Thank you." She raised her eyes to his. "How are you going to help me?"

He kissed her hand three times instead of answering. "I'll be in touch."

Brand leaned against the door and flashed a grin at the woman sorting papers. "I see your organizational skills haven't improved."

"Brand!" Delight lit up her face before she arranged her features into a disapproving frown. "What are you doing here? Come to rub my nose in your latest acquisition?" She patted her hair as she spoke; reassuring herself the elegant bun was still in place.

He moved forward and offered his hand. "*Chéri*, Isobel. You wound me. Can't I visit an old friend just because I want to?"

Isobel Guittard let him kiss her hand, making a point to count her rings afterward. "That's twice you've insulted me. You must want something."

Brand gave his head a cheeky toss. "You know me too well, *chéri*. But I think you'll like this favor."

Isobel watched Brand work the party. The man was smooth, she'd give him that. If she fawned over clients the way he did, she'd be thought of as an air-headed bimbo. She had to maintain a strict level of professionalism. People thought her cold and calculating. She didn't mind; she had little time for socializing. But his cavalier attitude was aggravating to someone who had to study and work and fight for every business opportunity. It all came so easily to him.

This gallery showing wasn't her purview. The large pieces on display appealed to egotistical buyers with little regard for the aesthetics or history of the work. No wonder Brand was right at home.

Her eyes narrowed as he strutted towards her. Not many men could get away with looking like a peacock. She took a sip of her champagne and licked her lips. "Having fun?"

Brand gave her one of his infuriating grins. "Of course, *chéri*. Aren't you?"

Isobel snorted. "If you count getting felt up by handsy old men." She brushed her loose hair over her shoulder. "Oh, wait. You do."

His grin just broadened. "Now, now. No need to pout just

because I see more action than you do."

"Some of us have standards." Isobel gestured to the artwork, so different from her usual offerings. "Why did you ask me here, anyway?"

Brand abandoned his half-empty glass on a passing tray, scanning the room looking for his next victim to prey upon. He shrugged, almost turning his attention back to her. "After the Ysillis incident, I figured you could use a change of clients."

Isobel threw her drink in his face. "Bastard! How dare you—" She punctuated that by slapping his face, the sound echoing loudly in the suddenly quiet gallery.

Brand fished out his pocket square and wiped the drips from his face. "I think it best if I leave." He nodded at the man hurrying over to usher him out and left without further scene.

Isobel sat at the bar across the street from the gallery, toying with her empty glass. It had been a busy evening. She huffed a sigh and raised her head to signal the bartender.

"May I buy you a drink?" Rutherford Shelton didn't wait for a response before he took the next barstool. "Ketel martini, three olives." He looked at Isobel expectantly.

"The same." Isobel smoothed her hair and made an effort to sit up straight.

"Rutherford Shelton. And you are Isobel Guittard." He offered his hand.

Isobel shook it, trying not to wince at his grip. "You were looking at the Neiman. Did you buy it?"

He gave her a toothy smile. "I'm considering it."

She knew that type and almost felt sorry for the dealer. "Do you have others?"

"The Grand Prix." Shelton lifted his drink. "To getting what you want."

Isobel raised her own glass. "I'll drink to that." She took a large gulp; she'd need it to tolerate his brand of bullshit.

"And what is it you want?" Shelton set his glass down on the other side of hers, moving into her space.

Isobel laughed nervously and leaned away. "Well, that's quite a question, Mr. Shelton." Unlike Brand, her version of personal service didn't extend to the bedroom.

"My friends call me Ford. And that isn't an answer."

She took a drink and weighed her options. Pleased with the response she came up with, she looked him in the eye. "Well, Ford, I want to surround myself with beauty."

His smile widened, revealing a dimple in one cheek. He smoothed his tie. "Then we want the same thing." He tipped back the rest of his drink and ordered another. "I couldn't help but notice your run-in earlier. What did that man do to make you so angry?"

Irritation rose once again. "Brand? Clearly you don't know him or it would be obvious. The man's a complete prat."

"Who is he?"

"Jules Brand is a constant obstacle to my goals. He's an art dealer." She shook her head. "But let's talk about something more pleasant. What do you do besides collecting art?"

He seemed to warm to the topic. "I make a great deal of money. Investments."

They chatted, mostly about Rutherford. Deep-sea fishing, Grand Prix racing, golf. His houses in the Hamptons and Bel Air, his apartment in London, his cars.

Isobel was still sipping her second drink, now warm and sour from the olives, while he was on his fourth. He reached over and moved her necklace, straightening it. "Tell me, Isobel. Do you know a woman named Mirella di Fiori?"

Isabel frowned and readjusted the necklace. "She's a serious collector." She gave him a thin smile. "Mostly of husbands, but other things, too. Art, jewelry, music boxes. Why?"

"Because I think she and that Brand fellow are plotting something." His eyes were dark and had taken on a dangerous edge.

"Oh?" Isobel pushed away her drink as if that could help her regain her senses.

Shelton nodded. "I saw them together a couple weeks ago."

The thought of Brand brought a sneer to her face and irritation to her voice. "I knew he couldn't finance that on his own."

"Finance what?"

"Cesare Varano produced a series of paintings, each featuring a different season. One of my clients has Winter and Spring. Mirella owns Summer." Her eyes narrowed as her anger built up. "I told you Brand likes to get the best of me. He must have found Fall."

"How much is something like that worth?"

Isobel raised her glass and gave him a delicious smile. "He's a relative unknown but my sources say he's about to explode. Let's just say my finder's fee will keep me surrounded by beauty for a long time."

Brand took the shopping bag from Katarina and slipped his arm around her waist. "You see, I told you this would make you feel better."

"I don't see how this is going to help." Katarina brushed a strand of hair off her face, a futile exercise in the afternoon breeze.

"Now, now. I've been very busy and I deserve some fun, too." Brand pulled her in front of a jewelry store window. He admired their reflection as he asked, "See anything you like?" They did make an attractive pair.

Katarina bit her lip, hesitating before pointing to a pair of emerald drop earrings. "Those are quite pretty."

"When this is over, you'll be able to have the whole set if you like. You'd be stunning in emeralds." He raised his hand to tame more errant tresses and let his fingers trail along her jaw.

"Thank you." She smiled broadly. "Thank you for not suggesting I let someone buy them for me."

"You're an amazing woman, Kat. You deserve to be more

than someone's accessory." He wrapped her hand around his arm as they continued walking. "If anything, handsome men should accessorize you."

She laughed. "Someone like you, perhaps."

"I do fit that description." Brand stopped at the corner and raised his hand to signal a taxi.

"And so modest. What's next for the plan?" Katarina kissed him on the cheek.

The taxi pulled up and Brand opened the door, handing over Katarina's shopping. "Next I check my hooks to see if I've had any nibbles." He gave the driver Katarina's address. "I'll be in touch, darling."

As the taxi drove off, Brand checked his watch. Shelton wasn't the only one with a fondness for expensive timepieces.

"Late for an appointment?"

Brand's head jerked up to see a large silhouette nearly blocking the sun. "I beg your pardon?"

"You're going to be late, if I see you with my wife again." The hulking shadow came into focus. Shelton.

"You must be mistaken." Brand took a step backwards, glancing around for exit options.

"I saw you." Shelton moved closer, edging Brand towards an alley.

"Ah, but as I understand, you're separated, therefore, she's not your wife anymore." The alleyway was dark and devoid of witnesses and entirely filled with substances that could ruin a nice suit. Brand tried to side-step but was thwarted by a large arm bracing against the building, blocking his way. "And I really do need to make my next appointment."

"Stay the hell away from my Kitty if you know what's good for you."

Shelton's arm drew back and Brand instinctively covered his face. He wasn't one of those men who could sport a broken nose with style. Luck was with him, for a given value of luck, and Shelton's fist hit him in the stomach.

Brand felt the air rush from him. The afternoon went dark

and he doubled over, clutching his mid-section. He really should say something witty, about Shelton hitting a man for a change, but his head was spinning and his lunch was threatening to revisit. He coughed, staggering back against the rough wall of a building.

By the time he regained his senses, it was far too late for repartee. Shelton was gone.

The phone rattled on the nightstand. Brand pulled the covers over his head and hunkered down. It stopped. A moment later it started again, this time clattering against a water glass. Brand groped for the offending device and pulled it into his cocoon, answering with a non-committal grunt.

"He's getting worse. You said you were doing something."

Brand could barely understand the woman through the sobs. "Calm down, darling." The voice finally registered through the fog of sleep. He sat up and rubbed his hair and sniffed deeply. "Kat." He cleared his throat with a drink of water. "Are you all right?"

"Yes, I'm ... He was here! He barged his way in."

Brand started leafing through his closet. "Is he there now?"

"No. He's gone."

"Lock the door. I'll be there as soon as I can." Brand blew out his cheeks as he tried to decide what the hero of this piece would wear.

Brand knocked on the door to Katarina's new apartment less than an hour later in a tomato-red silk shirt under a dark brown suit. If Rutherford was going to show up and punch him in the face, he didn't want bloodstains to ruin his outfit. "It's Brand. I'm alone."

The door opened enough for Katrina to confirm his statement before she released the chain.

"Are you all right, darling?" Brand checked the locks himself before turning to Katarina, putting his hand at the small of her back to guide her toward the threadbare sofa.

Her eyes went wide and she jolted away from his touch. Brand raised his hands in a gesture of apology and stepped back. "I'm sorry, Kat. I didn't mean—"

Katarina flung her arms around his neck and buried her face against him, trembling. Brand laid his hands on her shoulders lightly and murmured into her hair.

"It's all right, darling. You're safe now." He eased into a fuller embrace. "I'm here."

As the trembling subsided, she took a shaky breath in. "I feel a fool."

"Shh. It's over now." Brand pulled back and gave her a reassuring look. "Take a deep breath and tell me what happened." He gave her hands a squeeze and let go so she could talk.

She seemed to need to move and took a few steps to the door. "He came in and I was telling him to leave. He said he just wanted to check on me, make sure I was okay." She paced the carpet as she spoke. "I mean, as if he ever cared when he was knocking me around—"

"Kat. He looked around?" There wasn't much to see in the small apartment. The seating area opened into a kitchenette. Brand recognized the plates hanging on the wall. The bedroom was neat, the bed made.

"Yes. He told me to make coffee." Katarina pulled on her fingers, moving toward the kitchen.

Brand looked at the empty pot, the lid open. "But you didn't."

"No, he didn't want it." Her face made an O as she remembered. "He used the bathroom and left."

"What terrible manners." Brand gave her his charming smile. "You make wonderful coffee. Would you mind?" He gestured to the device.

Katarina shot him a strange look but returned to making coffee. "What do you think he wanted?"

Brand shot his cuffs and gave his head a toss. "Just to bully you, darling. Don't worry. We're right on schedule and he'll be out of your life soon enough."

She nodded and filled the carafe. While she was busy, Brand slipped into the bedroom. And there next to the open bathroom door was the painting, the initials CV in the corner.

Brand groped for the buzzing phone. This was getting to be a bad habit. "Time's it?"

There was a pause before Katarina answered. "It's two in the afternoon! Were you sleeping?"

"Late night." Brand pushed his shoulders up against the headboard and squinted at the day.

"I can't believe what he did! He tried to take my painting!"

"Darling, you know I don't like discussing your ex while I'm naked and thinking of you." He grinned at the strangled noise of frustration. "How about I pick up some dinner later and you can tell me all about it." He thumbed the connection closed and turned off his phone. Everything else could wait until later and he flopped back down to sleep.

It was nearly nine that night by the time Brand knocked on Katarina's door. A jaunty knock, carefree and playful. He was in far too good of a mood to take Katarina's scowl personally when she yanked the door open. "Wine?"

"Where have you been? I've left a dozen messages!" Katarina was wrapped in a thick wool sweater and tight jeans.

He breezed past her and started rummaging the kitchen for a bottle opener. "Sorry, darling. Some of my stops took a bit more time than I'd anticipated. Glasses?"

Katarina produced a pair of thick goblets and set them in front of Brand. She closed the drawers he had left open and handed him a corkscrew. "What stops? Brand, I've been so —"

"Here, try this." Brand poured as he spoke. It was a good bottle, one that deserved more attention than the previous owner would have bestowed upon it. He poured a smaller glassful for himself. "Good, hmm?"

Open delivery containers littered the counter. Brand touched his pendant as he noted how well the wine would complement the food he hadn't bought. He walked to the sofa, moving a decorative pillow as he sat. "Now, tell me what had you so upset earlier." He looked her over. "You look no worse for wear."

Katarina stared at him, but followed. She took a gulp of wine then set it aside. She rubbed her palms on her thighs and took a deep breath. When she looked at Brand, her eyes were full of fire, the gold sparking like embers. "That son of a bitch tried to take my mother's painting in the settlement."

Brand put his wineglass safely out of range on the low table. "Is that all? After a dozen messages, I expected something dire."

A manicured hand lashed out and Brand gripped her wrist, moving his head back. "Now, now, darling." He grinned as she growled at him. He loosened his grip and brought her hand to his mouth to kiss as he stared in her eyes. "You'll have to learn how to control your emotions if we're going to succeed."

She yanked her hand away and rubbed it but not before Brand had seen her eyes darken in response. "You're a bastard."

"Yes, but I'm told my father had his reasons." Brand refilled their glasses and handed over Katarina's. "Close your mouth before you catch flies."

Katarina dropped her head and tucked a strand of hair behind her ear. "Mirella used to tell me that when I was a girl."

Brand reached over to touch her chin, coaxing her to look up as he smiled. "And me, when I was a boy." The roller-coaster of emotions was taking a toll and her eyes were glistening.

Her face crinkled in pixie-fashion, a far more attractive look than the previous one. "I think you'd better tell me what's going on."

Brand smoothed his shirt and gave his head a toss. He looked across to the window and debated moving to the more dramatic location. The view was horrendous from this shabby apartment, however, so he stayed put. "I've spent the last month dropping hooks for our Rutherford. I've had a few nibbles but nothing solid until today."

He glanced over to see if she was following. "Now we know what he wants and," he paused to grin. "We can let him have it."

"Oh, no. He's not getting—"

Brand stilled her agitated hand. "There you go again, letting your emotions get in the way." The fire was back in her eyes as she glared at him. "We still have a lot of work to do, darling. And I need you to be clear-headed." He stroked the skin at her wrist as he explained what would happen in the next few days.

Understanding finally dawned and Katarina took a drink of wine to let it all sink in. Brand waited, his pulse racing, fingers twitching with the urge to touch his pendant.

"Are you sure this will work?" Her teeth worried at her lower lip.

Brand leaned forward, cupping her face with his hand, and nibbled at that lip himself. "Oh, yes," he whispered. "I know exactly what I'm doing."

The two couples faced off across the conference table: Rutherford Shelton with his lawyer on one side, Katarina Shelton (soon to be Parras once more) and her lawyer on the other.

Papers changed hands. Katarina read over the documents and was about to sign when she saw her mother's painting listed among Rutherford's assets. "No, that painting is mine. My mother gave it to me, not you."

"The pre-nup you signed says you get what you came into the marriage with, sweetheart. Nothing more. I'm being generous with the clothing." As he spoke, Rutherford's lawyer tried to stop him.

Katarina was more willing to heed her counsel and listened while the woman whispered in her ear. After a bit of back and forth, her lawyer addressed his. "Gifts received by one spouse are considered separate property and are exempt from the pre-nuptial agreement."

A whispered conference led to another proposal. "We're willing to offer fifty-thousand dollars."

"I'm not selling my mother's painting for—"

"A hundred thousand."

"Rot in Hell!" Katarina glared at Rutherford.

They had another whispered conference. The lawyer didn't look too certain of his client's judgment when he made the next overture. "Five-hundred thousand."

"Let me have a moment with my client please, gentlemen."

When Katarina's attorney joined the men in the hall, she told them to have the paperwork on her desk by morning.

Brand opened the champagne and brought the bottle to his nose to inhale the musky fragrance. None of that cork-popping showiness; this wine was worthy of a far more dignified treatment. He poured it into flutes and handed one to Katarina.

"Here's to a job well-done. You were magnificent, darling." Brand lifted his glass and clinked it gently to hers. They were in his hotel room. Bare hangers and full suitcases signaled his imminent departure. He was going to miss this place.

"Thank you. I had a good teacher." Katarina sipped her champagne and made a small noise of enjoyment.

A hurried knock interrupted them. Brand opened the door. "Isobel. You look like you could use a drink. Will champagne do?" He gestured her inside with a broad grin.

"Your celebration is premature, Brand. I told you that idiot was trouble." Isobel nodded greetings to Katarina and tossed her purse on the nearest flat surface.

"Which idiot is that, *chéri*?" Brand handed her a glass, entirely unperturbed by her distress.

She tipped the glass back and took long swallows then held it out for more. "Rutherford D. Shelton. The D stands for Dick-head."

"Actually, I believe it's for Destry." She blinked at his retort and he grinned. "Go on."

"He won't sell the painting. Not to me, not to you." Isobel sat down on the edge of the bed. "We're both screwed."

Her expression turned petulant and Brand laughed. Isobel looked from him to Katarina. They were both laughing at her. "What did I miss?"

"He has a fake. I had one knocked up, just in case. Kat still has the original." Brand took a thick envelope from his valise and held it out. "You've been very helpful. For once."

"Wait, what about my buyer?"

"That would be me. My apologies for the ruse. I'm sure this will compensate you for your time."

Isobel snatched the envelope and drained her glass. "If I find out you've sold the original, I'll expect a cut. And you owe me a favor, Brand. Remember that."

He took the empty glass and lifted her hand to his mouth. "Of course, *chéri*."

Isobel snorted and tossed her head, looking at Katarina. "Be careful of him. That charm hides a multitude of sins."

Katarina offered her hand to shake. "Thank you, Ms. Guittard. I won't forget this."

Isobel shot a look at Brand as she left. "Thanks for the tip about the Cezannes, by the way."

"Any time." He shut the door and reached out to Katarina, closing the distance between them. "What do you want to do now?"

She went to him, backing him up toward the bed. "I want you to tell me how you knew he'd go after my painting and how you knew he'd keep it."

When his legs hit the edge of the bed, he fell backwards, his hand at her waist to bring her along. When she laughed in delight, he kissed her neck, nuzzling against the sweet-smelling skin. "I told you. Men like him are very predictable and easy to manipulate."

Katarina writhed against him. "What about when he finds out there is no series?"

Brand chuckled. "Then he'll also find out who CV really is. Who could he tell without letting on you'd gotten the better of him?" He smiled up at her when she lifted her head.

"You're amazing. We have a half a million dollars thanks to you. I'm so happy."

"That's what I'm here for." To prove it, he kissed her, thoroughly and with every attention to her needs. After all, that was his first Rule: Keep the mark happy.

THE BRIDGEMASTER'S DAUGHTER
BY JOHN RYERS

Neloria hurled a throwing knife at her father's head.

Not really, but it's who she'd always pictured during practice. Wood splintered from the strike and Neloria spat at the target dummy's feet. Her father and brothers were cutting down men across the Artisean Toll, a bridge at the southern edge of their land, but not Neloria. She was stuck in the training field under a half-moon sky, and that's where she'd stay until they returned.

Neloria pried the dagger out of the dummy's head with a grunt and cursed, knocking the target to the dirt. They'd all return with bloodied swords and crimson-stained shirts, and all she'd have to show for her efforts was a bit of dust and sweat. Two of her brothers were older and, of course, entitled to defend the bridge, but her third brother was five years younger. Only fourteen, yet Father had no problem sending him to the Toll. She could fight as well as any of them, but not once had she been to the bridge except by armored escort in the light of day.

Neloria leaned against the wooden fence that surrounded the field and let her mind wander. Father's manor sat empty across the field, save for a few servants preparing a victory feast in the kitchen. Roasted duck and herbed potatoes wafted in the breeze, a smell that made both her mouth water and her blood boil, for it was a smell that reminded her she was not where she needed to be.

Her eyes travelled up the stone wall of the manor to the candle-lit window of Father's study. How long would she need to train before he allowed her to fight at the Artisean Toll? How long would it be before she returned with a blood-soaked shirt of her own?

A shadow flitted past the study window. Neloria straightened her back and squinted. No one was allowed into that wing of the house because that's where Father kept his prize: a sky shard he believed allowed himself and just a handful of men to hold the Toll against any that would seek to claim it. A prize that someone was about to take, or try to.

Neloria slipped the knife back into her sleeve and leapt over the fence. She dashed across the grassy field, keeping her eyes on the study window. The candle went out as she reached the side door. Whoever had the audacity to steal from her father would rue their decision to ever set foot in his home.

Neloria stopped at the door and caught her breath. Though time was short, bursting through the door and huffing up the stairs would only give her away, and there were at least a dozen different ways out of the manor the thief could choose. One more deep breath and she stepped inside.

The servants never saw her enter. It was a skill Father was quick to teach, as sneaking up on an opponent was the easiest way to gain the upper hand. Their voices were loud enough to cover her footfalls as she crept up the winding stone steps leading to the pitch black second floor. Fifteen steps up, half a dozen strides down the hall and third door on the left was Father's study. She'd memorized it as a child so she could find her way there in the darkness and sneak a peek at his prize.

The study door was slightly ajar, and she eased it open without a sound. Everything seemed in place and the study appeared empty, but it was hard to be certain in the dark. Father's prize remained untouched upon its pedestal: a sky shard the size of a man's fist with a single sliver of moonlight striking it from the window.

The hairs on her neck tingled; something was wrong. She

remembered as a child how the moonlight refracted through the shard, casting a rainbow of colours across the far wall. Even when the moon was nearly blotted out by clouds, the colours sparkled. Now there was nothing. The moonlight was strong, but it passed through father's prize as it would a simple piece of glass.

Neloria's breath caught in her throat; it'd been switched with a copy.

Something struck her in the back, and she stumbled forward. The thief pushed past her and instinct kicked in. Neloria swept her foot out, catching the man's shins. It sent him sprawling into the hallway with a grunt, and the sky shard flew from his hands, bouncing down the hall toward the steps.

The thief leapt to his feet without a sound and ran after the prize. Neloria gave chase. She could let a knife fly into the shadows but, if she missed, it'd only give the thief more time to escape. She knew the layout far better than he did, so a single hesitation was all she needed. When he paused to feel for the first step, she lunged for his waist, tackling him into the open stairway.

A tangle of arms and legs tumbled down the steps, and when they reached the bottom, the thief lay still. He wasn't dead, but he'd wish he was by the time Neloria was through.

Neloria checked the rope around the thief's wrists as he began to stir. He looked about the same age as her oldest brother and had neatly cropped hair with a clean shaven face: the picture of innocence.

She'd moved him out of the manor and into the servant's house across the training field after their tumble. Father used it during the harvest for extra servants, but with summer just beginning, it'd be the perfect place to hold a would-be thief without worry of interruption.

Finally he woke, his steel grey eyes darting around the tiny shack lit only by a single candle. He struggled to stand, straining hard against the rope around his wrists.

"Don't bother," Neloria said. "It's a kryllis knot. Few have ever freed themselves from it."

"Where am I?" he asked.

Neloria crouched down in front of him and drew a throwing knife from her sleeve. "I ask the questions, understand?"

He nodded, continuing to scan the room.

"Who are you?" Neloria said.

"No one of consequence," he replied with a wink.

Neloria pressed the tip of her blade through his pants, just above the knee.

"Quillfayne," he said with an eye-clenched grimace. "Korsen Quillfayne."

Neloria jumped to her feet, and he smiled. "You've heard of me then?"

She had. Word had travelled from the north that Quillfayne was working his way through Bitterfen, stealing artifacts and treasures along the way. The name Korsen Quillfayne was synonymous with infallibility; known for never failing a job and yet here he was, subdued and sitting on the floor of a servant's hut.

"Seems I broke your streak," Neloria said.

Korsen gave a short laugh. "That's not all you broke, sweetheart. Next time you wanna roll with ol' Korsen, just ask. No need to throw us down a staircase."

Neloria rolled her eyes. This was the infamous master thief of the realm's underworld? If Father could only see it now.

Neloria tapped the knife against her palm, thinking. Father was the most superstitious man she knew, and if he learned that his precious sky shard had been disturbed from its pedestal, by Korsen Quillfayne no less, he'd have a fit and be inconsolable for days. He was still at the Artisean Toll with her brothers, but they'd be back soon. If any of them saw Quillfayne here, they'd slit his throat on sight.

"You look perplexed," Korsen said. "Anything I can help you with?"

"You can shut your mouth for a start," Neloria said and he

did just that, feigning innocence as he lowered his head. She'd like to cut the smugness off his face, but there was a far better way to deal with him. He'd stolen from some pretty ruthless men in the past month, one of whom was Lord Nevarus, holder of Bitterfen's capital city, Stillwater. He'd placed an exceptional bounty on Korsen's head, one her brothers spoke of trying to claim if they'd ever had the chance.

"Do you know of Lord Nevarus?" Neloria asked.

Korsen's face paled.

"Thought so," she said. "Then you're aware of the price he put on your head?"

He was. Everyone was. Lord Nevarus was not a man to cross, and those that did often found themselves hunted right out of Bitterfen. For whatever reason, Korsen had decided to stick around despite the bounty. This would benefit Neloria in more ways than one: returning Korsen to Lord Nevarus would show Father she was fully capable of handling herself, and the reward would be enough to hire a permanent garrison to guard the Artisean Toll. A garrison she'd be happy to command as reward for her actions.

Korsen looked nervous.

"This is what's going to happen," Neloria said. "We're going on a little trip to Stillwater to see your friend."

Korsen swallowed hard.

Getting him there alive would yield thrice the reward his corpse would, but the road to Stillwater, despite being quick, was wrought with danger. Besides the treacherous environment itself, there'd be others that would hope to claim the bounty for themselves.

Korsen had a faraway look in his eyes. Neloria snapped her fingers to bring him back. "If you run, I'll break your legs. If you scream, I'll break your face. Get it?"

The arrogance fell from Korsen's expression, and his eyes grew worried. "You don't want to do this," he said. "We'll never make it through the marsh with that bounty on my head."

"I can deal with whatever Bitterfen throws at us," Neloria

said.

Quillfayne squirmed where he sat. "Look," he said, "if you're that desperate for coin, just let me take the sky shard to my client, and I'll give you the reward. You get rich and I'll happily maintain my image of infallibility. It's win win, really."

Neloria hit him in the jaw. "I'm not just doing it for the coin. And didn't I tell you to shut your mouth?"

"You keep asking me questions," Korsen said and spat blood. "I didn't wanna be rude, sweetheart."

"Call me sweetheart again and I'll cut your tongue out."

Korsen nodded. "Fair enough. What should I call you, then?"

"Preferably nothing at all, but if you must, address me as Lady Neloria Starsis."

"Of course, my Lady," Korsen said with a light bow.

The gallop of horses sounded outside. Father had returned with her brothers from the Toll, but if they knew of her plan, they'd take over and she'd be back in the field killing target dummies.

She peeked through the window toward the stables. Father had already dismounted, and her brothers weren't far behind. Coming away with another victory, all they'd care about now was food and drink and bragging about how many men they'd killed. Now was the time to leave.

She'd sneak across the bridge with Korsen while the others ate and head north along the marsh ridge to Stillwater. Father wouldn't know she was gone until morning, and by then she'd be halfway to Lord Nevarus.

Korsen was dragging his feet. Not literally of course, but for someone so nimble and sure-footed, he was doing a damn good job of delaying their walk across the Artisean Toll. Perhaps it was the blood.

The cobblestone bridge was slick with it, even though the

bodies had been dumped into the raging torrent beneath it for disposal. Father always left a few dismembered limbs scattered about as reminders to those brash enough to attempt a second attack.

The Artisean Toll was the most important part of Father's land and the source of all his wealth. Some thought it fair to claim the bridge as their own, but everyone that tried had failed. The Toll had been passed down by his father's father after its construction, and it was the only way to cross the channel that split the marshlands of Bitterfen in half. Its toll was steep, but unless you wanted to circumvent the channel and wade through a mire of waist–high muckwater, you paid it.

Two armored guards stood at the exit gate, wiping blood from their swords. On their own they weren't enough to hold the bridge, but they could ring the warning bell and alert Father. He and her brothers were efficient killers, much like Neloria, and winning was never a question, but using the bounty on Korsen for a permanent garrison would allow Father some peace. Perhaps it'd loosen his grip on her reigns too.

"Stay close and keep your binding concealed. Let me do the talking," Neloria said.

Quillfayne smirked. "Wouldn't dream of interrupting, Lady Starsis."

"Halt," one of the guards said. His eyes widened when he noticed who it was. "Lady Starsis. Apologies," he said with a bow. "Has your father sent for something?"

"Father says it's time I see what happens to those that seek to claim the bridge. A storm is coming, and he asked that I see the blood before it's washed away." Neloria nodded back to Korsen who stood silent. "This is my bodyguard, Tobo."

The guard raised an eyebrow. "We weren't told of this addition to the family guard. Does he have his papers?"

"Father's drawing them up in the morning. He's in the middle of dinner, but I can interrupt it if you need to see them."

Both guards answered with a quick head shake, and Korsen gave a quiet laugh that only she could hear. They bowed and let them pass. Korsen did a convincing job of acting the protector while Neloria took in the carnage strewn about. One day she'd play a part in it.

"Tobo?" Korsen asked once they were off the bridge.

"My childhood dog."

"I'm honored," Korsen said.

"Don't be. He was a mangy little thing that stunk and gave me fleas on more than one occasion. And he was rather annoying. Seemed a fitting name for you."

Korsen laughed. "All the same, Nels, you pulled that little lie off like an expert. You'd make an excellent procurer of goods one day."

"Procurer of goods?" Neloria said. "That's a long way of saying dirty thief."

"I'll have you know I bathe daily," he said. "In steaming, rose-petalled water with a goblet of bitterscotch in hand."

Neloria rolled her eyes. She wanted to crack him in the head again, but that'd only make him walk slower than he already was.

Thunder rumbled above, and the clouds blocked out the moon. They'd need to hurry lest a bogflood wash Korsen and his bounty into the blackness of Bitterfen's marsh.

Neloria dashed across the marsh as fast as she could. The storm had hit earlier than expected, and the water had already reached their knees. Korsen wasn't far behind, but the lead rope she'd attached to his bindings kept snapping taut, and he'd complain every time she yanked on it.

"Don't stop," she called back through the downpour.

"This would be a lot easier if you untied me," Korsen shouted from behind.

Bitterfen was hard enough to navigate during the dry season, if you could even call it that. Throw a summer storm into the mix and it made travel nigh impossible. There were very few areas of Bitterfen not submerged, but a group of hills in the distance would provide the elevation they needed until the bogflood subsided.

Her brothers had spoken of an inn on the other side of the hill, and if there was any truth to it, they'd take refuge there until the weather eased.

"Lady Starsis," Korsen yelled.

She ignored him and pushed through the water. Lively music sounded through the storm. The inn was close.

"Hey, sweetheart!"

"What?" Neloria snapped and looked back.

A wall of rolling water nearly ten feet high rushed toward them. She tied the lead rope around her waist and ran back for Korsen who'd already toppled over. She was only steps away when the bogflood hit and pulled them both under.

There wasn't time to take a breath. Murky water filled Neloria's mouth and marshweeds tangled her arms and legs. Korsen hadn't fared any better, and the torrent tossed them both around like rag dolls. Korsen's boot connected with the side of her head, and the surroundings blurred.

A lungful of water and a desperate reach for the surface was all she could manage before everything went black.

Droplets from a fleeting storm fell on Neloria, and the light of mid-day warmed her face. A gentle breeze carried the distant cry of gulls, but the sound of Korsen heaving up a mouthful of bog-water squelched the serenity.

He wiped his mouth with his wrists still bound with the kryllis knot and grimaced. "Welcome back."

"You saved me?" Neloria asked.

Korsen nodded and heaved another round of brown water. "Don't go getting sentimental," he said, lifting up the lead rope. "I didn't have a choice. Don't suppose this makes us even?"

Neloria shook her head. Even if he hadn't done it just to save his own skin, she couldn't let him go, not with them being so close to Stillwater.

Music erupted from the other side of the hill. Neloria dragged Korsen to his feet, and they staggered to the top of the mound. The bogflood had forced anyone in the immediate area toward it like rats to a life raft. Dozens of travellers bustled outside the inn, and the stable overflowed with horses.

Korsen took the lead and ambled toward the inn. Nearly drowning had exhausted them both, and there'd be no threat of the masterful Korsen Quillfayne making a run for it; he could barely walk.

He stopped at the door and fumbled with a pocket on his coat, twisting his bound wrists into awkward angles and finally producing a couple of coins between his fingers.

Neloria gave a short laugh. "Who'd you nab those off of?"

"You," he said. "When you were talking to the bridge guards."

Neloria felt the coin purse she'd hidden on herself before they left. Sure enough it was light by two.

Korsen nodded toward the inn. "Can I buy you a pint?" he asked with a wink.

They'd made decent time, and there was no point in passing out from hunger before even reaching Stillwater. She hadn't eaten since before the bridge attack, and after surviving a bogflood, a brief reprieve from their little trip was in order.

Inside was no less chaotic. A minstrel played his tune as loudly as he could upon a tiny stage in the back corner while men and woman crowded the room, shouting orders for ale and meat. Before there was even a chance to look, Korsen whistled at her over the crowd. He sat at a table in the corner with a man passed out at the foot of his chair. Whether he fell from it himself or had a helping hand from Korsen didn't matter at this point; it was an opportunity to sit.

Korsen lifted his bound hands and mouthed something to a barmaid across the room. She nodded with a knowing glance and disappeared into the crowd. Moments later, she returned with two frothy mugs and a plate of something that resembled meat.

Korsen lifted the mug with his hands, struggling to angle it toward his mouth. Half the contents spilled down his chin as he drank. He dropped the mug to the table and wiped his face with his arm. "I saved you from drowning. I found us the best seat in the house, and I bought you food and drink. Are the bindings still necessary?"

Neloria nodded with a laugh. It was hard to believe this was the infamous Korsen Quillfayne. The stories of some of the jobs he'd pulled over the years were impressive and yet, here he was, soaking wet with bog-water and ale, looking more like a vagrant than the master thief he claimed to be. It was a wonder if any of the stories were even true, or if he'd made them up just to appear more capable than he was. He took another awkward sip, spilling more ale and for a moment, she almost felt sorry for him.

Korsen stopped and looked past her, his eyes widening. "Are you armed?" he asked.

"Of course," Neloria said. She had a throwing knife concealed in each sleeve of her coat and with father's training that was all she'd ever need.

"We might have a problem," Korsen said and nodded toward a man across the room who had his eyes fixed on them. He was large and barrel-chested with a thick, black beard and crooked nose that looked as if it'd been broken at least a dozen times. A pair of scrawny men with scraggly beards and dirty clothes joined him on either side, and he smiled with a mouth full of golden teeth.

"Who's that?" Neloria asked.

"Trouble," Korsen replied, keeping his eyes locked on the man. "His name is Nox Tyrane. He's one of Lord Nevarus's hired goons. I saw him outside before we came in, but I thought he was leaving. He's probably just here for the music."

Nox stood from his chair and headed toward them with his lackeys in tow.

"Music, eh?" Neloria said. "Looks like we're about to dance then."

Korsen laughed. "Well put, but all the same, we should

probably go."

Quillfayne was more of a coward than she'd first thought. Scrapping didn't seem to be his strong suit, but this was exactly the sort of thing her training had prepared her for.

"I could take all three with a single knife," Neloria said.

"You might have to," Korsen said as Nox arrived.

Nox leaned over the table, gripping its edge between his massive hands. His two friends moved around behind them, one stopping behind Korsen, the other behind Neloria, so close she could smell the stink of his garlic breath.

"Well, well, well," Nox said. "The legendary Korsen Quillfayne, all wrapped up and ready to go. I trust he wasn't too much trouble for you, sweetheart?"

"Don't call her that," Korsen said. "It puts her in a mood."

"Apologies of course," he said with a light bow, "but he's wanted by Lord Nevarus, and I intend to deliver."

"I'm aware of this," Neloria said and shook a knife loose from her sleeve. It dropped quietly into her hand. "That's why he's coming with me."

Nox scowled then nodded to garlic breath behind Neloria. The man grabbed her shoulder, and Neloria spun up from her chair, slashing him across the face. He fell into the corner, clutching the wound, and Korsen jumped up, driving his head into the other man's chin. Nox reached for something behind his back, but Korsen lunged forward, smashing his head into Nox's nose. Blood exploded from the impact and Nox stumbled back over a chair, but it wasn't enough to topple him.

Neloria hurled the knife at Nox's head, but he got a hand up and took the hit in the back of his arm. She landed a kick to his leg and that finally put him down.

Korsen and Neloria hopped over chairs and tables and burst through the front doors as the patrons cheered them on.

"Over there," Korsen said, pointing to a large black destrier. "Nox's horse can hold us both. Take it."

Ever the thief, but he was right. They needed a quick escape, and Nox's steed would get them to Stillwater in a fraction of the time. Neloria knocked a couple patrons out of the way and grabbed the animal which still had all its tack in place. The saddle was large enough, as Korsen said, and once she'd secured herself, she yanked him up by his bindings.

Neloria snapped the reins. They tore past the inn, down the hill and back onto the marsh ridge path. They'd reach Stillwater within the hour.

Neloria yanked on the reins, and Nox's horse slowed to a stop. She'd always heard the stories about Stillwater but never saw the sunken city until now. What used to be the entrance to the city was now a hundred feet below the mire, and the rest of it rose into the air like a ship in mid-sink. The current gateway was nothing more than a gaping crack in what used to be the upper wall.

The path into the city was lined with extinguished torches marking a narrow ridge of solid ground barely wide enough for two wagons to pass each other. Murky water of unknown depths awaited any foolish enough to stray from the road. Korsen looked terrified.

"Where are the guards?" Neloria asked as they approached the wall.

Korsen shook his head. "Stillwater doesn't need them. The danger isn't outside the city, it's inside. Lord Nevarus gives sanctuary to people far worse than me and far more lethal."

Korsen's assessment of the city wouldn't deter her from the task. In a short little while, he'd be Nevarus's problem, and she'd be happily returning home. Nox's horse however, seemed to take heed to the warning and refused to move any further once they'd entered the city.

"You don't have to do this," Korsen said.

Neloria slid off the saddle and reached up for him. "You think I survived a bogflood and a bounty hunter just to turn around now?"

Korsen didn't answer.

Evening came on quickly as they continued toward Nevarus's keep on foot, working their way up steep cobblestone streets that seemed to lead into the sky. Dark shadows bled across the thoroughfare, concealing twitchy looking characters that skulked around the unlit shops and dwellings. Some locked eyes on Korsen as they moved past and others just grumbled incoherencies.

Quillfayne remained close. His eyes were wide and darted toward any new noise. For someone who spent most of their time in the shadows, he certainly looked uneasy about their surroundings.

When they reached the street that lead to the keep, Korsen planted his feet.

Neloria tugged on the kryllis knot. "Let's go."

"Wait," Korsen said, struggling against her grip. "You see that door over there. The one with the triple rose carved on it?"

The door was nearly hidden. Set into a stone wall that followed the street. It was covered with moss and worn from the weather. The carving of the triple rose was barely visible.

"What about it?" Neloria said.

"It's an Undalorian Rose: a triple blossom with a single thorny stem. It's the symbol of freedom, and it'll take us straight out of the city."

Neloria crossed her arms. "You still think I'm gonna let you go, don't you?"

"Just hear me out. Through that door is a tunnel that leads under the city wall and into the shallows of the marshland. A brief swim to the marsh ridge after that and it's home free. If you untie me and let me go, I'll never return to your father's home again."

"Sounds like you've done this before."

"Many times," he said. "I've been chased out of Stillwater more times than I can count, and not once has that Undalorian Rose let me down." Korsen did his best to look as charming and innocent as possible, but she wouldn't buy it. The moment she released him, he'd be through that door and halfway back to the sky shard before she could ever catch him.

"No deal," Neloria said and shoved Korsen forward. "Now go before I club you and drag your sorry ass the rest of the way.

His protests grew louder the closer they got to the gates. When the gatekeepers approached to halt them, he fell to his knees and sobbed. The guards looked down at Korsen with amusement, then up to Neloria. "State your business," one of them said.

"Lady Neloria Starsis to see Lord Nevarus. I have Korsen Quillfayne in my custody and wish to claim his bounty."

Korsen lowered his head, sniffling like a scorned child. The guards laughed, shaking their heads. "Follow us. Lord Nevarus will be most pleased to see Quillfayne back in Stillwater."

The guards stopped just inside the gates. Lord Nevarus was in the gardens with a servant, sniffing at some flowers growing from an archway. He was fat and red-faced and waddled along with a limp. When the guards signalled him and he saw Korsen, a wicked grin stretched across his face. He sent the servant scurrying off toward the keep and approached.

"Lady Neloria Starsis," the guard said.

Nevarus gave a light bow. "My Lady."

"I bring you Korsen Quillfayne and wish to claim the bounty."

Nevarus laughed. "She certainly gets right to the point. Did Quillfayne harm you, my dear?"

"Harm me? No."

"He never used a pistol?"

"No."

"Never threatened you with blade or bow?" Nevarus asked, almost like he'd hoped Korsen had done any of those things.

"Gods and spice, she said no." Korsen was suddenly standing, coiling up the rope that'd been around his wrists the whole time. "Stop being such a cheap bastard. I told you I could get her without a weapon. That's an extra twenty silver you owe me."

A shiver ran up Neloria's spine.

Lord Nevarus cursed under his breath and tossed Korsen two coin purses. He held them to his ear and gave a light shake.

"Excellent."

Heat flushed Neloria's face. "You were never there for the sky shard."

Korsen looked over and shot a wink. "I could buy a hundred sky shards, sweetheart. I simply needed to get your attention."

Neloria let her knife fly at his face.

Korsen caught the blade and twirled it between his fingers. "If nothing else I've admired your spirit."

"Why the ruse?" Neloria asked.

Korsen shrugged. "I could've drugged you; gods knew I had enough toxins to choose from. But then I'd have to drag you through the marsh which would be absolutely dreadful on my back, not to mention a single scream could reach your father if you ever woke up early. No, it was easier to simply let you lead yourself here."

Her shoulders sank, and her limbs went numb. How could she have been so blind?

"Did I miss it?" a gruff voice called out from the stables.

"She still looks shocked," Korsen replied and appearing in the gardens was Nox Tyrane.

Blood still caked his face, and his nose had swollen to twice the size, but he wore a jovial smile. "Clocked me pretty good back there, Korsen. And after I saved your useless hide from the bogflood."

"Thanks for that," Korsen said, tipping an imaginary hat. "Now stop your whining. It wasn't as bad as the last job. I knocked you out with that one, remember? How's the arm?"

Nox held his arm up and examined a bloodied bandage around Neloria's knife wound. "I'll survive. She's got a decent throw though," Nox said.

Korsen, Nox and Nevarus laughed about the whole ordeal, and Neloria's blood caught fire. "What do you want with me?"

Lord Nevarus raised an eyebrow and stepped closer as Korsen and Nox divided up their coins in the background. "Nothing at all, my dear. In fact, once the trade is made and the papers signed, you're free to leave."

"What trade?"

"You for the Artisean Toll of course," Nevarus said. "I'd grown tired of sending simpletons to claim it for me and, to be honest, it was becoming a rather expensive endeavour."

The servant Nevarus had originally sent off returned with a roll of parchment and handed it to him. Nevarus unrolled it and held it up to Neloria. "This is an agreement written in my own blood. Your father will sign the bridge over to myself in exchange for your freedom."

"We'd take it back the moment you looked away," Neloria said.

"Oh, but you wouldn't. I know how superstitious Lord Starsis is, and he wouldn't dare break a blood pact lest a thousand years of torture befall his soul. No, my dear, I think the bridge will stay in my control quite easily."

Korsen walked back over to Nevarus and threw his arm around the Lord's shoulder. "What's the next job?" he asked.

Nevarus shook his arm off with a look of disgust. "There isn't one. Now that I'll control the Artisean Toll, your services are no longer required."

Korsen sneered. "You promised ten contracts. That's a lot of coin you double-crossing bastard."

Neloria smirked. "How's it feel, Quillfayne?"

He looked unimpressed then glared at Nevarus. "I promise you'll regret crossing me."

"Guards!" Nevarus called out and the gatekeepers answered the call. "Escort Quillfayne and his brute off the property."

The guards grabbed Korsen, but he pulled out of their grip with ease. "That won't be necessary, gentlemen. We'll leave without trouble," Korsen said, then stopped at the coil of rope on the ground. He picked it up and held it out to Nevarus, pulling it taught. "At least let me return the favour to Lady Starsis before I go," he said.

Nevarus rolled his eyes. "Make it quick, I don't want you anywhere in sight when Lord Starsis arrives."

"Very well," Korsen said and secured Neloria's hands behind

her back. Whatever knot he'd used was far too loose to do any good. Korsen stalked around her, like a lion eyeing his kill. "I'll always remember the time we shared," he said then stopped behind her. His hand brushed hers, and the cold steel of her throwing knife slipped into her palm.

Korsen came back around in front. "Your beauty is unmatched, my Lady, like an Undalorian Rose," he said with a wink and gave the slightest nod toward the exit.

Nevarus huffed while reading over his blood pact. "Bloody hell," he said, never looking up. "Get out of my city, Quillfayne."

Korsen leaned in and kissed Neloria's cheek. "Make it count," he whispered, then left the property with Nox.

She would.

Neloria focused on Nevarus's neck. She shook the rope from her hands and let the knife fly. He looked up in shock as the blade found his throat, and Neloria turned on her heels, running toward the gate. There was no time to stand around and bask in the glory of duly dealt justice, but as she pushed through the Undalorian Rose door and dashed down the tunnel to freedom, her lips curled into a smile at the sight of her blood-stained shirt.

DANGERS OF TENSIRE

BY RYAN TOXOPEUS

Grodurs Whiteskull, chieftain of the ursine Whiteskull tribe, crouched behind a hilltop. Below, the merchant forces built and fortified their town—Phaelan's Rise—on the eastern shores of Tensire. It was mostly a collection of sod huts surrounded by an earthen dike and trench with iron spikes. In the middle of the town were large wooden buildings, constructed from what little timber had been available nearby when the merchants landed. As if it had not been bad enough years ago when the Iltherians had drained the land of its magic, now the merchants of Phaelan's Republic were coming to plunder the continent.

The ursine tribes had been killed and enslaved by the Iltherians, and Grodurs had heard rumours that these merchants were out to do more of the same. However, where the ursine had been viewed as a threat by the Iltherians, the Republic thought of them as a nuisance to be removed so the merchants could steal valuable resources. Grodurs growled low in his throat when he saw leporine pelts being carted into town.

"I will not allow this to happen to my people," Grodurs said.

Petey Furnax, a small, brown-furred, fox-like creature beside him, glared. "The loss of a few filthy leporine is not our concern. We will make Phaelan's Rise appear a name in jest. Don't let your rage spoil our plans."

"Your plans," Grodurs corrected. Giving the small vulpine

control over the situation was a risk, but what choice did he have? His own people had failed to be effective against both Iltherian and Republic invaders, thus far, while the secretive vulpine had remained mostly untouched. Or so they said. Grodurs wasn't sure he could take Petey at his word.

A moment of silence passed between the two before Petey looked up at Grodurs with mischief twinkling in his eyes. "There are many of them. The cost will be high. But I know someone who has lost much to these invaders already, and she will be more than willing to help. Despite great personal pain, she has trained in their ways, and will be invaluable to your cause."

"I will pay whatever price you require," Grodurs whispered. Soldiers with muskets patrolled the perimeter of the town, and he could not fathom how they could hope to match such power. The ability to kill from afar seemed an insurmountable obstacle. Even as he fumed at his own impotence, another ship appeared on the horizon, steaming toward the town. "When do we begin?"

There was no answer.

Grodurs looked down where Petey had been a moment before, but there was no sign of the vulpine. A chill ran up his spine, and the great ursine chief could find no evidence that the vulpine had ever been there.

But on the wind, he finally heard the soft reply. "Soon."

Jebeddo Raulner stood on the railing of the ship, partly to avoid the frantic movements of the much larger humans and dwarves who milled about, preparing for landfall at Phaelan's Rise. The captain of the ship stood in the middle of a circle of would-be colonists and adventurers, seeking out the bounty of this new land. Tensire was rumoured to be wild, with vast fields untouched by industry. Perhaps a year ago that had been true, but looking out over the town, at least this corner had been tamed—partially. But most importantly, Tensire was supposed to be rich with the strong yet lightweight metal, mithril. The reward for finding new veins was enough to send hundreds of people to Tensire's shores in search of their fortune.

Unlike anything he had ever seen before, the town of Phaelan's Rise stretched on and Jebeddo had no difficulty seeing over the squat sod buildings. Closer to the middle of town there were two wooden structures that stood taller than the rest. A rough earthen wall surrounded Phaelan's Rise, and a trench on the outside was filled with iron spikes.

As the ship docked, the captain let out an ear piercing whistle to draw the attention of the many adventurers from Phaelan's Republic and beyond. Listening intently, Jebeddo wrinkled his nose at the first job, which involved slaughtering leporine for their pelts. Killing animals was certainly against his moral code as a druid, even if they were mindless savages. The next job was to deal with an ursine chieftain. The ursine, like the leporine, were a species closer to animal than human, but rumoured to be sentient with their own culture. "Dealing with" something natural sounded like there might be some wiggle room to negotiate. After hearing the other options, his mind was still set on the ursine.

A bulky human warrior holding a glaive stood near the rail and cast a glance at Jebeddo. "Unless I miss my mark, you looked interested in the ursine. I'm Idnatius, mercenary. Sounds like a good job. More of a challenging fight than the little rabbits."

"We don't need to fight," Jebeddo insisted.

"Wouldn't hurt, though," someone on his other side said, and he glanced at the speaker. The deep elf wore a hood over his sensitive eyes, but his black skin gave away his identity.

Jebeddo huffed. "Zacnefron, I'm sure you would enjoy hunting leporine."

"Sure," the deep elf said, a sly smile creeping over his face. "More enjoyment making you squirm, though."

A squirrelley—a halfling with flaps of skin connecting his trunk and arms—bounded over and sat on the rail beside Jebeddo. "Did I hear you guys say you're going for the ursine chief? I bet he'll have something shiny!"

Hope for a peaceful resolution faded fast and Jebeddo sighed. It would be up to him, and him alone, to try to steer the others away from killing the ursine on sight. After all, more than rewards and treasure, the ursine might have valuable knowledge of the natural world. Tensire was an unknown place, full of wonder. If he could discover the secrets of the land, perhaps he could start fresh here and build a new druidic order.

One step at a time. First, the job.

When the gangplank dropped to the dock, people flooded off the ship. Not far from the dock, they found a blonde dwarf with a sign that read, "Ursine." Beside her stood a creature that was about the same height as Jebeddo with dark brown fur covering its pointy face. Its black nose twitched as they approached, and his small brown eyes were moist.

"You here for the ursine chief?" the dwarf asked. When they all nodded, she said, "Good. I'm Deputy Hammerstrike. This here vulpine is Petey. He'll tell you more. Between the constant leporine attacks and everything else going on around here, I just don't have time for this." Without another word she left.

"Thank you for coming!" Petey said, his voice trembling. "I've been living up north in a new outpost that Phaelan's Republic is constructing near some forest. My wife is pregnant and was a passenger with a merchant to come here for medical attention. However, the cart came under attack by Chief Grodurs Whiteskull, a particularly large and foul-tempered ursine. I tracked them a short ways, but they are too many for me to handle alone." He patted a pistol on his hip, which looked absurdly large on his small frame. "There will, of course, be a reward for killing Grodurs."

Jebeddo's heart sank at the words. So much for diplomacy.

"Show us the way!" Idnatius said, and the other three followed their vulpine guide.

An hour north of Phaelan's Rise, Jebeddo had almost given

up hope of finding any wildlife that could help them. The grass on either side of the road was taller even than his human companion, Idnatius, and it was rare that any animals would come near. Of those that did get close enough for him to call, all the field mice and chickadees he had spoken with had no idea about the ursine.

Finally a little brown mouse had something informative to share. "Oh! Ursine big! Saw them fight. Scary!"

"Did you see which way they went?" Jebeddo asked.

"Not far!"

And sure enough, a short distance away, a broken down cart was halfway into the grass on the side of the road. Three dead bodies sprawled nearby: two guards and the merchant who had owned the cart.

Zacnefron looked inside the cart and asked, "What had they been carrying?"

"Timber," Petey answered. "Wood's hard to come by nearer to Phaelan's Rise, so that's why they set up the outpost further north."

"Just your wife missing?" Idnatius asked.

Petey shook his head. "There were two other passengers as well. A human and a dwarf."

"It looks like the ursine only killed those who might have fought back," Jebeddo said, hoping to quell any growing bloodlust.

Idnatius nodded. "Maybe."

"Which way did the ursine go?" Jebeddo asked.

Pointing west, deeper into the mainland and into the tall grasses, Petey said, "That way. I tried getting a feel for the surrounding lands, but am too short to see over the tall grasses, even on top of a hill."

"I can help with that," Jebeddo said. He said farewell to the little mouse, and called upon magical fae that looked like chickadees to blend in with the natural wildlife. "Go. Look for any signs of the ursine."

"In the meantime, we should start travelling," Petey implored.

"My wife could be in distress as we speak! I shudder to think of harm befalling our litter."

Walking in the long grass unnerved Jebeddo. The way it swished around them, or crunched underfoot for his larger companions, made it difficult to hear and impossible to see. While normally at home in natural surroundings, he worried that an attack was imminent at all times.

He was relieved when his chickadees returned to announce that they had not found anything up to the first hill, which was still about an hour away. While there were spots of flattened grass far to either side, there were no signs of trouble in the direction they were headed.

Finally at ease, Jebeddo dismissed the fae creatures and tried to enjoy the trek.

Four hours later, the group stopped short of a stand of small trees. Nothing had gotten in their way, but now the soft roars of the ursine language were easy to hear, if not understand.

At least they hadn't gotten louder, indicating that Zacnefron was still undetected. Lief, the squirrelley, had offered to go ahead and scout the location, but Zacnefron had smirked, assured them all he would be unseen, and left before anyone could argue.

When the deep elf returned a few minutes later, his skin was covered in a sheen of sweat, but he appeared not to notice. "I count twelve ursine," he whispered. To Petey he said, "Your wife is unconscious. The dwarf is bound with rope. The human has been mauled to death."

"So much for only killing those who fought back," Idnatius said.

Jebeddo hung his head. Peace was no longer an option. Petey fidgeted with his pistol, appearing eager to kill the ursine.

"The prisoners are near the southern edge of the camp. I think I can sneak in and get them out, undetected," Zacnefron said.

Leaping at the chance to avoid further bloodshed, Jebeddo

said, "Do it. I'll get closer to the edge of the treed area with some wolves ready if things go badly."

"I'll go around the other direction," said Lief, and headed out of sight to the north.

Idnatius tapped his heavy armour. "I'll hang back."

While he wasn't as stealthy as his roguish companions, Jebeddo managed to step quietly enough to remain undetected by the ursine. Near the edge of the grass, he peeked out and gulped. On the north side of the camp, a huge black ursine with a white skull painted on his face was talking to two other ursine.

Jebeddo hoped Zacnefron was as sneaky as he claimed to be, because fighting the leader of the Whiteskull clan was not something he wanted to do. As though on cue, Zacnefron's dark form slinked soundlessly from the grass toward the prisoners. Without drawing attention to himself, Zacnefron nudged the dwarf, who appeared not to have been tied up after all. Scooping up Petey's wife, Zacnefron started back to the grass with the dwarf following close behind. It was then that Jebeddo noticed the ropes on the ground where the dwarf had been. Had the dwarf already freed himself before his rescuers arrived?

The dwarf stumbled. It wasn't much, but it was enough to draw the attention of the ursine. Even as they howled in outrage, Jebeddo sent his eight fae wolves charging forward. Zacnefron ran past him, the dwarf pale and wide-eyed right on his heels. A gun went off beside him, and Jebeddo saw Petey's lips curled back, revealing a row of small, sharp teeth.

He's lost his mind, Jebeddo thought. "Get out of here, Petey! Everyone's running!"

In the stand of trees, the wolves did their job. An ursine warrior fell to the ground, two wolves leaping on top of it. The leader, Grodurs, had a wicked looking Warhammer in one hand, and a rough wooden shield in the other. But his attention was captured when a small golden object zipped through the air, right into Lief's waiting hands. Almost everyone is running, he thought.

Grodurs spun and struck Lief with his hammer, battering the

little squirrelley before he had a chance to flee. A wolf went down, and Jebeddo fled to the east. While the wolves were powerful, more ursine were charging into the fray, and the fae beasts wouldn't last much longer.

Howls from both sides of the fight continued in the background, and Jebeddo counted the yelps of fallen wolves. He felt the spell dissipate after the eighth fell. He hoped that would be the end of it, but it was not long before he heard the ursine charging after him.

And they were gaining fast.

Pausing long enough to lay down a magical carpet of spiked stones, Jebeddo dared not stay longer. Fortunately Zacnefron came back to check on him and added his own touch to the cunning trap: caltrops. Any ursine stubborn enough to continue after them would be in serious pain.

In a shorter amount of time than he would have liked, Jebeddo heard shrieks close behind him. With any luck they would stop.

But someone was still coming. Grodurs. It had to be. Too slow to get away from the enraged chieftain, Jebeddo leapt aside, dug in, and prepared a spell for the instant the chieftain came into view. Zacnefron had a similar idea, and waited in the long grass, blades sheathed but ready.

Idnatius readied his glaive for the charging chieftain.

Grodurs screamed with murderous intent when he saw the human warrior waiting, but he missed the small gnome and stealthy deep elf to either side of his path. Jebeddo unleashed a thunderous explosion, and Grodurs stumbled to the side, right into Zacnefron's waiting weapons.

But the ursine did not wince or cry, instead launching into a rage-fuelled offensive. His hammer smashed into Zacnefron, battering the deep elf who spun away with the force of the blow. Idnatius charged and stabbed the ursine, drawing his attention. Petey's pistol fired on the opposite side from Jebeddo, and he hoped the vulpine was a good shot, and wouldn't accidentally hit him.

With the chieftain ignoring him for the moment, Jebeddo summoned flames to his will, and sent the ball of fire rolling at the ursine. The smell of singed fur filled the air, along with burning grass. Before the fire had a chance to spread, Jebeddo summoned more magic to snuff the flames. The last thing they needed was to be fighting the terrifying ursine in the middle of a grass fire.

Grodurs spun and swung, landing blow after blow against Idnatius and Zacnefron, but they were also scoring hits in return. However, the cuts only seemed to anger the ursine, whereas Idnatius and Zacnefron were slower to recover after each heavy impact.

Thinking the fire rolling across the ground was a bad idea, Jebeddo changed his strategy and threw fire through the air against Grodurs. While the first blast hit the chieftain, a second flew wide and ignited the grass on the other side. Again Jebeddo was forced to take his attention from the fight to douse the flames. Arrows joined the fray, and Jebeddo was heartened to know that Lief had escaped the ursine camp to rejoin the fight. But even with an arrow sticking out of him, Grodurs continued to battle with impossible fury. Getting angry at the stubborn tenacity with which the ursine battled, Jebeddo fired up at Grodurs's head, only to miss again. Another blast from Petey's gun sounded louder than the previous ones, and the vulpine cursed and shouted that his gun had exploded.

Idnatius and Zacnefron grimaced with every attack and movement, and blood matted Grodurs's fur from countless wounds. How could the chief still stand? He raised his hammer high, preparing a death blow against Zacnefron, when Jebeddo channeled his own frustration and anger into a powerful lightning bolt from the blue sky. The arcing white light hit the ursine chieftain's war hammer and burned through his body.

Finally, the huge ursine toppled.

But so did Zacnefron and Idnatius, for the blast injured them as well. Swearing at his stupidity, Jebeddo added irritation at his own brash actions to his list of things to be mad about. Spells of healing brought his companions back from the brink, but the gnome druid was not done yet.

Concentrating on maintaining his control over the deadly power overhead, he stalked back to the stand of trees. When he got there, the remaining ursine were gathered, nursing their sore feet. They looked up as one when Jebeddo stepped out of the grass.

Pointing a shaking finger at the ursine, he shouted, "Die!" The ursine ran the other way, but Jebeddo unleashed a blast of lightning into their midst. Two ursine fell dead and others screamed, their fur scorched. Into the long grasses on the other side of the trees they ran.

Jebeddo raised his hand toward the grass and let loose another lightning bolt, which ignited the grass in the area and felled more ursine. With a wave of his hand, he doused the flames from the lightning, but he could not spot the fleeing survivors.

"Wow," Idnatius said, holding a blood streaked hand over his chest, where his armour was dented. "When you give up on diplomacy, you really give up."

Lief stumbled into the area, a large bulge under his cloak. Jebeddo asked, "What's that?"

"Dragon statue!" Lief replied, holding the golden figure out for them to see. "Can you believe my luck? They had it just sitting out in the open!"

Indeed, such a treasure would be worth a great deal back in town. The people back in the republic would pay a small fortune for such a fine looking specimen.

It wasn't long before Zacnefron joined them, Grodurs' severed head hanging from his hand. "Are we done, or going after the rest of them?"

"Please, we need to get back," Petey said, nursing his injured hand. "My wife…"

"I think the ursine got the message," Idnatius said. "Let's go back to Phaelan's Rise and get our reward!"

It was late when they returned to town, but the people were still abuzz. Apparently the leporine had attacked Phaelan's Rise with a stolen cannon while Jebeddo and his companions had been away. Grass near the town had been cleared away, too, although there were whispers that some of it was an uncontrolled burn, started by the leporine.

Jebeddo escorted Petey and his wife to the middle of town, where the medical hut was located. When they got there, he offered to help in any way, but the midwife took one look and waved him away. "We've helped birth many babies. You look like you need sleep more than anything."

It was hard to argue with their assessment. After walking for over ten hours, with brief stops for food and fighting, he ached all over. When he got to a hut they had claimed, Zacnefron was waiting for him, wearing a grin. "Two pounds of ivory each for Grodurs's head. Not bad!"

Jebeddo's stomach turned when he received his share of the bounty. From what he had seen, there were no large plains animals in the area, which would make the ivory a rare commodity. As unpleasant as it was to receive trophies from dead animals, Petey understood the need for trade goods to use in the barter economy. Maybe he could buy some supplies to make potions of healing to rid himself of the burden.

"How's Petey's wife?" Lief asked.

Jebeddo shrugged and laid down on a bed roll. "Still unresponsive. Alive, but I'm worried about her. Even my healing spells didn't rouse her."

"I'm sure the medics in town will be able to help," Lief said, stifling a yawn. He placed his dragon statue on his bed roll, curled up around it, and threw his cloak over it, leaving himself exposed. "We make a good team. Can't wait to see what the morning brings."

Jebeddo felt like he had barely closed his eyes when the sod hut shook with a thunderous boom. It reminded him of his thunder wave spell, but much, much more powerful. Suddenly alert, he leapt out of bed and ran for the door.

Smoke rose into the early morning sky from the middle of town. There was no sign of the sheriff's building or the barracks. Stumbling into the street, Jebeddo ached from the previous day's adventures. His foggy mind had trouble comprehending what he was seeing. He went closer to the area to find flaming bits of debris scattered in a wide area.

Without thinking, he used his magic to snuff out nearby flames. He spotted the sheriff near where his building had been, and asked, "What happened? Who did this?"

"No idea," the sheriff answered. "I'm a bit busy trying to figure that out. If you want to help, start looking around for anything suspicious. Check around town for missing people. Get the injured to the medic hut."

Jebeddo gathered his wits and saw that Lief and Zacnefron had already taken to the roofs, searching for further trouble. Idnatius just stared wide-eyed.

Moving through the debris, Jebeddo checked the bodies in the streets, finding most were already dead, Deputy Hammerstrike among them. A few were only unconscious, and after sending them some of his own healing magic, he signaled for them to be taken to the healer's hut. He wasn't strong enough to do it himself, but Idnatius was more than capable. He dragged one person's limp form to the medical hut, and Jebeddo gasped when they entered. Everyone inside was dead. Each victim showed signs of strangulation or slash marks.

Also concerning was that there was no sign of Petey or his wife.

When they found Lief and Zacnefron again, the deep elf was wringing his hands uncontrollably, his skin still covered in a sheen of sweat.

"No sign of Petey, and the medics are dead," Jebeddo said.

"I'll ask the guards at the gate if anyone saw him and his wife leave," Zacnefron said, and left.

Back near the leveled sheriff's building, Jebeddo found the

sheriff in the area that would have been between his building and the barracks. "Find anything?"

"Yes," the sheriff said, pointing to scorch marks on the ground that were more easily visible as the sun began to rise. "Someone used detonation cord to set off several barrels of black powder around town."

Together, they followed the trail to the medical hut.

"H-H-How big... how big a bundle would someone need to get enough detonation cord to do this?" Lief asked.

The sheriff shrugged and held his hands a short distance apart. "If it was tightly wound, not a great deal."

"About the size of a belly with a litter of babies in it," Idnatius whispered.

There was no doubt in Jebeddo's mind. They had escorted Petey and his wife into the heart of town with enough detonation cord to level the place. But why go through all that deception? Petey had been in town when they arrived. Couldn't he have done the damage without their aid? Something wasn't right.

Zacnefron came running, wringing his hands, but despite the nervous twitch, his voice remained calm. "The guards say no vulpine left the town."

"Maybe they're still here, planning another attack," Idnatius said.

Looking all around at the sod buildings, Jebeddo had an idea. He approached the medic's hut and placed his hand on the sod. Casting a spell to speak with plants, he asked, "Do you know where the vulpine went?"

"You're on the wrong side of this," the grass replied.

Jebeddo stepped back, his face screwed up in confusion. "What?"

"Look at us. Do you think we like being shaped into buildings? Your people come and tear nature apart."

Shaking his head, unable to rid himself of the feeling that the grass was right, he focused on the task at hand. "Where did the vulpine go?"

But the sod hut remained eerily silent.

"Well?" Lief asked.

"It... it said we're on the wrong side of the conflict."

Lief rocked back on his heels and looked all around them. The chaos continued, although the fires were extinguished, and bodies were being transported out of town. "Maybe that's the truth." The squirrelley held up his arms, showing off his skin flaps. "I mean, I'm closer to them than I am to the people here in Phaelan's Rise, aren't I? We came here to find mithril, but it looks and sounds more like an invasion. I... I don't want to be on the wrong side of a war, again."

Whatever war the rogue alluded to was lost on Jebeddo, but he understood the sentiment. The more he thought about it, the less he liked their situation.

"Have you checked the walls?" Idnatius asked the sheriff, who shook his head. "Just a quick look. Haven't had time for anything in depth. Why?"

The four companions exchanged a look and Lief said, "We'll check it out."

Together they started examining the earthen wall, looking for any signs of a disturbance. As hard as Jebeddo looked, he saw no sign of any claw marks to indicate the vulpine had scrambled over the wall. Pausing, he noticed one of their number was gone. "Where'd Lief go?"

Backtracking, they found Lief coming out of a small hole in the bottom of the wall. "Good job, L—"

The squirrelley drew his bow, and wrapped a rag around an arrow. "If anyone wants to stay with Phaelan's Republic, now's the time to make your decision."

Idnatius shrugged. "I got my payment for the job I was given." Both Zacnefron and Jebeddo stood firm.

Seeing they were of one mind, Lief lit the rag on the arrow and bent low, aiming into the tunnel. His shot flew true, and a violent explosion ripped the wall asunder, sending chunks of debris in all directions. In the aftermath, Lief cried out, "There they go! We'll get them!" and charged through the hole in the wall.

Jebeddo followed, unable to believe what had just happened. Never in his wildest dreams had he considered that his life would lead to treason against the republic. The ground outside the wall was smooth, the trench filled in with earth. Had the vulpine done that? Was another attack coming, now that Phaelan's Rise had a gaping hole in its defences?

Fearing the worst, Jebeddo did his best to keep up with the others as they ran north.

Their nervous conversation ended abruptly when the broken down cart came into view on the side of the road. Petey sat on top of it, his tail swishing rhythmically between his dangling feet. He smiled when he saw them.

"I'm glad you all came to see reason," the vulpine said, and he dropped from the cart to the road.

Lief stepped forward and spoke in an accusatory tone. "You set off all that black powder!"

"So did you," Petey countered.

That stopped Lief in his tracks. Jebeddo asked, "What happens now?"

"That's entirely up to you." Petey held up three fingers, and ticked them off with each point. "You can go back empty handed and report that you couldn't find me. You can try to kill me, like you did Grodurs, and hope for another small reward. Or you can come with me. Together we can find the ursine and figure out what to do next to resist Phaelan's Republic."

"Do you think the ursine will forgive us for killing their chieftain?" Idnatius asked.

Petey nodded, his features somber. "Grodurs Whiteskull understood the cost involved in our grand deception. Even though I told him there was a good chance he would die, he sacrificed himself to bring ruin to Phaelan's Rise. We had to be as convincing as possible not only to get the detonation cord into the city, unchallenged, but also if we hoped to convince the good people there to join us." He looked pointedly at them.

"I killed more than just their chieftain," Jebeddo said, his stomach sinking in a sickening lurch. "I killed more of them. I was so angry. They'll never forgive us."

Petey walked over to him and rested a paw on his shoulder. Staring into his eyes, Petey said, "They trust me. I will tell them what happened, and they will forgive you. Trust me. The ursine are a reasonable people."

Even so, guilt gnawed at Jebeddo. If they forgave him, he was not sure he could ever forgive himself for losing his temper and murdering the ursine who had turned and run from him.

When they agreed to join Petey and return to the ursine, his wife strolled out of the grass, no sign of pregnancy to be seen.

"Have your litter, then?" Idnatius said sarcastically.

"They came out with a bang," she replied with a sly smile.

She was a little shorter than Jebeddo, a fact that hadn't had time to settle in his mind, since she had been carried away from the ursine camp, all the way to Phaelan's Rise. In the light of day, seeing her walking, her bright red fur smoothed down, and her tail swishing side-to-side, he felt a sudden longing he hadn't expected. He asked, "What's your name, anyway? And are you even Petey's wife?"

Looking over her shoulder at him, her lips turned up in a coy smile. "Felicia."

That expression set his heart hammering. "Beautiful name for a beautiful woman," he said.

She looked him up and down with an appraising gaze and grinned. "Thank you." If he hoped for more, she wasn't going to give it to him, and she continued west.

Hours passed in relative silence, until they met up with the surviving ursine warriors. Most of them bore scars from their battle, first with the wolves, and then with Jebeddo's lightning bolts. Seeing the burns in their flesh brought on a fresh wave of guilt.

"I'm so sorry," Jebeddo blurted out, and he fell to his knees before the huge bear folk. "I'm sorry we killed your leader. I'm sorry I came back and killed more of your people. I had no idea."

One of the ursine stepped forward and bent down, using a large claw under Jebeddo's chin to lift his face. "Chieftain Grodurs knew the risks. Petey told us his plan, and that it might require death to fulfill. Chieftan Grodurs believed the risk was worth the reward. If we can be rid of the invaders, his sacrifice will not have been in vain."

Lief said, "What's the plan now, then?"

"We wait," Petey replied, and all of them stared at him in disbelief. "It is our hope that they will leave on their own, now that their defences have been compromised."

Shaking his head, Lief said, "The Republic wants the mithril too badly to just give up. How did that 'wait and see' attitude work for you when the Iltherians invaded the west coast?"

"Not well," Petey admitted. "But I will let you in on a secret: there is no mithril."

Jebeddo balked at the news. How could it be possible that the Republic would send so many people to a distant land without any hope of succeeding in their mission?

Petey continued. "Think about it. Mithril is a metal found deep in the earth, often in mountainous regions. Do you see any mountains around here? It's all hilly grasslands. This isn't a mining area!"

"But then why would they send so many people here?" Jebeddo asked.

Lief paced back and forth, clasping his hands behind his back. "Land. I've been around the world, and the first thing that struck me about Phaelan's Republic was how everything felt cramped. I bet they see Tensire as the perfect place to expand to. You heard how they talk about the mutates here! They're riling up their people, telling them that this wild land is inhabited by savages. We wouldn't feel guilty about taking land away from beasts, would we?"

Jebeddo nodded, wondering what other lies he had been fed by the Republic.

"We need a plan," Lief insisted. "We need to follow up that attack with more. If we can scare them out of Phaelan's Rise now, we might have a chance."

Zacnefron grinned. "We could go back, screaming about a giant ursine army coming."

"I like it," Idnatius said. "But they might not buy it."

"We'll rough each other up before we go back!" Lief closed a fist and punched the air. "A few bruises and cuts to really sell it to them."

"And," Zacnefron added, "the ursine could come in behind us and make some noise. It'll be dark by the time we get back."

But the ursine each took a step back, casting quick glances at each other. Leaderless, none showed a willingness to be the first to speak up. Finally an ursine covered in dark brown fur from head to toe said, "We fear the guns."

"That's fair," Idnatius said.

That was, after all, the reason Phaelan's Republic had the weapons. Not only were the firearms lethal at long range, but they made a tremendous noise with each bullet fired.

Puffing up his small chest, Lief said, "They won't shoot us. We'll go back and scare them away."

"Before you go," the brown ursine said, although he paused and looked down at his feet. "If you could... we understand you claim the golden dragon statue that you won in combat. However, it holds great sentimental value for us." He blurted out the rest. "In years past, we served a dragon, before the Iltherian dragon hunters came to these lands. Our master was slain, and that statue is a reminder of the glory our people once knew."

Lief hefted the statue in both hands and looked at it with open longing. But after staring at it briefly, he held it up to the ursine, who took it in one great paw and bowed to Lief. "Thank you, little one. You are honourable."

A wicked grin spread over Lief's face. "We'll see if the people at Phaelan's Rise feel the same way when we're done with them."

Darkness had settled over the land, and Jebeddo crept

through the long grass, surveying the town. The earthen wall on the north side remained down, although there was evidence of rebuilding beginning. Guards posted in the hole were alert, with lamps blazing beside them offering plenty of light all the way out to the long grass. Perhaps it was a good thing that the ursine had not come along, for they would make easy targets without the cover of darkness.

Beside him, Zacnefron crouched low, and Jebeddo saw three lines of blood shimmering in the small amount of light that filtered through to their position. The ursine had helped maim them before they left, ensuring that the wounds looked legitimate. Anyone who gazed upon their faces would see the scratches made by large ursine paws. They had intentionally shredded their clothing, which Jebeddo had told them he could fix with simple spells of mending after they were done their deception.

Further to the side, Jebeddo heard Lief's soft voice whisper. "Go!"

As one, the four companions burst from the grass and sprinted for the hole in the wall. They shouted loud, but each yelled something different so that their voices wouldn't be easily understood. The initial response from the guards was to raise their muskets, but when they saw the runners weren't mutates, they looked at each other with confusion.

Finally when Idnatius came close, he yelled, "An ursine army is coming!"

"We must flee!" Zacnefron added.

Jebeddo shouted at the top of his lungs. "To the north! To the outpost!"

Staring at each other, uncertain what to do, the guards had the decision made for them when civilians heard the ruckus.

After countless attacks by the leporine, the citizenry was in no state to handle the idea of large, angry savages coming to slaughter them. News spread through the town almost instantaneously. The four companions fanned out through the streets, each feeding the fear. People screamed and grabbed whatever they could carry before running for their lives.

There was no ship in the harbour—what luck! Jebeddo thought—so the people headed for the gate or the hole in the wall. Brandishing torches and lamps, they fled, and Jebeddo watched with awe as the lights slowly faded into the distance.

The town had emptied out far faster than he could have hoped. The people had swallowed the lie whole, and he doubted anyone remained at all.

Gathering together in the middle of town, the companions grinned at each other. They spent the rest of the night snooping through huts, stealing what was left behind, and rasing the town to the ground.

Petey and Felicia stood in the shadows, grinning as people fled Phaelan's Rise. "I couldn't have hoped for a better outcome," Petey said. "That said, we have to look ahead, and there are potential pitfalls that await us."

"Such as?" Felicia raised an eyebrow, and Petey didn't appreciate her doubt.

"For instance," he said, trying and failing to keep the anger from his voice, "Why did you choose to tell them your name is Felicia? That's too close to the last name I used. If we wind up crossing paths with any would-be investigators from our previous exploits, they might find that Felicia the vulpine might just be Felix the vulpine."

"Then let them see me, and know that I am not you," Felicia said. She was so thick sometimes that it hurt Petey to interact with her.

"Druids can change their forms, my dear," he replied. The sickly sweet tone of his voice did nothing to allow his meaning to slip into her skull. "Those who know of what I have done will believe you are me, just in another guise. Do I need to think up aliases for you in advance, to avoid future problems?"

She hung her head, but still peeked up to watch the nearby sod houses tumble. "I'll use something totally different next time." She paused. "Maybe Petra!"

Unable to take any more, Petey turned away from the chaos and headed back toward the ursine camp. Behind him he heard Felicia's soft steps falling in line.

"What's your next plan, anyway?"

Petey smiled. "For now, we work with the ursine and this new group. I have plans for them when they return. Our next moves will require subtle manipulation. Give them a little bit of what they want, and see how deep they will travel into the depths of depravity. Let them call us the 'Resistance' if they wish. I already have plans for the druid. See if you can't find a way to use your charms against one of the others."

"The squirrelley is kind of cute."

That could work, especially seeing how the gnome had shown interest. Was he falling for Felicia enough to drive a wedge into the party dynamics, if the squirrelley reciprocated Felicia's interest? Petey couldn't wait to find out.

Jebeddo felt invigorated upon his return to the ursine camp. Having thwarted Phaelan's Republic, he felt that the juggernaut had been dealt a serious blow. More ursine had joined the camp, and a dozen towering warriors had now gathered. With them was a tiefling dressed in leather armour and carrying an assortment of weapons—but it was not the demon-spawns outfit that made him stand out. With red flesh and thick horns like a goat's, the tiefling radiated power.

Before Jebeddo could inquire about the demon-spawn, Petey approached him and took him aside. "Well done in Phaelan's Rise. I have already heard of your success, and the ursine are talking amongst themselves, looking to press the advantage. With the northern outpost in ruins, the refugees from Phaelan's Rise will have no defences. True, they still have their guns, but most of their black powder was destroyed. If we can attack them, they will be unlikely to ever return!"

"That sounds like a good idea," Jebeddo said. "Any news

from the council of druids?"

Petey's mouth twitched, and he put an arm around Jebeddo's shoulder, steering him away from the others. In hushed tones he said, "I have heard back from the druid who looks after the waters on the coast, and while there is good news regarding a sea creature that can help us, you probably won't like the cost."

Steeling himself for the worst, Jebeddo was still unprepared for what Petey said next.

"There is an ancient being of immense power that guards the waters. It is said it used to live off the west coast, but was driven off by Iltherian invaders. The druid has found it living off the eastern shores now, in the deep waters below where the Republic ships sail. It is willing to help us," Petey paused and looked around to make sure no one was eavesdropping, "but it requires a sacrifice. It needs to devour a child, if it is to help us."

Jebeddo shook his head, unable to comprehend the revolting request. "A child? I can't do that."

"I thought you might not have the stomach for it," Petey said, nodding knowingly.

"It—" Jebeddo hesitated, trying to find the words. "It goes against my sensibilities. It feels evil."

Petey said, "As a fellow druid, I understand the need for balance in all things, as you do. However, in this case I think the ends might justify the means. Think of the ruin we could bring upon the Republic fleets. They wouldn't dare bring more people to these lands. Besides," he waved his hand toward the east, where the refugees of Phaelan's Rise would be, "the Republic children, driven from their homes by your own actions, won't live long without shelter."

"A Republic child would suffice?" Jebeddo started to put the pieces together in his mind. If they were going to assault the refugees anyway, leaving them defenceless, would it matter if the child died sooner or later? Was death from exposure and starvation better than death in the belly of an ancient being? "Would the child feel any pain?"

"Of course not," Petey scoffed. He pulled back and scowled

at Jebeddo. "I'm not a monster. The child would feel nothing. But the ancient sea creature did specify that the sacrifice should come from those it will hunt, so only a refugee child would help our cause."

Turning inward, Jebeddo contemplated the options before him. If he didn't take a child, the Republic would return, and perhaps with greater forces. He had seen the steam-powered cities of the Republic, and if they brought their ingenuity and greater technology with them, the Tensirians might not be able to unseat the republic a second time.

"I'll do it," he said.

Petey placed a paw on Jebeddo's shoulder and nodded, his mouth drawn into a grim line. "I know you do not make this decision lightly. You've done the right thing. Now, gather with the others. I believe the Whiteskull and Clawed Fist tribes are prepared to speak."

A dozen ursine warriors stood before them, shoulder-to-shoulder, a shared look of determination on their faces. Jebeddo stood beside the devilish looking tiefling, who also waited to hear what the ursine tribes had to say.

A tall, black-furred male named Ragorith from the Clawed Fist tribe spoke first. "You did well scaring off the people in Phaelan's Rise, and we thank you. However, they still pose a threat to our people. While their main stores of black powder are depleted, they still have their guns. We need to strike while they are disoriented."

A brown ursine from the Whiteskull tribe, Fawlin, stepped forward. "It has also been decided that this hunt will determine who is to be the next chieftain of our respective clans. Our six best warriors from each tribe stand before you, and when the attack is over, only one of us will remain from each tribe. If the hunt is called off, and more than one warrior from a tribe still lives, they will fight until only one remains. The survivors will be the chieftains and return to our tribes, far to the south, where all the ursine gather."

While Jebeddo was unfamiliar with specific ursine traditions, it wasn't uncommon for animals to undertake such barbaric practices. It wasn't his ideal way of determining leadership, but he also recognized it was not his place to interfere.

"What can you tell me about the golden dragon statue?"

The question came from Zacnefron, which puzzled Jebeddo. Why the sudden interest, he wondered.

Even more interesting, one of the Clawed Fist tribe members shook his head and closed his eyes. That gesture seemed to go unnoticed by the other ursine.

Fawlin addressed Zacnefron. "The statue is a reminder of the great dragon our tribe served, before the Iltherian dragon hunters killed it."

"I know that," Zacnefron said with a sigh. "I mean, where did it come from?"

The ursine muttered confusedly before Fawlin replied, "We don't know. Grodurs was our chieftain, and the secret of where he got the statue from may have died with him. Perhaps he told one of his wives."

"Where are they?"

"Back in the main camp," Fawlin said. "Why do you ask?"

"Just curious," Zacnefron said, unconvincingly.

Whatever the reason behind the question, Jebeddo got the feeling the Clawed Fist had planted it in the deep elf's mind. In his awkward way, Zacnefron had called attention to what likely should have been a more subtle request for information. Jebeddo made a mental note to ask Zacnefron for more information later.

"If there are no further questions, daylight will be scarce soon. If we leave now, we might arrive at the refugee camp by nightfall, and take their guards by surprise."

A full on frontal assault against a group of soldiers armed with muskets sounded dangerous. Surprise would give them an advantage, at least at the beginning. Idnatius offered to stay behind, citing the fact that he wasn't cut out for a stealth assault mission. Jebeddo hoped not to feel the sting of any bullets.

Magical darkness hid everything and Jebeddo wondered how much further they had to go before they would spring their trap upon the Republic guards. He held tight to a rope, as did the Whiteskull clan ursine behind him. Up ahead, he occasionally heard sounds of the tiefling and the six Clawed Fist ursine moving through the long grass. If it weren't for the rope connecting the groups, he was certain they would have wandered in different directions.

Leading them forward, Zacnefron was not covered in a globe of darkness, but relied on his natural stealth to keep him unseen.

The rope went slack, and Jebeddo stopped. That was the sign that they were close. While Zacnefron scouted the base, they would sit and wait.

"What's going on?" Lief asked beside him. Jebeddo nearly yelled with surprise, because he had not heard the squirrelley approach. Indeed, he could not remember the last time he had seen Lief. "I missed the meeting, and the next thing I knew you guys were gone!"

Jebeddo shushed him and whispered, "Nice of you to join us. We're going to attack the refugees from Phaelan's Rise, and kidnap a child."

"Kidnap a child? Why?"

"That's a long story, but I need to bring a child to Petey, who will take it to the council of druids. There's a sea creature we'll sacrifice the child to, and it will destroy Republic ships that come to Tensire."

A long silence followed the explanation, and Jebeddo said, "Lief?"

"Yeah, I heard you," came the reply. "I... I get it that I wasn't there at the meeting, but can we discuss this? Sacrificing children is dark."

"These kids won't last long anyway, with nowhere to call home," Jebeddo explained. "And we'll stop more Republic forces from landing and attacking the inhabitants of these lands."

"There's got to be another way."

"Well, if there is, I don't know what it is."

After a brief pause, Lief said, "I can't join this fight. I'm heading back to camp."

"Lief!" Jebeddo hissed, but the squirrelley didn't respond. "Great," he muttered. The rogue's bow would have been a welcome addition to the fight. He was about to let go of the rope to go find Lief when Zacnefron touched his shoulder and made him jump.

"I already told Alz'hared what I found, but I'll tell you and your group, too."

"Alz'hared?"

Zacnefron sighed. "The tiefling. Honestly, people say I'm rude, but at least I know his name!"

"Go on," Jebeddo said, biting his tongue.

"They've put together pathetic defences. Some charred timbers have been stacked into low cover. There's two barriers nearby, with two guards crouched behind each one. A little further back are two more defensive positions with a couple more guards behind each. I'm pretty sure there were more than just eight guards for all of Phaelan's Rise, so expect more in the camp itself. Maybe they're going to get some sleep. The campfires are starting to burn low, so we can attack soon."

In position, the tiefling and deep elf dropped their magical darkness, and everyone crouched down in the grass to wait. The guards behind the barriers lit torches and stuck them into the defences. As the campfires in the back flickered out, Jebeddo marvelled at the size of the camp. If the ursine could break through the surrounding soldiers, the camp itself would still pose a threat from sheer numbers if the colonists turned on them.

Finally the signal came, a sharp tug on the rope, and the Clawed Fist tribe charged forward across the grasses that had been cleared around the fallen outpost. They held their roars until the guards spotted them in the dim torch light, but by that time it was too late. Zacnefron thrust his blades into the back of a guard who had been lining up a shot on an enraged ursine and the guard went down. The other guard on the left side of their approach attempted to fire, but his musket exploded in his face. Before he could recover, he was mauled by several sets of claws.

Jebeddo stood back and watched the Whiteskull clan sprint past him, heading for the fortification on the right side. The two guards there fared better, rattling off two shots into an approaching Whiteskull ursine and dropping it. When the warriors got closer, the republic guards thrust with their bayonets, injuring two of the ursine before being overwhelmed.

Two more guard posts remained further afield, and the sounds of their guns firing shook Jebeddo. Even so, he moved forward and spotted a group of people just beyond the last two fortified positions. Unleashing his magic, he surrounded the people in a wall of wind. Two of the people trapped inside attempted to escape, but the first was thrown back into the group, and the other got tossed through the air to the north and smashed into a tree. No one else attempted to get away.

But there was something strange about the whole situation. As more gunfire sounded, and ursine and Republic guards cried out in anguish, Jebeddo stalked forward and noted that there were only adults caught in his windy prison. And looking deeper into the camp, no one remained. How was it possible for a camp of that size to empty out so quickly?

Jebeddo summoned his fae wolves, and the eight creatures followed his command, charging off after the scent of the refugees. It didn't take them long to turn north, toward the woods, and Jebeddo smiled with the knowledge that the colonists couldn't hide from him.

But that smile disappeared when the forest lit up with flames that immolated the summoned wolves.

"Zacnefron!" he called out, and caught the deep elf's eye. The second guard post on the left was already dealt with, and the elf nodded and ran to the north to find out what had happened.

To the south, the last fortified post was in a pitched battle with the Whiteskull tribe down to only two members remaining in the fight. Jebeddo ran forward and as he did, he lobbed a ball of flame at the nearest guard. The soldier screamed and fell back into the other, both of them on fire.

More gunfire sounded from the camp, with four soldiers who had not been at the defensive positions lining up and taking shots at the larger gathering of Clawed Fist ursine. With their attention focused in the other direction, Jebeddo and the two remaining Whiteskull ursine charged and broke their formation long enough for the Clawed Fist to arrive and kill the last soldiers.

The resistance dealt with, Jebeddo looked to the north, but there was no sign of Zacnefron. Had he met the same end as the summoned wolves? Jebeddo pointed to the woods and said, "We still need a child! Follow them!"

The ursine roared their approval, and the half dozen remaining warriors ran ahead. Jebeddo used his magic to change his form into a large bear and loped ahead of the ursine, with Alz'harad taking up the rear. The trail turned west, inland, and Jebeddo started following it, but the ursine charged north through unbroken foliage.

Alz'harad jogged up to Jebeddo and asked, "What's going on? Why are they going north, if the trail goes northwest?"

Unable to speak in his bear form, Jebeddo grunted. In the end, he decided to trust the keen senses of the ursine and ran after them. It was good that he did, because they did not run far before the trail started up once more. Had someone covered the tracks of the colonists? But how had they made the false trail in the other direction look so convincing?

Whatever the ruse, it wasn't long before Jebeddo heard the sounds of fleeing colonists running through the dark forest. It was impossible to move quickly, especially for those humans who would be unable to see well in the dark, so it wasn't long before the ursine were almost on top of them.

The colonists in the rear stopped running and formed a line, two deep. Armed with improvised weapons, they leaped to attack their pursuers. Jebeddo wasted no time, reverting to his gnomish form and unleashing a blast of thunder that knocked the colonists back, shattering bone with the force of the attack. Even so, the colonists outnumbered the ursine, and through sheer attrition they managed to take down two of the mighty Clawed Fist ursine before they themselves were killed.

And among the dead there were no children to be found. Wouldn't it have made sense for the children to be stragglers at the back of the pack? How was it that he still hadn't found any!

The remaining four ursine roared and continued the hunt, with Jebeddo and Alz'harad following close behind. In a few moments they were once again near the back of the fleeing refugee pack, and once again those in the rear turned to fight. As before, they died, but not without taking another ursine with them, and injuring both Jebeddo and Alz'harad.

Panting with exertion, Jebeddo shook his head, unable to comprehend how he had not completed his mission. Not that he had ever kidnapped anyone before, but he had thought it would be a simpler task than this.

The ursine convened, and Ragorith claimed the title of Clawed Fist Chieftain. There were only two remaining Whiteskull ursine, and no more will to continue the pursuit in case they all perished against the colonists. Facing each other, the two ursine launched into a vicious battle against each other, and in the end only Fawlin remained.

Thus decided, Ragorith and Fawlin congratulated each other on becoming the chieftains of their respective tribes, and the four of them turned back to find Zacnefron coming late to the fight.

"Sorry, there was a false trail that ended in nothing. I heard fighting this way and came as fast as I could. Pity I missed the fun."

"Fun?" Ragorith asked, rising to his full height and towering over the deep elf. "Ten ursine are dead, and many more colonists. I do not think we can call what happened tonight 'fun.'"

"My apologies," Zacnefron said with a bow. "Shall we return to camp?"

Jebeddo followed behind the others, disappointed that he had failed to find even one child in the entire refugee camp. There had been children in Phaelan's Rise, hadn't there? Not that he had paid much attention, but what were the odds the entire town had been made up of adults? No, the medics had said they had helped women give birth when Felicia had pretended to be pregnant. There must have been children.

A soft whimper broke through his ponderings, and he turned toward the sound. Again he heard it. Was someone crying in the forest?

Motioning for the others to follow him, Jebeddo followed the crying until he found a young boy sitting on the ground, clutching his ankle. Tracks ran off in this direction, all around the child.

He snapped his eyes up and peered into the distance, but saw no signs of anyone nearby. Had someone intentionally taken the children away from the adults to hide their escape? Did they know Jebeddo had been sent to kidnap one of them, or an inherent need to protect their young from any threat?

Alz'harad knelt beside the boy and smiled, showing his pointy teeth. "We're not here to hurt you. What happened?"

The soothing tones of the tiefling's voice appeared to help settle the boy, who leaned back against the tree and wiped away his tears. "Pa said monsters were coming for us. The kids were sent this way, and the adults ran the other. But I tripped on a tree root and got left behind."

"We have a camp nearby," Alz'hared said. "If you let us take you there, we can tend to your wounds."

"O-okay," the boy said. "But I can't walk."

Once again Jebeddo shifted into the form of a bear, and Alz'hared helped the child up onto his back. The walk was slow, so as not to jostle the boy too much, but it worked. The boy rambled on about how amazing it was to ride a bear, and he spoke about his father who was looking for mithril so they could be rich when they returned to Phaelan's Republic. When they returned, they would get a big house, and his mother had promised him a pet leporine.

The boy prattled on, and Jebeddo was glad to be in his bear

form because if he had tried to converse with the child, he was certain his voice would have broken, and his resolve along with it. The ends justify the means, he told himself, imagining Republic ships sinking to the bottom of the ocean. He was saving all the native inhabitants of Tensire. This was just one boy.

And all the others we just killed, he thought.

Shaking his head, he tried to drive the negative thoughts out. This was what the druid council had requested. This was what the ancient sea monster needed. It was his duty to bring the boy and end the greater threat.

The rest of the way back to the camp, he did his best to ignore the voice of the boy who rode on his back.

Exhausted and weary of listening to the little boy prattle on, Jebeddo perked up when he saw Petey waiting for their return. Jebeddo lowered his head and the boy slid down into Petey's waiting arms.

The child wore a big smile and shouted, "Again!"

But Petey ignored the request and instead bowed to Jebeddo. "You have done well. I will bring the child to the sea, and his sacrifice will bring peace to Tensire."

The boy's eyes went wide. "Wait, what?"

"Sleep," Petey said, and touched the boy's forehead. The child slumped to the ground, and Petey spoke to Jebeddo. "Go with the ursine to their camp. I will catch up with you soon."

A last bit of resistance to the plan flared in Jebeddo's mind and he couldn't keep quiet. "You're certain the boy won't feel any pain?"

"As I said before, I'm not a monster," Petey replied. "He will sleep, and be blissfully unaware of his fate." With that, he turned into a giant bird, picked up the unconscious boy in his talons, and flew away to the southwest.

Satisfied with the response, Jebeddo and the others set up camp to get some much needed rest. Even with that first long sleep, the next two weeks were full of walking through long grasses, which was not so much physically exhausting as it was mentally draining. Seeing the same sights as far as he could see was monotonous. He found his attention often being drawn to Lief and Felicia, who were enjoying each other's company more than a little. They made no secret of their nightly trysts, after Lief had discovered that Felicia and Petey's marriage had been a sham to allow them to blow up the buildings in Phaelan's Rise.

The fact that Felicia had chosen the halfling over him irked him more than a little. It shouldn't have mattered. After all, he had only just met her. Yet the swish of her bright red tail, and sparkle in her eyes were alluring in ways he had never before imagined. What did Lief have that he didn't? Try as he might, Jebeddo couldn't see anything special about Lief, and that fact left him grinding his teeth at night, as he listened to their intimate interactions in the distance.

By the time they found the southern woods that bordered the mountains, Jebeddo was only too happy to go off on his own to try to learn more about the council of druids that Petey had spoken of. But when he started asking around the ursine camp, none had heard of the druids, although they had some of their own.

Meeting with the Whiteskull druids, he hoped to learn new secrets to advance his craft, only to discover that he already knew all they did, and then some. Although he had set out to learn, he wound up sitting for days, teaching. He was thankful for the distraction, and soon Felicia was out of his mind.

At the start of their third day in the ursine camp, Zacnefron approached Jebeddo, his hair in disarray, his lips pursed. When Jebeddo asked him what was wrong, Zacnefron snapped, "I've been looking for two whole days for a wife of the old Whiteskull chieftain who might know something about that golden dragon statue, and the only wife I've found so far knew next to nothing about it! I need to give it a rest. I thought since the Clawed Fist ursine trusted me enough to ask me to do this, the other ursine would like me, too! I swear they had me running in circles, when they'd even bother to talk to me. Please tell me we have other plans to distract me from this."

"No plans that I'm aware of," Jebeddo said. "The ursine druids are good students, and I'm afraid I haven't put much thought into what we should do next, now that we're far from the ruins of Phaelan's Rise."

Alz'hared sauntered over, a smile on his face. "We could always attack that Republic outpost I heard about to the east."

"Anything!" Zacnefron pleaded.

"Plus, did you know there's some kind of plant-guy here? He's got a magic bowl that lets him mix potions faster than normal."

That piqued Jebeddo's interest. He had been brewing some potions in his spare time to supply his companions, and speeding up the process would be most welcome. "Where's this plant person?"

"Over in the mountains south of the Clawed Fist tribe. I got some free healing potions for helping out Ragorith in his quest to become the next chieftain."

"A magic bowl?" Lief appeared beside them. The stealth the halfling possessed was unnerving, and Jebeddo shot him a glare. If the look bothered Lief, he didn't show it, instead saying, "I haven't seen much in the way of magical items in my travels. Mostly the Iltherians destroy them."

"That's what One Who Loves Bears said," Alz'hared confirmed. "Apparently his whole race is magical by nature—not surprising, really, seeing how he's a walking plant—and they have been hunted by the Iltherians in their jungle homes. That's why One Who Loves Bears is here with the ursine."

"At any rate, I like the sounds of this raid against the Republic outpost," Lief said.

Alz'hared said, "With how easily we dealt with the refugees and their soldiers, it should be an easy task. And it would allow the ursine to march in numbers against the town further north."

"Will the ursine come with us?" Jebeddo asked.

With no one knowing, they searched the Whiteskull camp for Chieftain Fawlin. But the ursine shook his head at their idea. "We fear their guns. If we try to attack in numbers, they will mow us down."

"What they need is for us to show them that the Republic soldiers with guns don't need to be feared," Zacnefron said.

Chieftain Fawlin shrugged his great shoulders. "Their people killed nine of our mighty warriors who battled to become the chiefs of the Whiteskull and Clawed Fist tribes. The story has already been told. They will fear the Republic soldiers."

Attacking an outpost without any help sounded like suicide, but then Jebeddo was struck with inspiration. "Are there any large, scary animals near the outpost?"

Fawlin gazed off to the east and nodded. "Large bears and wild cats roam the mountains south of the outpost. Why do you ask?"

"I'll bet they're not too happy with the Republic outpost there," Jebeddo said to his companions. "I might be able to talk them into joining us in our assault."

Zacnefron started toward the mountains and called over his shoulder, "Anything!"

After a two day trek through the mountains, Jebeddo looked down upon the outpost near the coast. While not terribly large, he spotted at least a dozen soldiers patrolling the walls. Who could tell how many more lived in the large stone building, or in the tall tower beside it?

But the defences appeared incomplete. Stonework had begun at the base of the tower, but most of it was wood. The walls were in a similar state, with piles of stone blocks starting to overlay the wooden base. That would actually make scaling the walls easier, if they could climb the piles and jump the rest of the distance.

Lief said, "I could glide in from this height, and probably hit their tower. Start a fight inside the outpost before they even know anything's happening. Then you guys could charge in when they're distracted."

"Let's wait and see what kind of help we can find," Jebeddo said. "Alz'hared, can you give me some help amplifying my voice?"

After the tiefling cast a spell on him, Jebeddo turned up to the mountains and shouted in the languages of the bears and felines, "Come to me, and you might be free of these invaders on the coast!"

His voice boomed, and the others moved away from him, glancing around in all directions. It was some time before the bushes and trees began to rustle, and a dozen large brown bears came out to stare at Jebeddo.

Perhaps this had not been his wisest plan.

But the bears didn't turn on him. Instead, they sat down and listened intently.

"Thank you for coming. Am I right in assuming the people below are causing you grief?"

The largest bear spoke for the group. "They slash and burn our forest to the west of their fort, and cut away the mountain. They destroy our homes, so we have answered your call. What do you propose?"

"We plan to attack the outpost," Jebeddo answered, his voice smaller than the bears, but no less forceful. To show any signs of fear or doubt would only drive this potential help away. "With the outpost destroyed, the ursine to the west will march against the Republic settlement further north, and all of us can be free."

"We fear their guns."

Again with the accursed guns! Jebeddo said, "What if we can even the battle field, and open their doors? Would you and yours charge into their outpost and tear them limb from limb, alongside us?"

The bears exchanged long looks before the leader said, "Yes."

"Excellent! Thank you!" Jebeddo reverted to the common tongue and addressed his companions. "We need to get the front gate open, and then the bears will charge in."

"If we wait until nightfall, I can sneak over the walls and open the gate from the inside," Zacnefron said.

"Then my plan to soar down to the tower will act as additional diversion to help our deep elf friend," Lief added.

"I'll join Zacnefron in scaling the walls with my spider climb spell," Alz'hared offered.

Jebeddo nodded. "I will add my lightning bolts, and bring down their tower."

The plan was set. All they needed to do was wait for nightfall.

But the night brought a surprise of its own. From a room at the top of the tower, a great beam of light shone down on the grounds outside the outpost walls. The spotlight moved across the ground at an alarming pace, making a stealthy approach by Zacnefron and Alz'hared impossible.

But by the light of the moon, Jebeddo watched the small halfling soar with his hands and legs stretched out, gliding down from the mountains to the tower. Jebeddo ducked back behind the trees at the edge of the forest when the beam of light came back, narrowly avoiding detection.

He would just have to trust Lief to get the job done on his own.

When the spotlight passed by again, Jebeddo leaned out to look at the outpost. Lamps on the wall provided plenty of light for the guards up top, but they were nowhere near bright enough to illuminate the entire approach to the gate.

His eyes were drawn up to the top of the tower when the spotlight ceased its movement. A moment later, Lief leaped out of the tower, a rope in hand, and the spotlight went out.

"Now!" Jebeddo hissed.

Zacnefron and Alz'hared sprinted across the hundred foot expanse to the outpost walls. Jebeddo stepped out from the trees and pointed at the tower, where he saw Lief circling back and into another room further down the tower.

Not my fault he went into danger, Jebeddo thought with a sneer. A blast of lightning hit the spot in the tower where the wood met the top of the stone construction. Although he had hoped for the wood to explode with the attack, he only left a black scorch mark on the side. Damn!

And then the second surprise came when a cannon fired from the same room Lief had just flown into. Jebeddo watched in wide-eyed terror as the cannon ball flew in his direction.

The projectile hit a tree behind him and flames erupted everywhere, blowing down nearby trees. Jebeddo was engulfed in fire, and cried out before he could douse them with his druidic magic. But it was not enough to undo the full scale of the damage, and he heard the bears he had hoped would help them roar in anguish. The sounds of them crashing away through the woods made Jebeddo's heart sink.

Worse, the light from the fires in the woods illuminated the area between the trees and the walls, and the soldiers up top fired their muskets down at Zacnefron and Alz'hared.

Jebeddo unleashed a second blast of lightning into the room where Lief had been, hoping to ignite the black powder for the cannon, but again the bolt appeared to have little effect.

A second cannon a floor beneath the first fired, but this time Jebeddo managed to flee. The blast at his back sent him flying through the air, and he had the wind knocked out of him when he hit the dirt.

He looked up to see Alz'hared had scaled the wall, only to be rushed by four soldiers with bayonets. They each pierced him, and he slumped down on top of the wall. Zacnefron had gained the top of the gate, but other guards were waiting there for him. Soldiers to either side fired their muskets, while those closer to him rushed with their bayonets.

Jebeddo's heart fell along with Zacnefron's body. The deep elf hit the ground outside the gates and didn't move.

With a final attack, Jebeddo cursed when his bolt of lightning did no obvious damage to the tower. He shifted into the form of a giant snake to attempt to escape into the woods. Around the flaming trees he went, and deeper, but he could not have known the long range of the cannons, or the anger of the Republic gunners. After a pause, the first cannon fired again, dropping flaming death on Jebeddo. Writhing and screaming, he tried to flee as another cannon ball obliterated the trees around him with a gigantic blast.

The pain was too great, and he was forced to shift out of the snake form. Not that his gnomish body was faring much better. As he ran, he shifted again, this time into the form of a wolf. With greater speed, and terror driving his limbs, he darted through the dark forest. Behind him, another cannon ball exploded, leveling the forest, but he grew hopeful since the strike was so far behind him.

No more explosions sounded, but Jebeddo did not stop running all through the night.

Petey watched the fiery destruction rain down on the hapless adventuring party. When fireballs erupted in the woods, he squealed with glee, wondering if the clever shape shifting druid could escape immolation.

At his side, Felicia shook her head. "Is this all necessary? Couldn't we again infiltrate the Republic and level the outpost from within?"

"The less we interfere, the better," Petey replied. Another cannon blast was followed by an explosion that lit up the night. In the aftermath, Petey delighted at the squirming form of a giant snake shifting into the small form of a limping gnome. But when Jebeddo shifted into a wolf and ran at breakneck speed through the trees, the next cannonball didn't come anywhere near the mark, and the gunners gave up on trying to find the elusive enemy in the thick woods.

He found Felicia staring at him when he turned his attention away from the carnage below. She said, "All we do is interfere.

Why, you interfered with the plans of the Iltherians by bringing me over to your side, and I haven't known you to stop ever since."

Sighing, Petey rubbed his paw over his face. He needed to get the lies straight once more to keep her loyalty. Thus, he started at the beginning, to remind himself of all the steps of his deception. "As the only non-human in the Iltherian forces, you told me you already felt like you didn't belong with them. They only wanted to train you to infiltrate the mutate camps across Tensire and destroy their magical artifacts that might be used against them. I was not 'interfering' by agreeing with your own sentiments. It was not as though I had to work particularly hard to convince you to leave them behind and join me—a magic user—your sworn enemy." He saw her frown, and knew that she was remembering a flicker of her past that might not have lined up with what he said. Was she remembering enjoying the slaughter she had brought to the old druid council? Alone, she had torn through their ranks, and she slowed for only an instant when she spotted him there. That pause, caused by seeing a vulpine like herself, had given him the time he needed to begin to weave his web of lies.

He pressed on, rewriting her history. "I brought you to my fortress and showed you my secrets. You helped me by single-handedly stealing Iltherian tapestries depicting their slaughter of our people, and those make excellent additions to our historic halls. That was your decision, because you wanted to remember the awful hell they put you through, in training you to destroy magic. You did not wish to forget the threat they pose to us."

Felicia nodded, and Petey breathed a little easier. By weaving the truth in with the lies, he had carefully manipulated Felicia into being his ally. She needn't know that he had encouraged a group of fae creatures and magical plants to distract the Iltherians, so she could enter unopposed to take those tapestries. Had she run into her fellow Iltherians, they might have triggered Felicia's real memories of having willingly joined them, and she would have been lost to him. While it had been a risk, he had felt the need to push her to give her real memories to blend with the lies.

It was handy having someone as strong as her on his side. Soon he knew he would need her special talents, if he was to be successful in fully turning the fleeing druid below to his cause. Jebeddo had proven himself a worthy apprentice, doing what "needed to be done" in order to advance their cause. Jebeddo needn't know that the boy he had kidnapped to sacrifice to the non-existent sea monster had been placed on a spike outside the ruins of Phaelan's Rise to unnerve those who would undoubtedly come to repopulate the town.

The rest of Jebeddo's allies could die for all Petey cared, but if he could convince a Republic druid to join his cause, the entire Republic could crumble from within. That kind of chaos made him smile. It was time to show them his real power.

Upon returning to the ursine camp, Jebeddo was unsurprised when the ursine made the decision to abandon any ideas of attacking the Republic outpost. For the moment, the republic's foothold on Tensire would remain. But there was hope, since there were other ursine and mutate tribes in the surrounding regions. Chieftain Ragorith let him know that the ursine would appreciate any help that he could offer in seeking out allies, once Jebeddo had recovered from his injuries.

Later that day Lief returned to camp as well, and they traded notes on what had transpired. Apparently Lief's plans in the raid had gone off perfectly. Upon landing on the Republic tower, he had gone into the spotlight room where the guards bought his lie that he was a scout for the Republic. When they weren't looking, he hooked his grapple to the large filament in the spotlight and leaped from the tower, tearing the filament loose. He had then circled around using his wing flaps to enter another room in the tower and set off a cannon prematurely, before they had time to aim it.

Jebeddo couldn't believe his bad luck that the cannon had still managed to hit him when the weapon had fired blind! But his thoughts turned to Felicia, and he wondered if it was true that it had been an accident at all. Had Lief taken an opportunity to rid himself of a potential rival, like he had when he struck the tower with lightning bolts while Lief was still inside?

Shaking his head, Jebeddo tried to put the thought out of his mind.

Idnatius, who had made himself scarce of late, had been off looking for allies already. So it was that Lief and Jebeddo were joined by a human rogue who referred to himself as the Phantom Shade, a quirky dwarf who introduced himself as the Lord Admiral H.D., a lupine warlock named Nyx Bloodfang, and Patches the ursine ranger. Especially odd was the "animal companion" Patches referred to, who appeared to be a human named Edmund. Patches was unwilling to elaborate on the relationship.

The group was preparing to leave to find more allies when Chieftain Ragorith approached. His attention darted around the encampment before his gaze finally settled on Jebeddo. "One Who Loves Bears has been killed, and his magical mixing bowl destroyed."

Seeing the looks of confusion on the faces of his new companions, Jebeddo explained that the plant-creature had been important in creating potions for the encampment. Together they decided to take the short hike up the mountain to where One Who Loves Bears had lived. Its crumpled body was still there, beside its mixing bowl which had a hole in the bottom. A quick spell to detect magic determined that it no longer held any power.

Worse, One Who Loves Bears showed signs of necrotic damage around the stab wounds that covered its spindly body.

"Iltherians," the group agreed unanimously. The necrotic damage was a telltale sign that the anti-magic zealots were in the area.

Phantom Shade scoured the area, and Nyx attempted to sniff for clues about the killer. Neither was particularly successful, with Nyx grumbling about smelly bear-people all over the place, but they decided the only direction that made sense for the killer to run was up a nearby mountain path, away from the ursine encampment.

Jebeddo, Phantom Shade, and Lief took point, sneaking up the path in search of anyone who might be waiting to ambush them. However, there were no signs of fresh tracks, so the group reconvened. Frustrated by the murderer's easy disappearance, they decided to continue south into the mountains to look for stragglers from other tribes, or new allies.

Not wanting to waste their time, the Lord Admiral H.D. cast a spell to help them divine whether they would find an ursine to the south within the next two days of travel. After receiving confirmation that their trek would not be in vain, they continued on their journey.

The next afternoon they came across an ursine draped in robes, slumped against a tree. His fur was matted with blood, and one of his eyes had been torn out. The ursine ranger checked to make sure he was still alive, and Jebeddo stepped forward to touch the unconscious figure with his healing magic.

But when he neared, the injured ursine reached up and grabbed his forearm, one angry eye glaring at him. Jebeddo quickly squeaked, "Healing!" and the ursine held him there, scrutinizing him, before letting go. With the worst of his wounds mended, the ursine rose to his feet, slowly.

"I'm Patches," the ranger said. "Who are you?"

"Brodur," the ursine replied. He patted his robes and cursed. "My spell components and wand are gone."

That didn't sound right to Jebeddo. "What happened?"

"Vulpine," Brodur spat. "Two black little devils came out of nowhere and attacked me."

The companions exchanged confused looks. Lief asked, "Why didn't they finish you off?"

"They left me for dead in the middle of nowhere, didn't

they?" Brodur replied. "I guess I was just tougher than they thought."

"And they were black?" Jebeddo asked. From everything he had heard and seen, vulpine fur tended to range from white, to brown, to red. Maybe Brodur was mistaken. Perhaps he had not gotten a good look at the ambushers.

But Brodur nodded. "As night. They carved me up and beat me pretty badly. Worse, my spells didn't seem to work on them. I think one of them might have been a spell caster too, and dispelled my efforts."

"If they attacked and left you for dead, they can't be far," Phantom Shade said, peering across the mountain terrain. There were only a few scraggly trees and bushes in the area, leaving few hiding spots. Examining the ground, he pointed back south, the way they had come. "I think they went that way."

Jebeddo, who had spent time in the mountains while recovering from the failed attack against the outpost, had discovered panthers in the area. Using his magic, he summoned eight fey panthers. He let them smell Brodur to pick up the vulpine scent and sent them running, commanding them to spread out and cover as much area as possible.

An hour later, only four returned, and the party decided the direction the other four hadn't returned from was the path they needed to follow.

"I'll come with you, if you don't mind," Brodur said. "Perhaps I'll find my missing gear, and some revenge."

Four sets of panther tracks converged on a plateau, but they vanished without a trace. Jebeddo realized that if Brodur had his magic cancelled by his attackers, it would make sense that they could remove his summoned animals without difficulty.

The plateau offered a scenic view of the mountains that surrounded them and the forest to the north where the ursine camp was located. A waterfall fed a small pristine lake on the plateau, although there were no rivers flowing from the lake. Sensing something was amiss, Jebeddo checked behind the waterfall and found an opening.

"Who wants to go first?" Jebeddo asked.

No one volunteered. In fact, Brodur outright refused to go in at all, and said he would head down the mountain to the ursine camp. Apparently the underground was no place for one of his people, a remark that made Patches growl and stomp forward into the tunnel.

Jebeddo followed close behind, but stopped when he heard the Lord Admiral emit a low whistle behind him. The dwarf ran his fingers over the tunnel walls, feeling the smooth edges of stone blocks. "It mayn't be dwarven work, but it's good. Very good."

The hall turned in a slow descent, plunging them into darkness. Fortunately most of the party possessed some level of dark vision, allowing them to see in the lightless tunnel. But Phantom Shade stopped when he could no longer see. Jebeddo unpacked his rope and gave one end to the human. "Follow my lead, and we can save our torches."

"I have lots of torches," Nyx said, opening his pack and showing them off. "I got caught in the under dark without light once. Never again."

Even so, they decided to use the rope for the time being. If they ran into trouble, they could light the torches later.

The floor was slick with water from the falls behind them, but the slope was not so steep that anyone fell. When they finally reached the first chamber, each of them let out a soft sigh of relief that there had been no traps.

Before them stood a stone tablet, taller than Jebeddo, but with few words carved into it. The text was alien to him, and none of the others in the room could decipher it, either. Nyx stepped forward and said, "I have a spell that will help, but it will take time."

Jebeddo looked around the room and saw no doors. "I think we can give you all the time you want."

While Nyx began his ritual spellcasting, Patches pointed up. About twenty feet up was a hole, and there were small handholds going up the wall. Too impatient to wait, Patches scrambled up and disappeared through the hole.

It was not long before Patches returned to the opening. "It's just a hallway. I mean, there are no exits except this one."

Phantom Shade shook his head. "Probably a secret door," he said, before climbing to join Patches.

"There we go," Nyx said, after some time had passed. "This tablet offers a warning that intruders should leave, or forfeit their lives. Pleasant."

"That's it?" Jebeddo asked.

Nyx nodded, and Phantom Shade called down to them. "Found it! At the end of the hall, there's a door that was disguised. But the release is just a stone on the door frame. Easy enough to figure out."

The group climbed into the tunnel, and sure enough the door opened at the slightest pressure on the stone the rogue had found. Another tunnel went off to the right, and they followed it to another end. Lief saw straight away that it was the same situation, and the second door popped open, leading to a third hallway. At the end, another door.

That door led them into a chamber, with walls covered in murals. Straight in front of them, there were images of vulpine battling with all manner of deep-dwellers: dwarves, deep elves, and monsters the likes of which they had never seen. To the right of the door they had just used to enter the chamber, there were images of vulpine battling surface dwellers, including humans with glowing green blades—Iltherians. The wall they had come from also contained murals of vulpine fighting each other. And although the fourth wall was left entirely blank, raising their suspicions, they found nothing untoward about it.

Nyx announced that his ritual spell would last for quite some time, and he was still able to read the text on a tablet in the middle of the room. "This is an ancient vulpine fortress, and these walls depict the battles they have fought against a host of enemies."

"Ancient?" the Lord Admiral said, wiping a finger over some of the tiles that made up the murals on the walls. "If this work is so old, where's the layer of dust? 'Tis clean!"

Jebeddo scuffed his foot on the floor and found no dust there, either. Something wasn't adding up, but he couldn't figure out what was going on.

During a brief discussion of where to go next, Lief joked that they should take half the party one way, and the other half could go the other. Unwilling to split up, they decided to go through the tunnel where the wall held images of the surface battles.

The stonework tunnel brought them back up into another chamber, where burnt tapestries hung on the walls. Jebeddo rushed forward to take a closer look, but leapt back when one of the stones on the floor gave way beneath him and dropped into darkness.

Jebeddo stepped forward and gingerly tapped the stones until another one plunged below. Putting his ear to the new hole, he waited until he heard the sound of rock smashing into rock. "That's a long drop. Lucky I was quick on my feet," he said. "This could take a while to figure out how many of the blocks are safe to step on."

A snort behind him brought Jebeddo's attention to Patches, who was unrolling his own length of rope from his pack. "No need to be slow about it. We can go gnome fishing."

Being a good sport about it, Jebeddo allowed Patches to loop the rope around him. A quick sprint across the room was cut short when several of the stones gave way, and Jebeddo lost his footing before reaching the far wall. He hit the end of the rope and dangled there, staring into the pitch black below. Out of the darkness rose the point of a stalagmite, which would have impaled him had he fallen much farther. It wasn't long before he felt the rope being hauled up, and he was set loose again and again.

In just a few minutes, the entire floor was tested, revealing a large circular gap in the middle of the room. Wary of falling to their dooms, they made sure to watch their steps as they examined the burnt tapestries. The artwork depicted battles where Iltherians slaughtered vulpine. Near the far tunnel, Nyx shook his head as he read a small plaque underneath a stone bust of a vulpine. "Lord Frederick the Great led his forces against the Iltherians, and is said to have defeated a dozen of their warriors single-handedly before falling in battle. His battle cry was 'Death to all invaders!' Perhaps they helped slow the spread of the Iltherians in Tensire long before resisting Phaelan's Republic."

From what he had seen of Petey and Felicia's resistance, however, Jebeddo had a hard time picturing them battling out in the open like that. Vulpine weren't overt warriors.

Or maybe they had been, until they lost to the Iltherians. Perhaps they had been forced to change their tactics. Jebeddo used his magic to create a small yellow flower, and placed it on top of the bust. These vulpine had suffered great losses at the hands of many enemies.

Down another hall they found another empty chamber, this one lacking any decoration at all.

"If this is a fortress, where are the defenders?" Lief asked.

It was a fair question. There was no sign of anyone living in the fortress, other than the absolute lack of dust anywhere. Was there a custodian of the fortress keeping it clean? Lost in thought, Jebeddo stepped forward to test the floor when the rope that he had been using to guide Phantom Shade fell to the floor, neatly severed by a wall that had appeared from nowhere.

"Hello?" he called out, hitting his fist against solid stone. He was alone.

Hoping it was a spell, he quickly cast his own to dispel it, and breathed easier when the wall vanished. "Thank goodness," he said with a sigh.

"What was that all about?" Phantom Shade asked, groping blindly in the dark.

Jebeddo took up the shortened rope and handed one end to the rogue. "Just a spell. Nothing to worry about."

Two exits were present once more, one straight ahead, and

one to their left. Nyx lifted his snout and smelled the air. "I smell something down the hall straight ahead. Leporine? Maybe ursine, too, although it's difficult to tell with Patches standing so close."

"Let's check out the exit on the left first, then," Lief said. "We'll save the mutates for later."

Inside an adjoining room they found more murals. The one on the far wall was done in darker stone, and the details were difficult to make out without light, so Jebeddo moved close to it, with Nyx at his side.

Just as he started to make out an image of a town with buildings, the wall exploding, and people fleeing, the floor gave out from under him again. Although he managed to leap away, Nyx was not so lucky, and plunged down the dark hole.

"Nyx!" Jebeddo cried out, falling to his knees at the edge of the pit.

Nyx's echoing voice came back up to him. "I'm all right! I managed to cast a spell of flight before I fell too far. I just want to look around down here quickly. It's ... strange."

"Strange how?"

But Jebeddo's question went unanswered. Several moments passed before Nyx flew up through the hole again. Nyx choked on his words. "That room is some sort of hellish trap. In the middle of the room was a huge stalagmite with stone blocks littered around it. Presumably from the first floor that gave way under you, Jebeddo. There are more stalagmites and stalactites around the chamber, and what I thought were natural pillars. But I saw arms and legs sticking out of the middle of some of them, as though the stone ceiling and floor had come together to crush people. What kind of magic could do such a thing?"

"Druidic," Jebeddo whispered. He had heard of druids who had dedicated themselves to the earth and could perform amazing feats. It couldn't be Petey, could it? He tried to think if he had ever witnessed Petey use any forms of earth magic, but nothing came to mind. Besides, he wasn't black like Brodur had said his attackers were. There must be another vulpine druid here. Although the dark mural of Phaelan's Rise cast doubts on that thought. That attack was only a little over two weeks old. Not ancient history at all.

"Well, whatever it is, we should take a look!" Lief said. "Come on, Nyx!"

Although he appeared uncertain, Nyx took hold of Lief, and they flew down the hole together to investigate.

"Looks like Lief finally got his way and split us up," the Lord Admiral said, his tone full of doubt.

"Should we continue on without them?" Phantom Shade asked.

Patches nodded. "I want to see what that ursine smell is about that Nyx mentioned."

Leaving unsaid the possibility that Nyx and Lief might not return from wherever it was they were headed, Jebeddo agreed with Patches and the four of them made their way back to the other room and started down the other tunnel, which wound deeper and deeper into the mountain.

Jebeddo stared up at the walls, his heart hammering in his chest, nausea threatening to empty his stomach. Ursine and leporine heads adorned the walls, mounted like trophies.

And one of them was black with a white skull.

"Take him down," Jebeddo whispered.

Patches took Grodurs' head off the wall and put it on the floor, where Jebeddo could examine it.

"Who is it?" Patches asked, growling.

Although the name under the head was unreadable to him, and Nyx was off with Lief, Jebeddo had no doubt this was the dead chieftain of the White Skull clan. But how was that possible? They had been two weeks north of this place when they had killed Grodurs. The dark mural came back to haunt him, and he shook his head in denial, looking up at the other heads that acted as vile decorations.

"He was the chieftain of the White Skull tribe, which is a

part of the larger camp, now," Jebeddo said.

"I can speak with the dead," the Lord Admiral offered, kneeling beside the head. "We will only get a few questions answered, but it might be enough to figure out what's going on here. So long as he's cooperative, of course."

"Do it," Patches said forcefully.

When the spell was cast, Grodurs' face animated and his mouth closed.

"Hello," the Lord Admiral started. "Do you know any black vulpine?"

"No."

The dwarf sat back and thought carefully. "Have any vulpine passed by this way?"

"I don't know."

"His dead eyes might not have seen them," Jebeddo said with a sigh, rubbing his face in frustration. They were getting nowhere.

"Who killed you?" the dwarf asked next.

"He did." The ursine's eyes turned to Jebeddo.

Patches roared and pulled out his swords. Holding his hands up, Jebeddo squeaked, "It wasn't my fault!" When Patches didn't immediately attack him, Jebeddo blurted out the whole story about saving the prisoners, Grodurs chasing them, and how it had all been part of a larger plot to destroy Phaelan's Rise by Petey and Felicia.

"Two vulpine," Patches said, his mind going in the same direction Jebeddo's was. Who else could have mounted Grodurs' head and brought it to a vulpine fortress? He hoped he was wrong, and it wasn't Petey and Felicia who had lured them here.

"Is that story true?" the Lord Admiral asked Grodurs.

"Yes," Grodurs replied. He then closed his eyes, and appeared to fall asleep.

"I won't get any more out of him," the Lord Admiral said. "Should we continue on?"

Jebeddo turned back to the tunnel, wishing Nyx and Lief would return, but there was no sign of them. "Yes, let's push on."

A short hallway brought them to a room littered with a variety of artifacts. Weapons and armour were heaped on the floor, and atop one of the piles was a large Warhammer that looked familiar to Jebeddo. Sure enough, it was the weapon Grodurs had used to beat his companions nearly to death.

"There's magic items in here!" the Lord Admiral shouted, his voice echoing. He clapped his hands over his mouth, then offered a muffled apology. He rummaged through the piles and pulled out a dagger and a metal bar that was attached to four long metal claws. "These are magical. If you don't mind waiting, I can cast a spell to identify what properties they possess."

Again Jebeddo stared back at the hallway they had come through. He waited in silence to see if there were any sounds at all in response to Lord Admiral H.D.'s outburst, but everything was silent. "Go ahead," he said. If Nyx and Lief are still alive, it will give them time to catch up to us again."

The Lord Admiral sat on the floor and began his ritual.

"Standard sorts of enchantments," the Lord Admiral said. "They'll be a bit better in combat than a non-magical weapon."

Phantom Shade picked up the dagger and said, "Hope you don't mind."

"Patches?" Jebeddo said, pointing at the claw weapon. "Unless I've missed my guess, that belonged to the old chieftain of the Clawed Fist tribe."

Taking the claw in hand, Patches wrapped his fingers around the bar and admired the craftsmanship of the wicked weapon. "I'll take it for now," he replied.

"Take what?" Lief asked, skipping into the room.

Patches held up the claw for Lief to admire, but Jebeddo was more interested in where the halfling and lupine had gotten off to.

"There was a huge chamber full of spikes and pillars that we flew across to another tunnel, which led to this boring room with some benches, but then we found something amazing!" Lief paused for effect. "It's the largest room we've seen so far, probably a hundred feet across, and eighty tall. There were veins of silver and gold running through the walls. That find alone would be worth a fortune!"

Nyx chimed in, "There was also an obelisk with more writing on it. The room was called the War Hall, and apparently dwarves tunnelled into it while seeking new mineral veins. War erupted between them, and a vulpine named Fayra the Bold marched all the way to the dwarven city of Helbolf and gave her life to collapse the tunnels."

"Interesting," Jebeddo said. The corroboration with the murals that the vulpine had been at war with their neighbours left him feeling unsettled. Was that why this place appeared to be abandoned? Had the vulpine simply had too many enemies trying to kill them?

"Anyway," Lief said, "we climbed up a wall to another tunnel and it brought us back to the room with the murals of their enemies. It was easy from there to find our way back to you."

"Now that we're all back together, we should proceed deeper into the fortress," Nyx said.

Another tunnel led to a room with a narrow stone staircase that hugged the walls of the room and spiralled down further than their dark vision could see.

"Anyone have a shield I could borrow?" Lief asked. After receiving one from the Lord Admiral, he placed it on the stairs and jumped onto it, riding it at breakneck speed out of sight. Not long after, he called up, "I made it! It's not too much further down from where we could see."

Making their way down carefully, nobody toppled off the edge of the staircase, and soon enough they reached the bottom, again faced with two choices. One smelled more strongly of vulpine.

Going the other way first, they came out of a long tunnel into the room Nyx had discovered with the stone pillars, stalactites, and stalagmites. Since Nyx had already explored that area, the group turned around and headed back for the tunnel that smelled of vulpine.

On the other side of that tunnel was a large staircase that headed deeper into the mountain, but off to the side were apartments. Long unused, the beds remained untouched, cabinets bare, and they were about to head down the stairs when Lief called out that he'd found a secret door.

Adjoining the apartments was what must have been a large barracks. Weapons and armour crafted for the small vulpine adorned the walls, but what caught Jebeddo's eye was a switch on the far wall. His gnomish curiosity got the better of him, and he ran over to pull the switch down.

He jumped back in case the switch was for a trap and immediately regretted it, as he found himself falling down a hole.

Thinking fast, he changed his shape into that of a cave bear and plugged the hole with his girth. Head up, he roared plaintively, hoping someone could help him out. His rear was starting to get cold, and he feared what might be below.

Instead of help in the traditional sense, he heard Lief shout, "I can handle this!" and the next thing he knew, the halfling had jumped down the hole and landed on him. Jumping several times, Lief unstuck the bear, and they fell the remaining distance into a frigid room. Large flanks of ice-coated meat hung from hooks in the ceiling, and rows of stone chests contained what appeared to be freezer-burned food. After a quick check, they decided to leave the storage room and try to find the others.

A tunnel took them up to another room with only one other tunnel to choose, as another option had collapsed. This new, long tunnel took them up to another set of empty apartments, and they met back up with the rest of their group.

"Just empty apartments back that way," Patches said, motioning to another tunnel from the higher level. That left just one more direction to try.

The tunnel on the lower level of the apartments was long, and led to a small room with a plaque on the wall that Nyx read, and said, "Overlook." The far end of the room opened into a huge chamber below them. Water fell from the ceiling into a pond below, although one side of the room remained dry. At the far end, they could see a shadowy figure standing near a gleaming vein of metal.

Nyx lit a torch and threw it below so Phantom Shade would be able to see, but the flames died when the torch splashed into the pond. Throwing another lit torch out further, this one bounced off the floor, half way between them and the figure, offering no clue as to who it was.

Not waiting for the others, Lief leaped out of the opening and glided down to the floor. Jebeddo cursed at the halfling's impetuousness, as the others set a rope onto a hook so they could get down more safely. But Jebeddo didn't wait, instead leaping far off to the side, and diving head first into the pond. The cool, refreshing water might have made for a pleasant place to swim, were it not for the dread that clutched at his heart when he surfaced and heard a familiar voice speaking to Lief.

Petey.

"... if you join me—for real this time—in wiping out our true enemies."

Lief shook his head. "Look at this place. Your people have lost so much already. Stop this pointless fighting, before you join those who lived here."

Silence greeted his statement, and Jebeddo dug his bear claws against the bottom of the pond, slowly making his way closer to where Petey was.

Finally Petey responded. "You should join me. If we were on the same side ..."

"And what side is that?" Lief asked.

"My own," Petey answered with a devilish smile. "What? Do you honestly believe the ursine are with you? And you battled against Phaelan's Republic! You have no one."

"That's where you're wrong," Lief said. "I have my side." Without warning, Lief drew back an arrow and fired at Petey.

Oh no, Jebeddo thought. If they killed Petey, Jebeddo might never meet the druid council. For a moment, he thought about joining Petey, at least long enough to stop the fighting. But Petey had accepted the arrow in his leg, and lifted his hand. With that motion, Jebeddo felt his weight shift, and his body hurtled up toward the ceiling.

"Fools!" Petey cried. "I will not die here, in this lightless cavern. You should have joined me."

They all crashed into the ceiling with jarring force, except for the Lord Admiral, who had stayed behind in the Overlook with Patches' companion. Thinking fast, Jebeddo reverted to his gnomish form and ran to find a spot over deeper water. If Petey thought to drop them to the floor, he didn't want to get even more hurt. Patches and Nyx saw him and did the same, while Lief ran closer to the edge of the cavern where Petey was, and spread his arms to glide down.

Seeing that the reversal of gravity was only in front of the vulpine, Jebeddo summoned a swarm of small poisonous snakes on the ground around Petey's feet. If this was how it had to end, then so be it.

But with his next spell, Petey summoned slabs of stone, the first blocking off the Overlook's opening and cutting off the Lord Admiral from the battle. But more slabs snaked out under Nyx and Patches, with walls sprouting out of the end. With that spell cast, gravity returned to normal, and Jebeddo plunged into the pond. But Patches was stuck behind an L-shaped stone wall so he couldn't see Petey, and Nyx remained up there as well. Taking advantage of having the high ground, Nyx unleashed a blast of energy at Petey, but a collective gasp rang through the chamber when a second, red-furred form leaped from the shadows and snared the spell with a renik dagger.

Felicia stood before Petey and aimed her glowing blade at Jebeddo, who had not the presence of mind to react as a beam of anti-magic blasted him in the chest and sent him to the ground. Dazed, he pulled himself up to sitting and watched the ensuing madness with a detached sense of wonder.

How had Felicia learned to snap magic out of the air with an Iltherian weapon? Weren't all Iltherians human? He watched as she ran forward, snaring more spells out of the air, and slashed her blade across once, twice, and shattered the magical dagger that Phantom Shade had only recently pilfered from the artifact chamber. Her blade soaked up the magical energy from the destroyed weapon, and with a howl she thrust the dagger at Jebeddo, releasing another attack.

With the pain of the first attack still fresh in his mind, Jebeddo rolled aside and the beam sizzled across the stone where he had been. Getting onto shaky feet, he looked over to see Patches—on the ground now—come up behind Felicia and plunge his swords into her back.

At some point during the fight, Petey had fallen, too, multiple arrows piercing his body. The last one stuck out of his eye.

"I don't understand," Jebeddo wheezed, shuffling closer.

"He lied to us," Lief said, pulling the arrows from Petey's corpse. "He attacked that ursine, Brodur, and lured us down here through these empty halls. He had no intention of helping the ursine. He just wants them dead, along with everyone else. But now he's the one who's fallen."

Lied to us. The phrase bothered Jebeddo more and more as he thought about it. How many lies had Petey woven? If Felicia was an Iltherian agent, had she killed the dendobrium, One Who Loves Bears? The wounds certainly matched what she could do. The vulpine hadn't joined them on their attack against the Republic outpost. Had Petey wanted them to fail? Grodurs had died believing in their quest to destroy Phaelan's Republic, but in truth Petey had eliminated those he saw as enemies on both sides, leaving the ursine weaker. Had he known the ursine warriors would battle to the death to see who would become the next chieftains of the White Skull and Clawed Fist tribes?

What of the child he had kidnapped for the council of druids to sacrifice to the ancient sea monster? Was there even a sea monster at all? Was there a council of druids? What had become of that child?

Rage burned inside Petey as he looked at that small,

crumpled form. He lost all control, and pulled out a stone knife. With wild fury, he slashed and cut and mutilated, until Petey's pelt lay on the floor.

When he looked up, most of the others stared at him with revulsion.

"I'm sorry," Lief said, shaking his head. "I think this is where we part company."

Jebeddo stared after them, but Lief, Patches, and Nyx climbed the rope to the Overlook and hauled it up behind them.

"You sure you're not coming with us?" Lief called to Phantom Shade, the only person who still remained below with Jebeddo.

"Nah," Phantom Shade replied. "Petey had that coming."

Without another word, the other adventurers left Jebeddo and Phantom Shade behind.

The torch went out, plunging them into darkness. Jebeddo's eyes shifted to dark vision, and he looked at his blood-spattered hands, his rage played out.

What have I done? He looked at Phantom Shade, who sat down in a pitch black that his human vision could not pierce.

Jebeddo had but one ally left.

He stared at Petey's mutilated form, and Felicia's nearby. The two of them had died together in this cave, to be replaced by Jebeddo and Phantom Shade, who had pilfered the renik dagger at some point. The unmistakable similarities between the vulpine and his own situation crystalized in his mind.

What have I become?

About the Authors

And now, about the Authors, in their own words. Please make sure to check out the ones you like and the ones that made you think.

◆ LINDA G. HILL

Linda G. Hill is a stay-at-home mom of three boys and the guardian of one beagle and two kitties. Author of the Gothic paranormal romance novel *The Magician's Curse*, and a romantic comedy novelette, *All Good Stories*, she concocts tales in her head 24/7 and blogs almost daily at lindaghill.com. She lives in Southern Ontario, Canada.

◆ LAURA JOHNSON

Laura Johnson is a fantasy writer and poet who resides in London, Ontario. Although her Psychology degree doesn't give her the ability to read minds, she does use it to flesh out her characters. Her writing lair is littered with dragon paraphernalia, emergency rations of dark chocolate, and enough books to fill a small library. At present she is working on a fantasy series that blends intrigue, mythology, and dark magic. Previously, her work has appeared in Folklore, a collection of poems and short stories about Scandinavian folklore, and two other Phoenix Quill Anthologies: *Heroes* and *Monsters*.

◆ TIFFANY WOODBECK

Tiffany Woodbeck is a fantasy author and lead editor at OWS Ink, living in Seattle, WA. When she's not writing or editing, you can find her gleaning random inspiration for other artistic pursuits from the people and settings around her. Formerly writing as Stephanie Reisen, she has one book published under her pen name. *Luck of the Grave* is the first short story in the Gravebound Souls series. Currently, she's reworking her entire brand, including the book, to be under her real name.

◆ DREW CARMODY

Drew Carmody is a writer of strange fantasy and science fiction. He is currently working on his debut novel, *Odd Jobs*, Book One of the Short & Sword series, a blend of Fantasy and Weird West. When not writing, Drew can be found engaging in all manner of nerdy pursuits in the general vicinity of Charlotte, North Carolina with his fiancé, his almost-stepson, three dogs, two cats and a ferret. He is also on a lifelong quest to find the perfect cheeseburger.

◆ P. A. CORNELL

P. A. Cornell began her early adulthood as a world renowned concert trianglist, a career tragically cut short by an accident involving her left baby toe, a coffee table leg and a handful of Legos. Following extensive therapy her parents encouraged her to follow in the family business, but "international super spy/ninja" lacked the excitement she craved. She turned instead to the world of fiction writing (some of this bio may in fact be fictional, though I'm not telling which parts). She currently works as a full-time writer and freelance editor from her home in Ontario, Canada, which she shares with her husband, three kids, and a cat with anger management issues. This is her second publication in a TPQ Anthology, following her short story *The Monsters We Create* published last year in *Monsters*. Follow her on Facebook (@CornellWriter), Twitter (@PACornellWriter) and on her Amazon author page.

◆ ISA MCLAREN

Isa McLaren is a freelance writer and customer service professional who enjoys casing museums and luxury condos and can craft a cocktail for any occasion. She is currently learning how to advocate for the dead and dying. She resides in the Containment Area for Relocated Yankees known as Cary, NC with her two burglar cats, Archibald Dortmunder and Bernie Rhodenbarr and can be found hanging around Twitter as @IWMcLaren. Isa's first short story, *Third Time's a Charm*, was published in the anthology *Den of Thieves*.

◆ JOHN RYERS

John hails from Ontario, Canada with his wife and twin daughters. He's written fantasy from a very young age, inspired by the impromptu stories told by his father at bedtime.

In January 2017, John released his debut novel *The Glass Thief*, and he has short stories published in the first two TPQ anthologies as well.

Find out more about John at: johnryers.com

◆ RYAN TOXOPEUS

Ryan Toxopeus, award winning writer of the Empire's Foundation fantasy trilogy, has been writing fantastic tales for two decades. In the last five years, he has published two novels (A Noble's Quest, A Wizard's Gambit), a novella (Demon Invasion), and several short stories both related to his larger fantasy world, and stand alone stories including Macimanito Môswa which won Honourable Mention in the L. Ron Hubbard Writers of the Future contest.

He lives in Guelph, Ontario with his wife, children, and several animals. He also works on creating games related to his writing.

Website address:
https://prcreative.ca/ryan/
Facebook fan site:
https://www.facebook.com/RyanToxopeusWriting/
Amazon author site:
https://www.amazon.com/Ryan-Toxopeus/e/B0095WNDXK/

About the Editor

◆ ASHLEY CYR

It didn't take long after graduating from the Queen's University for Ashley Cyr to jump into publishing with both feet. By day she works at an academic publishing house, while by night she is the Editor in Chief at Bushmead Publishing. She has served as editor for best-selling novels, and has served as primary editor for Heroes, Monsters, and Another Place.

You can follow the work that she does at Bushmead by going to www.bushmead.com

www.ingramcontent.com/pod-product-compliance
Lightning Source LLC
Chambersburg PA
CBHW060905250626
47159CB00008B/2881